Also by Cheryl Hollon

Webb's Glass Shop Mystery Series

Pane and Suffering

Shards of Murder

Cracked to Death

Etched in Tears

Shattered at Sea

Down in Flames

Paint & Shine Mystery Series

Still Knife Painting

Draw and Order

Published by Kensington Publishing Corp.

Draw and Order

Cheryl Hollon

KENSINGTON
PUBLISHING CORP.

www.kensingtonbooks.com

KENSINGTON BOOKS are published by

Kensington Publishing Corp.
119 West 40th Street
New York, NY 10018

First Kensington Books Mass Market Paperback Printing: July 2021

ISBN-13: 978-1-4967-2526-4
ISBN-10: 1-4967-2526-3

ISBN-13: 978-1-4967-2527-1 (ebook)
ISBN-10: 1-4967-2527-1 (ebook)

10 9 8 7 6 5 4 3 2 1

Printed in the United States of America

Dedicated to Ramona DeFelice Long
Author, editor, muse. RIP.

Cast of Characters

Miranda Dorothy Trent	Protagonist
Sandy	Miranda's male puppy
Iris Hobb	Cook
Lily Hobb	Cook
Austin Morgan	Local forest ranger
Gene Buchanan	Miranda's late bachelor uncle
Alfred Whittaker	Client #1—a freelance reporter
Ben DeBerg	Client #2—a criminal defense lawyer
Jennifer O'Rourke	Client #3—a jewelry artist
Kevin Burkart	Client #4—owner of a financial services business
Kurt Smith	Client #5—a cosmetic surgeon
Stephanie Brinkley	Client #6—a licensed pharmacist
Sheriff Richard J. Larson	Wolfe County sheriff
Felicia Larson	Coroner and sheriff's wife
Barbara DuPont	Forensic anthropologist
Howard Cable	Miranda's cousin
Ora Cable	Howard's mother
Roy and Elsie Kash	Miranda's neighbors
Tyler Morgan	Austin's sister
Doris Ann Norris	Receptionist
Dorothy Marcella Trent	Miranda's mother
Lance Campbell	Brewery intern
Anna Belle Cable	Howard's younger sister

Anna Sue Cable	Howard's older sister
Ron Menifee	Miranda's handyman
Andrew Perry	EMT #1
Scott Caldwell	EMT #2
Doc Watson	Local physician
John Latchy	Cousin of *Lexington Herald-Leader* owner

Chapter 1

Early Sunday Morning in November,
Miranda's Farmhouse

Short, earsplitting shrieks blasted from the fire alarm over the stove in Miranda Trent's farmhouse kitchen. She startled, fumbled, and then almost dropped the final portion of her scratch-made country-fried chicken onto the linoleum floor. She held the dripping, golden-brown breast in her tongs over the spattering cast-iron skillet. Like a waiting-in-the-wings vacuum robot, her puppy, Sandy, skidded into the kitchen, toenails scrabbling for footing, and added crackly voiced wolf howling to the smoke detector wail.

"Iris! Grab the stepladder and turn that screeching thing off."

The hot bacon-grease-and-butter mixture crackled like fireworks in the ancient skillet. A roiling plume of smoke rose from the angry frying pan. Miranda hurried to put the chicken on the draining rack, move the skillet to a back burner, and turn off the flame.

Grabbing a pot lid from the open shelf next to the stove, she slapped it over the still-sizzling skillet. Miranda sighed relief and wiped both hands on her logo-imprinted apron. She turned around to watch Iris Hobb, one of her local cooks, set up the stepladder right next to her huge commercial range. "I wanted crispy chicken, but I think I went a little too far."

Iris stepped onto the ladder, grabbed the smoke alarm, gave it a quick twist, took it off its mounting plate, and then removed the battery. The resulting silence was beautiful.

"Where's the fire?" Lily, the second cook and sister to Iris, walked in through the back door. She planted her hands on her hips. "I thought that thing only went off for a fire."

Miranda opened the window over the sink on the other side of the kitchen. "It was the crackling of the grease. The modern ones are sensitive to airborne particles." She flapped a kitchen towel toward the window opening. "Pump the back door open and closed a few times and help me clear the air."

The chilly morning rushed through the kitchen as Iris and Lily helped Miranda whoosh away the smoke. Meanwhile, Sandy, her fluffy blond terrier-mix puppy, ran around the kitchen begging to play and nearly tripping them all. He thought smoke clearing was a wonderful game.

After a few minutes of door swinging and apron flapping, the smoke in the kitchen dissipated and the burning smell faded. "Go ahead and put the battery back in. Maybe we've blown things out enough for the little beast."

Iris replaced the battery and the alarm didn't make a sound.

"Perfect," said Miranda. "Put it way over there." She pointed to the counter next to the sink. "We'll let it sit over there for a few days. If it stays happy, we'll remount it over the back door instead of over the stove. Southern cooking involves lots of bacon grease and butter so we do get a lot of spatter."

As the owner of Paint & Shine, a cultural-adventure tour business set in the Daniel Boone National Forest, Miranda wanted her clients to enjoy the best examples of Southern food possible. Her eastern-Kentucky farmhouse was normally the location for the meal. But today's offering was an old-timey packed lunch to eat out on the trail overlooking the cliff formation called Battleship Rock.

"Thanks for coming in early on Sunday, ladies."

"It's no problem," said Iris. "Although Grandmother Hobb was mighty upset with us."

"We take her to church every week," said Lily. "In fact, we're using this as the perfect excuse. We don't enjoy the fire-and-brimstone preaching anymore."

Iris added, "We never did, but now that we have a paying job, she can't say nuthin'." They smirked and winked happily at each other.

"Thanks. Iris, is the dining room ready for packing up the lunch boxes?"

"Yes, ma'am," said Iris. "We only needed the chicken."

"Great." Miranda grabbed the draining rack with the eight golden-fried chicken breasts and went into the dining room. On the large round table was an assembly line for packing each picnic meal into a vintage handwoven white oak basket. Miranda placed the chicken next to a roll of waxed paper.

"Okay, let's first wrap the chicken in the waxed paper and put it on top of the gingham square at the bottom of each basket, like this." Miranda demonstrated. "Then we put the green beans, pickled cabbage, pickles, and the mustard potato salad in the lightweight cardboard box." That idea was supplied by her mom. She had told Miranda that Tupperware containers hadn't been affordable for most farming families when reusable containers came to hand absolutely free. "Wrap the corn on the cob and the corn bread individually in aluminum foil. The cobbler gets wrapped in aluminum foil as well, and then finally, we put the lemonade moonshine cocktail in a mason jar."

"Won't the drink get warm?" asked Lily.

"It will be fairly cool up there, but I'm going to tuck in a few ice cubes. Realistically, if they want an authentic picnic experience, then lukewarm lemonade is what it must be."

"This pack is already heavy," said Iris as she hefted one of the backpacks with a Paint & Shine logo patch sewn onto the back. Miranda did the sewing herself and saved the cost of ordering them already attached from an imprint specialist.

"These clients have assured me that they are fit athletes and can carry more than twice the weight of these day-trip packs. We'll see. I mean, as a group they call themselves Risky Business Adventurers. That must mean something. This is my first remote-trail offering. I hope it's a success."

Miranda was anxious. As a way to calm her worries, she was taking extra food to feed Ranger Austin Morgan and extra drawing supplies in case some got ruined, and finally she packed some emergency equipment in case of, well, an emergency. She would make sure Austin knew about them. All that made her feel more confident.

Austin was her down-the-road neighbor. An experienced forest ranger, he was a vital, colorful, but unplanned part of her cultural adventures. He usually stopped by the trail overlook site she had chosen for the painting session and gave her clients a history of the area's geology. In addition, he knew a thousand tidbits of local lore to sprinkle into his ranger talk.

Iris wore a logo apron over a T-shirt she had embroidered with a strip of her namesake flower down one long white sleeve. She frowned. "You're going to have Austin up there, aren't you? You'll feel better after he arrives to give the group one of his ranger talks."

Miranda raised her eyebrows. "I will."

Iris continued, "You're worried that he might not make it all the way up the Indian Staircase to the view of Battleship Rock."

"He hasn't missed an event yet." Miranda realized that she sounded a bit defensive. Could it be that his part of her events was becoming important to her in more than a business way? "He must enjoy them." Or could it be that she felt grateful for his help solving the case of the murdered cook when she first opened the business last month? What a calamity.

Lily, wearing a T-shirt with lilies embroidered down the opposite sleeve to Iris's, slipped the last lunch basket into the sixth and final client backpack. "The lectures are part of his job, but he does seem keenly dedicated." Lily and Iris exchanged a knowing glance.

Iris looked up and down at Miranda's light jacket, logo shirt, sturdy jeans, and hiking boots. "Is that all you're going to wear? November weather can be pretty tricky up on the cliffs."

"Good catch. I forgot to pack my all-weather jacket and pants. Thankfully, they fold up into small self-contained packets. I'm also going to put in my emergency pop-up tent. Each of the backpacks already have a tiny survival kit."

"That should do it," said Iris.

Miranda's clients had requested a specific location for their cultural adventure. Given the distance of the hike and its remoteness, Miranda had chosen to provide a lesson in charcoal sketching rather than the normal activity of creating an acrylic painting of the Battleship Rock overlook. After all, everything hauled up to the vantage point had to be hauled back down.

Lily and Iris helped her load the pile of backpacks into Miranda's white van.

She was just about ready to leave when the phone rang in the living room. Iris dashed into the house to answer it before it rolled over to the answering machine. In another moment, she opened the screen door and yelled, "It's the distillery supplier. He says there's a problem."

"You mean another problem." Miranda glanced at her watch. She had a few minutes to spare. She went into the living room and picked up the phone. "This is Miranda Trent. What's the problem this time?"

"Good morning, ma'am. I'm the owner of Custom Metal Craft. I've run into an issue with your stainless-steel fermentation tank. It's not a serious one, but there will be a small delay."

"Another delay? You've missed every date that you've promised. Every date."

"Yes, ma'am, but your specifications are unique."

"Unique?" Miranda formed a fist and shook it at the phone. "What you really mean is that you have no experience with anything but the standard size of fermentation tank. Don't tell me this is the first special order you've ever built?"

There was absolute silence on the other end of the line.

Miranda placed her hand on her forehead and looked up at the ceiling. "This is your first special order, right?"

Again the silence drew out into a long pause. "Yes, ma'am. I don't know how I'm gonna make this up to you, but I promise that I will. Your fermentation tank is an absolute genius of a design."

"What is your new delivery date?"

"Miss Trent, I swear on the grave of my dear granny that your tank will be delivered on tomorrow."

She had no choice but to agree. She mentally calculated the impact of another day of delay to her production plans. It was disappointing. It appeared that the moonshine spirits of the mountains were plotting against her.

Her late uncle Gene Buchanan had left her the ancestral farm. But the will stipulated she had to establish a distillery to produce his legendary moonshine. The deadline for acquiring her license was at the stroke of midnight on New Year's Eve. It was still a few weeks until Thanksgiving, but time was getting tight.

She had so far endured delay after delay. First, from the county officials in getting the right permits. Then next, it was getting permission to upgrade the tobacco barn. More rejected drawing plans, more delays. Each of these issues was not catastrophic, but they added up to a significant financial risk if she didn't get production of her new moonshine started soon.

At the moment, she was still on good terms with the

owner of the Limestone Distillery over in the outskirts of Lexington. He was happy to supply her with as much moonshine as she could sell out of her little gift shop. He provided her with sampling supplies free of charge. That was how small distilleries helped one another.

Miranda went out to the van and called to Iris and Lily, "Don't forget to tuck Sandy up in his cage."

She started up the van and heard a ding. She let her head fall against the steering wheel. The "low fuel" warning symbol lit up and continued to ding.

Chapter 2

Sunday Morning, Hemlock Lodge

After stopping at the gas station at the Slade Hill exit for a fill-up, Miranda Trent arrived at Hemlock Lodge only a few minutes late. Set back into the cliffside of the Natural Bridge State Park, the lodge offered basic rooms with balconies that overlooked the mountainside. Miranda's tours started in the lobby in front of a two-story fireplace built with local honey-colored stone.

A roaring fire crackled as Miranda rushed over to a group of six people dressed in matching bright red T-shirts. Their high-tech outerwear proclaimed them ready for an outdoor adventure.

In general, there were two types of visitors to Hemlock Lodge this early on a Sunday morning. One, the church-going families getting a filling breakfast meant to last during a long service, or two, the hikers off to an early start on the trails.

Miranda made a beeline for the red shirts.

"Good morning, are you here for the Paint and Shine cultural adventure?"

The tallest man in the group smiled broadly and stepped forward with his hand stretched out. "Hi, you must be Miranda. I'm Alfred Whittaker, the unofficial leader of our little adventure group, which we've been calling Risky Business Adventurers."

Miranda shook hands in a strong grip to match his. "Good morning, I'm so sorry to be a little late. I hope you're all set to sketch the overlook at Battleship Rock."

There were nods and murmurs from the group. "We are," said Alfred, who returned to his spot across the room near the floor-to-ceiling windows.

"First, I would like to welcome you to a Paint and Shine picnic tour. This is a unique experience blending art, adventure, food, and drink in one package. Although you know each other well, I would like an introduction before we head out. Just your name and profession and where you're from if you don't mind. Alfred, you first."

He flashed a little self-possessed grin. "I'm a freelance reporter with the *Lexington Herald-Leader* and I live over near the Blue Grass Airport." He nodded to the short, bald, trim man next to him.

"I'm Ben DeBerg. I'm a criminal defense lawyer. My mother and I own a practice in Washington, DC." He glanced at the slender woman to his left.

"I'm Jennifer O'Rourke. I'm a jewelry artist." She pulled back her long brown locks to reveal a set of silver-encased amber earrings. "I own a shop over in Stanton, about twenty minutes from here." Her smile warmed her amber-brown eyes.

Leaning against the ledge of the window with his arms

folded and legs crossed at the ankles, a dark-haired man with a deep tan spoke. "I'm Kevin Burkart. I was born over in Stanton and I have a financial services business down in St. Petersburg, Florida. I love to hunt, fish, hike, and play electric guitar." He waved a hand to the sandy-haired, blue-eyed, stocky man next to him.

"I'm Kurt Smith. I own a large and, if I may say so, very profitable cosmetic-surgery and spa facility in Lexington." He looked over to his left. "You're next, Stephanie."

Stephanie narrowed her green eyes beneath a short fringe of auburn hair. "My name is Stephanie Brinkley. I'm a licensed pharmacist and I work over at Lexington's Saint Joseph Hospital."

"Thank y'all for that. My turn. I'm Miranda Trent, born here in Wolfe County. I was working as an artist in New York City when I inherited my bachelor uncle's farmhouse in Pine Ridge, Kentucky. Not only is this my dream job to teach art, but I'm in the process of turning the barn into a distillery and brewing up the secret recipes I found of my uncle's famous moonshine."

"Awesome," said Kevin. "I love 'shine. Good luck to you."

"Thanks. If all y'all would please follow me out to the van, we'll drive over to the trailhead, get our packs, and head out."

After she parked and got their permit at the Gladie Learning Center, the group picked up their backpacks and headed out onto the Bison Way Trailhead, which connected to the loop that led to Battleship Rock.

Miranda led the way and had asked Kevin, as the most experienced hiker, to bring up the rear. This not being a particularly well-traveled trail, the footing was tricky with the wet leaves from last night's rain. A comfortable bantering floated in the air among the group.

In about an hour, they were grouped in front of a vertical sandstone wall that had hand-carved footholds up to the summit. The cliff face was about twenty feet high and pitched up at about a forty-five-degree angle.

"Kevin, would you mind going up first? I'll hang back here and—"

"Good morning, can I help?" A tall figure in a tan uniform appeared at the edge of the group. He flashed a broad smile at Miranda, then stepped up beside her.

"You sure can." Miranda turned to him, mirroring his smile. "Folks, this is Forest Ranger Austin Morgan. He's the local officer in charge of this part of the Daniel Boone National Forest. He's also one of the founders of our local rescue organization. Expertise I'm certain we won't need given your adventuring track record."

Austin turned to her. "Do you want me down here or would you like for me to demonstrate the climb? I could also add a little history."

Relief swept through Miranda's tense shoulders. The wet rocks added a hazardous component that she wasn't certain she could in good conscience thrust upon her clients. Ranger Morgan's presence turned that uncomfortable situation into an educational opportunity.

Austin stood in front of the group and waited until he had their undivided attention. "These indentations have been a popular challenge here in the Red River Gorge since they were discovered. We're lucky it is still here. This area came very close to being flooded by a proposed dam. The locals made sure that the proposal was shot down. It is now a world-famous rock-climbing area and also known for excellent backpacking.

"History has it that these steps are the handiwork of a native tribe. They not only carved them into the soft sandstone but took advantage of a natural shelter in the cliff above us. There's plenty of evidence of their culture and lifestyle during their tenure here, including well-preserved clothing and household items. Sadly, the exact nature of the steps—who exactly built them and what they were for—remains a mystery. The shelter has dozens of pictogram images that tell of hunting feats."

"Has anyone documented the images?" asked Jennifer. "You know, an anthropologist or maybe an expert from the University of Kentucky?"

Austin wrinkled his brow. "Good questions. According to the Forest Service, there are over forty petroglyphs located in the Daniel Boone National Forest. There are many common themes or motifs, including turkey tracks, deer tracks, lines, and geometric designs. We've had visiting archaeologists and anthropologists try to answer this question, but their theories are all over the place. One study I find interesting suggests that the animal tracks were guideposts to important minerals or possibly silver deposits. Some say that they point to the Jonathan Swift mines. No one has yet found a silver mine based on the petroglyphs. No one who has let that be known, anyway. I think it's something that needs to be researched."

"Great," said Jennifer. "That's something I might be interested in, as well as sketching them to use as inspiration for my jewelry designs. I'm always looking for a unique vision in order to launch a new line."

Austin pointed up to the limestone steps. "Although the climb looks terrifying from this angle, it's relatively easy and your packs are light. The payoff is a spectacular cliff view as well as some archaeological artifacts in an excellent state of preservation. Let me start with a little basic demonstration."

Alfred interrupted, "We're all experienced climbers. Some better than others, but we are all at the intermediate to expert level."

"Well then," continued Austin, "who wants to go first?"

"Me, of course," said Kevin. "I always go first in our little adventures."

Miranda bit at the corner of her lip. *It looks like there are two leaders. One for travel arrangements and one as alpha male. I've seen this puppet leadership style before. It complicates everything.*

"Great," said Miranda. "I can watch then. I'm certainly *not* an expert."

Kevin put both hands into the carved-out openings and placed one foot into the lowest step. He hauled himself up about three feet. The next handhold was easy to reach so he made that one in his next move. The angle steepened and he stepped into the next foothold so quickly that he slipped and skidded down the surface about a foot.

Jennifer gasped and yelled, "Be careful. You're showing off and not paying attention."

Kevin recovered. "Don't get touchy. I'm just fooling around. I know what I'm doing." Then he raced up the staircase like a mountain goat.

Jennifer puffed a sigh of relief and patted her chest to indicate that her heart was still pounding. "You need to stop scaring us with your tricks."

Kevin turned to grin down at them. "Why? You fall for it every time. See, this is a piece of cake. You guys will be fine."

"Even so," Ranger Austin Morgan called up to him,

"caution is the best approach." Austin scanned the remaining hikers. "It means that you'll get to climb another day. Who's next?"

Alfred stepped up to face the sandstone wall. "I'll get up there so you have someone reliable to count on." He tackled the steps with deliberate precision and was soon standing on the upper level next to Kevin. "Oh, wow. The view is spectacular. This is so worth it."

"Okay, I'm ready to go next. I'm a pushover for a great view," said Stephanie. She inhaled a great calming breath and cautiously climbed the incline slowly, but with complete competence. When she straightened up, she yelled down to the others, "The climb is not as bad as it looks from down there."

Miranda turned to Austin and said in a low voice, "I think I should go up next to keep things in order up there. This group seems a little more daring than my normal type of clients."

Austin nodded and raised his eyebrows. "I agree." Apparently, he had noticed the same thing she had about the group's dynamics. They appeared to spur one another on to risky behavior.

"It feels like herding squirrels with cats," she whispered back. She shifted her heavy pack to settle it better and reached for the first set of indented handholds.

While reaching for the next recess in the sandstone at the point where the pitch was steepest, Miranda felt a sudden shift within her pack. It took her by surprise, but she automatically hitched up her shoulder to readjust the weight. Then she lost her footing. She yelped as her foot slipped out of the lower indention. She was hanging on to the cliff by one foot and one hand.

"Freeze, Miranda," yelled Ranger Morgan. "Don't

move. Hang on to the steps you already have." The force of his voice pierced her confusion and she stiffened in place.

"Now, grab a handhold and ignore your foot."

She did that and felt herself stabilize.

"Slip your foot back to where it was."

She explored the surface of the rock with her toe and found the foothold that had given her the slip. "I've got it now."

"Rest a minute until you get your bearings."

"I'm good now." Miranda refocused her attention to the remaining few handholds and climbed to the top in a tightly controlled set of cautious moves.

Kevin grabbed her hand at the top. "Are you okay? That was a little scary. You did great to recover so well. I've known seasoned climbers to freeze in place and then have to be rescued. Well done."

"Thanks." Miranda placed her pack on the ground, then plopped down beside it. Then she dropped her head between her knees gulping in air.

After Ben, Jennifer, and Kurt arrived at the top, Ranger Morgan climbed up and rushed over to Miranda. "Are you okay? Do you need a drink of water or something stronger?"

Miranda waved him away and grabbed the water bottle from her pack. "Thanks, I only need some water." She tipped back her head and downed most of the container. It was exactly the right thing for her. She hopped up and grinned. "Sorry about that. I'm a rank beginner in the sport of rock climbing. I think it may not ever be my sport of choice."

Kevin cleared his throat, "As we've mentioned, we don't need a climbing instructor. We signed up for the chance to draw this overlook in the open air." He walked over to the edge of the sandstone cliff. "This view is worth the trouble."

The group wandered over to stand next to Kevin. There was complete silence while they stared at the over-look.

The vista stretched for miles and revealed stony ridges exposed between the fading autumn beauty of scarlet maples. The breeze carried the fresh scent of the emerald-green pines.

Ranger Morgan cleared his throat. "This seems like the perfect time to give you the history of this spot." He moved so that everyone could see the view behind him. "The steps you just climbed are known as the Indian Staircase. This is the most panoramic view of the Red River Gorge geologic area. That prominent rock forma-tion in front of us is called Battleship Rock."

Ranger Morgan stepped back from the Indian Stair-case into a small clearing in front of another sandstone cliff face. "Back over this way is what is considered as convincing evidence that Native Americans inhabited this area. There's plenty of signs of their culture and lifestyle during their tenure here.

"Another view worth a look is northwest along the ridge to see the Frog's Head formation as well as another shelter called the Council Chamber."

Stephanie glanced back down over the top of the In-dian Staircase. "How are we going to get back down? It will be trickier to descend."

"Don't worry," said Miranda. "There's another trail down the other side of this cliff back here. It's not very well marked, but it's better than struggling to climb down with these loaded packs." She gave a sour glance at hers.

"We'll take that route after our sketching session. First, let's get set up for our picnic lunch. We'll do our sketching lesson afterwards."

Miranda spoke up, "Lunches are in your pack. Just find a place to sit and dig in."

Her clients spread out in a cleared area on the sandstone rock at the top of the Indian Staircase. It was a good choice.

"Austin, I packed a picnic for you if you can stay with us for a while."

"That's nice." He looked at the paper bag. "So that's why your pack was overbalanced."

Miranda frowned and looked down. "I'm so embarrassed. I should have set up a rope relay for the packs so that none of us would be overbalanced. I'll do that the next time—if there is a next time."

"Not liking this?" He lifted an eyebrow.

Miranda rubbed the back of her neck. "No. Yes. Maybe. I don't know." She scanned the area. "I feel the weight of the past here, and that feeling is even stronger near the Council Chamber."

"That's weird. I didn't think you were superstitious."

"I don't think I am." Miranda handed Austin his picnic. "Let me give my dining speech and we'll eat. There's a log over there that looks comfortable, okay?"

She walked over to the group, who had settled in a circle. "What we have here is a typical picnic that would have been popular in this area during the forties and fifties. Way before Colonel Sanders perfected his special recipe." That brought a chuckle. "Everything is locally sourced and prepared traditionally at my farmhouse. The beverage is a lemonade cocktail containing a home-brewed corn moonshine. Questions?"

"Who made the moonshine?" asked Kevin after taking a sip. "It's so smooth."

"That's my own concoction. I've resurrected my late uncle's original still equipment for small-batch brewing in the barn. My full-sized distillery is in construction. I'm hoping it will be ready for production for the Christmas holidays. That's a big season for spirits around these parts."

"This chicken is incredible," said Stephanie. "Can I have the recipe?"

Miranda scrunched her forehead. "I don't have a version I can hand out just yet. We're not really chefs around here and don't go by exact measurements. I learned how to make traditional fried chicken by watching my mother and grandmother."

"You should come up with a cookbook," said Jennifer. "I would buy one."

"That is a great idea. I'll add it to my list of items for the gift shop." Miranda paused, then smiled broadly. "Enjoy!"

She walked to the log, where Austin was halfway through with his chicken.

He mumbled around a full bite, "She's got a point." He rolled his eyes and took a swig of lemonade from the mason jar. "This is incredibly good. You sure your family didn't know Colonel Sanders?"

"Thanks." She sat down beside Austin and placed her picnic box on her lap. She didn't move.

"What's wrong? Aren't you hungry? That was a challenging hike."

"Sorry." She opened her lunch. "I'm still worried about something. I need to shake off a bad feeling." She reinforced that thought with a real shake of her head.

"Can I help?"

Miranda smiled at him. "Not yet."

In a few minutes, everyone finished and seemed happy with the meal. Miranda noted that the group were well versed in woodland manners. They each repacked the remains of their lunches back in the baskets. Miranda scanned the clearing. Not a single scrap of litter was to be found. She smiled and stood near the group.

Ranger Morgan raised his hand. "There's another artifact up here that you might like to see. It's been off-limits to the public for the last few years, but I have a key to the gate. Is anyone interested?"

A unanimous yes followed.

He walked over to the far edge of the clearing and skirted around a tree and several large boulders. An iron fence had been installed with a narrow gate a few yards in front of the opening to a shallow cave. The heavy padlock opened with a loud click, and Ranger Morgan pushed the gate open.

He pulled a small flashlight from his pocket and shone it on the walls. "This was most likely used as a weather shelter or maybe for ceremonial purposes. The local place name is the Council Chamber. Around these parts, no one can remember it being called anything else. There are some drawings here that depict figures in large groups, but it looks like they are celebrating successful hunts. The drawings are well-preserved and haven't been studied by any scientific or scholarly groups, so there has been no consensus. I keep waiting for someone to figure it out."

The group entered and several more flashlights appeared from various pockets and backpacks to light the little cavern. The walls were covered with faint images.

"These are amazing," said Kevin. "I've been up here several times, but I didn't know this."

"I definitely want to sketch these," said Jennifer in a reverent whisper.

Miranda followed up, "That's a great idea. If Ranger Morgan agrees, we could start our drawing in here and then move out to the overlook."

"Not this time." Ranger Morgan locked the gate and shook it to check its security. "I personally think that shelter was the primary purpose for this place. You could hole up here for quite some time and be just fine."

Miranda waved at everyone to hustle. "We need to get back on schedule. After our old-timey picnic we're running a bit behind. The last weather update I got before we left the Gladie Learning Center predicted wind and rain later today, but we'll be all right if we keep to the plan."

"Yeah, I saw that report, too," said Ben. "This is not where I want to be in a storm."

Ranger Morgan cleared his throat. "Well, I'm—"

Miranda interrupted, "Why don't you stay for a quick sketching lesson? You might enjoy it."

Austin smiled back at her. "I have to admit, I am curious about how you teach art up in the wilderness. I'll just watch from over here." He found a bit of wall and leaned against it with his arms folded across his chest.

Miranda turned back to her group. "The first thing and, in truth, I believe, the most important step is to get in the right place. Make sure you're comfortable, and we'll go through a few charcoal-sketching basics."

After a bit of bustle, everyone found a nice spot with a great view of Battleship Rock. They were chatting and lively mostly due to the relaxing effects of Miranda's lemonade cocktail.

Jennifer was the last one searching for a spot to take the drawing lesson.

"Come on, Jen," teased Alfred, "you're always the last one for everything."

"Keep your britches on. I want to get the best view of the petroglyphs and that beautiful red maple as well."

Kevin piped up, "Charcoal is black-and-white. You don't need to look for color."

"It inspires me," she shot back. Jennifer finally chose a large tree to lean against near the fence. It had a great view of a patch of petroglyphs.

"Let's make sure everyone has their materials. You should have a drawing pad, three charcoal pencils, a stick of white chalk, a blending stump, and a gray kneading eraser. Everyone good?"

"I don't think I have a blending stump, whatever that is," said Ben.

Miranda started to move toward her backpack for her backup supplies. She had at least two extras of each item she provided to her clients.

"Oh, wait. This must be it. Never mind." Ben held the three-inch stick of tightly rolled-up felted paper with two pointed ends up high and laughed it off. "My vision isn't great in the dark innards of my backpack."

"No problem. Anyone else missing anything? . . . No? Good. Let's begin."

The group caught on quickly after Miranda's demonstration of the basics of using the hard, medium, and soft charcoal pencils to outline, fill-in, and smudge shapes. Using special charcoal paper helped the beginners get a jump start with their sketches.

"Wow, these are fantastic. You guys catch on really quick." Miranda walked among the group giving pointers and praise. "Don't overwork an image. Tear off the sheet and begin another when you feel it's not quite done. You want to make sure your time out here is focused on the view and your emotional reaction to the setting."

Austin stood away from the cavern wall. "I need to get on back. Thanks for letting me watch. Y'all have a great time and be safe on your trek back down. Make sure you check back in with the nice folks at the Gladie Learning Center. This isn't a trail for beginners, and they keep track of everyone."

He waved farewell and headed toward the trail.

"Just a few more seconds, please. Miranda, is this right?" Jennifer called out to Miranda. "I'm not sure about this. My drawing is getting too dark and I don't know how to fix it."

Miranda looked at Jennifer's sketch of the distinctive petroglyphs. "You're right. It looks like you've just gotten a little enthusiastic with the soft pencil. Use the piece of white chalk to make some touches of contrast." Miranda tilted her head sideways. "I love the bleak tone. If that's what you're going for, you nailed it."

Jennifer grinned. "Thanks. *Bleak* is just the right word for how I feel about this place."

"Why is that?"

"Nothing, I'm getting a bit stiff sitting here. Leaning against this tree isn't as comfortable as I thought it would be." Jennifer struggled to get up and Miranda offered her a hand.

As soon as she grabbed on, Miranda pulled, but Jennifer's heel skidded on some leaves and they both fell onto the base of the tree.

"Ouch!" Jennifer yelped, loud enough for everyone to turn in their direction. "That hurt!" She scrambled up and looked at her hand. Blood was oozing from a dull scrape across her palm. "I'm bleeding!"

"Let me see." Miranda looked at the wound. "Hold on to your wrist as tight as you can. I've got a first aid kit to patch that up for you." She looked down, wondering how Jennifer could have gotten injured.

Poking up from the leaf litter was a sharp, brown stick-like object.

A shudder ran down Miranda's spine. That was not a stick. She picked up a nearby branch and poked at the leaves until more of the foreign forms were exposed. She felt a sick tingle in her teeth. The forms were not wooden sticks. One last scrape revealed a jawbone and a skull. They were human bones.

Chapter 3

Sunday Morning, Battleship Rock

Jennifer screamed so loud and so long, Miranda thought her ears might start to bleed. It was only the one scream, but the terrain spread the sound. An eerie echo played along the cliffs like shrill notes on a violin.

Everyone rushed over.

"What's wrong?" Alfred looked down at the bit of skull with an exposed fragment of jaw. "Is that an animal?" He turned to the rest of the group for what sounded like reassurance. "It's got to be a bear, right?"

Kevin peered at the exposed fragment. "Not with a jaw like that."

"That looks human." Kurt grabbed the long stick from Miranda and flicked even more of the debris away, exposing the full jaw and more of the skull. "It's human. I'm sure of that, but these bones have been here a long time."

"How long?" asked Kevin.

"Long enough to be discolored by the soil." Kurt shrugged. "I don't remember my forensics-class particulars, but definitely more than a few months—maybe years."

Jennifer began to shake. "Years?"

Miranda put her arm around Jennifer, who responded by going still and silent. "So, it's possible that this could be ancient?"

Kurt shrugged again.

"We need to call the authorities." Ranger Morgan appeared on Miranda's other side.

"Oh, I'm so glad you're here," she whispered.

His face was pale, but his expression firm. "I'll see if I can reach Sheriff Larson."

"Thanks." Still holding on to Jennifer, Miranda said, "Everyone, if you could return to the sketching site, that would be helpful. We need to stay out of the way." She looked at Kurt. "Take Jennifer with you. She needs some water; or perhaps some lemonade out of my pack. Oh, and maybe a blanket."

"I know that. Remember, I'm a qualified surgeon."

"Right, sorry."

Kurt took Jennifer by the arm. She quietly let herself be led away.

Miranda turned back to Austin, who was putting his cell phone away. "Any luck?"

"Yep. Oddly, cell signal is great up here—one of those freakish signal bounces. We must be within the line of sight with one of the newer towers. Sheriff Larson says he and the coroner are on the way."

"Good." Miranda half smiled. "We can drop this in his lap and not think about it."

After everyone had reassembled at the overlook, Miranda stayed behind. "Austin, this feels surreal." She looked at her watch. "It will be at least another thirty minutes before the sheriff and coroner get up here. I'm going to continue the lesson. I mean, since the remains are old, it's better to keep everyone focused on something other than this scary pile of bones."

"I think that's a good idea, especially if you can keep everyone calm. I'll stay here by the tree to discourage any more disturbance. Although over the years, that has already occurred."

Miranda lifted her eyebrows. "Do you know who it might be?"

"I've got a hunch, but I'm not saying."

"I'm not saying either." She sighed. Although it was a struggle, she led the group through several more sketches of the view. It was better than staring at death.

Chapter 4

Sunday Morning, Battleship Rock

Wolfe County sheriff Richard Larson appeared at the top of the Indian Staircase red of face and huffing like a blacksmith's bellows. Dr. Felicia Larson, the Wolfe County coroner and also his wife, followed him, not even breathing fast in spite of the large backpack she carried.

"You need to start working out, Richard. This is embarrassing."

He stood at the top, bent over, with one hand grabbing his side. It was a couple of seconds before he could reply. "I rarely find the need"—he gasped—"to climb a mountain in the"—he coughed—"regular course of my job."

"Since when have we ever had a normal day with our jobs?"

"Point taken." His panting eventually eased and his blotchy skin cleared back to his normal tanned features. "There's Austin."

"It looks like he's standing guard for me," said Felicia. "Aww. Good man."

They walked over to the tree. Sheriff Larson and Coroner Larson shook hands with Ranger Morgan.

The sheriff coughed again. "That's quite a climb. These folks have done this for one of Miranda's art classes? Really?"

Ranger Morgan nodded. "Yes, sir. Crazy, isn't it?"

The sheriff splayed his hands out.

Felicia sat her backpack down on a bare bit of sandstone. "You need to catch up with the times, Richard. This new style of touring is making a big difference in our part of the Appalachians. I think it's a wonderful idea as an adventure tour. Did she bring some of her grandmother's fabulous country-fried chicken?"

Ranger Morgan sighed. "Oh, yes. It's as good as I remember when I was a little kid." His family's farmhouse was right down the road from Miranda's. Their families had known each other for generations. "She's got the recipe down perfect."

Miranda waved at her clients to signal them to stay put, then she joined the officials. "You got here quick." She looked over at Felicia. "They're human, aren't they?"

"Yes, they're definitely human. The jawbone gives it away. You were right to keep everyone over on the other side of the clearing. Give me a few minutes to document the site as I found it, and then I'll see if I can identify this poor soul." Felicia pulled out her digital camera. "The discoloration can happen quickly in this kind of soil. These remains might not be that old." She took pictures of the entire site from the exposed skull down to where the leg bones should be.

Miranda, Sheriff Larson, and Ranger Morgan stood in a small circle unconsciously blocking the view of the bones from the adventure group. They looked at one another, then Miranda coughed and spoke in a kind voice. "A visual barrier is a bit late, don't you think? Everyone up here has seen the bones."

Sheriff Larson and Ranger Morgan both lifted their eyebrows.

"Habits," said Sheriff Larson. "They're like muscle memory and step in when you're not thinking."

Felicia put the camera down, then pulled on a pair of black latex gloves. Gently, she removed the forest debris around the middle section of the skeleton. "That's odd. There should be a billfold, or backpack, or at least a day pack right around here. No one with any sense would come up here without supplies of some sort." She craned her head back to look at her husband.

"Don't look at me like that. I like to travel light. We're only going to be up here for a short time. Besides, you've got enough gear in that pack to supply a marching army."

"That's not the point. For any hiker on this trail, I would expect a day pack of some sort. His day pack would have emergency supplies. He would most likely be prepared to spend the night in the mountains." She returned to the overgrowth and teased out a few more clumps of matted grass. After a few minutes, she sat back on her heels. "I don't get it. There are remnants of the jeans, underwear, socks, boots, and a flannel shirt, but no backpack or wallet. That's not right."

"Do you know if it's a man or woman?" Miranda's voice sounded a little louder than she intended.

"From the shape of the pelvis, I'm reasonably confident these are the remains of a male. These have been here anywhere from five to ten years. It's difficult to tell since this is a high-mountain microclimate up here on this overlook. It means that the aging profile will be slower than typical." She rose from the bone site and looked at her husband. "I'm going to need some high-powered expertise to nail this down. Actually, this is the perfect job for my friend Barbara."

"Your friend Barbara, as in the let's-stay-out-late-drinking-wine Barbara?"

Felicia smiled and nodded yes.

"Who's that?" asked Miranda. "How can she help?"

Felicia crossed her arms across her chest. "My friend is Dr. Barbara DuPont, forensic anthropologist and tenured professor at the University of Kentucky, in Lexington." Felicia reached into her backpack and pulled out her cell. "I'm calling her up here to help me with this identification. Not only is she an internationally renowned expert, but she would kill me if I didn't bring her in on this."

Sheriff Larson groaned. "Do you really need to do that? You know the state of our department's budget. She's expensive."

"Richard, you need to get serious about this. I know it's late in the fiscal year, but here we are with a complicated situation. Do you want to identify these remains? The fact that we haven't got a billfold, backpack, or gear with the bones tells me this isn't an ordinary situation. I don't have enough experience with bones that have been exposed to the elements. She does. I'm calling her." Felicia looked at her phone. "Wow, I've got a signal. You were right. This is an unusual spot." She stepped away a few yards to make the call.

Miranda turned to Sheriff Larson. "Lexington is about

an hour away, and then there's the thirty-minute hike up here. Basically, you're talking about at least two hours before Dr. DuPont can begin her examination. Do you need to keep my clients up here?"

"I don't think they have to stay, but I will need their local contact information just in case there are any clarifications."

"I've got all that from their application forms. I'll email them to your office." Miranda returned to the group and they began packing up. She handed the van keys to Kevin and watched while they took the easier trail back to the Gladie Learning Center. She returned to stand next to Ranger Morgan.

He frowned. "You're not going back with them?"

"No, I'm going to hang around for a little bit, if you don't mind." Miranda sounded as if she was trying to convince herself as well as Sheriff Larson. "I'm the one that found the bones. Dr. DuPont might have some questions about how that happened."

Sheriff Larson quirked an eyebrow. "Don't let your curiosity get out of hand. You two don't have to stay up here."

Ranger Morgan stood a bit taller. "This discovery is officially in my jurisdiction. I'm required to oversee everything and submit reports to headquarters. If you feel strongly that I shouldn't perform my duties, I'll give you my supervisor's number. Besides, if we need to remove these remains, you're going to need all the help you can get."

Sheriff Larson rubbed a hand across his chin. "Yeah. With two forensic experts on-site, they may want to take everything within ten feet of the remains." He turned to

Miranda. "You, however, can go on back. There's no need for you to stay."

"I want to stay." Miranda's voice cracked. She cleared her throat and then stood up straight and tall as she spoke. "I may have the best reason to stay."

"Why?" asked Ranger Morgan. "What do you mean?"

"The bones could belong to Howard Cable. He left early one morning for a hike in these hills exactly five years ago. He never returned."

Sheriff Larson and Ranger Morgan exchanged a glance.

"I remember that search and rescue effort very well. But why would you need to stay?" asked Sheriff Larson.

"I want to represent the interests of the family." She stared at the remains. "Howard was the only son of my mom's sister, Aunt Ora. He's my first cousin."

Chapter 5

Ranger Morgan climbed down the Indian Staircase backward. Dr. DuPont had texted Felicia that she would be there in about ten more minutes and would need help with her gear.

After Ranger Morgan had tied it to a sturdy rope, Sheriff Larson pulled up a black forensic-investigation case. They repeated the process for a backpack. Preceded by some serious on-the-spot rock climbing training, a sturdy woman with a bright shock of close-cropped purple hair arrived followed by a perspiring Ranger Austin. Sheriff Larson carried the equipment a handy distance from the remains and set it down.

"Thanks, that's considerate." Dr. DuPont looked at the view to Battleship Rock. "This is the first time I've been up here."

"Barbara!" shouted Felicia, and gave her friend a giant hug.

"Hi, Felicia. Sorry it took so long. I would have been here sooner if traffic wasn't such a disaster in Lexington."

"Why is that?" asked Miranda. "It's Sunday!"

"Today's the Bourbon Chase, that two-hundred-mile running relay that ties up the highways—it has checkpoints at five distilleries." Dr. DuPont stuck out her hand. "Hi. I'm Barbara. I don't think we've met."

"No, we haven't. I'm Miranda Trent. I discovered the bones."

Barbara grimaced, "Oh, I'm so sorry. That can be upsetting. Where are they?"

Miranda pointed to the tree.

Lifting her field case and backpack, Barbara made her way over to the site of the skeleton and stood for a moment. She stepped about six feet away and put her gear down. "You were right to call me, Felicia. This is definitely my specialty." Barbara looked up and pointed to a log about ten feet away. "You guys get comfortable over there. I don't want any more contamination than has already occurred."

Sheriff Larson smiled politely and led Felicia, Austin, and Miranda over to sit on the log. "Anybody got some water?" Sheriff Larson asked.

"You didn't bring any?" Felicia sounded exasperated and also tolerant. "Of course not. I did."

Miranda frowned. She thought it must be complicated to have a two-career law-enforcement marriage. Definitely something to think about if she continued to be involved with Austin.

Felicia dived into her pack and pulled out a Yeti thermos. The tinging of ice cubes inside the container echoed across the clearing. "You would forget your head if it wasn't attached."

She handed her husband the container and he took a long draft. "Thanks." She turned and raised her eyebrows at Miranda and Austin. They both shook their heads no.

Barbara had pulled on a white coverall and blue bootees and donned latex gloves. She was hovering over the leaf litter and carefully removing debris with a trowel. It looked like her favorite tool. The handle was worn and discolored and the point had been chipped. Her power of concentration was evident in her intense focus as she examined the bones. Miranda was convinced that an elephant could have walked by and Barbara wouldn't have noticed.

Felicia stared at her friend with increasing concern. "She's taking a long time." She turned to her husband. "Why do you think she's taking such a long time?"

"Honey, I have no clue. This is your bailiwick—not mine."

Finally, Barbara stood, pulled off her gloves, bootees, and coveralls, bundled them into a bag and stuffed the bag into her case. She walked over to the little group.

"So far, I've confirmed that these are the remains of a male about twenty-five years old. There is no identification. There is evidence of unusual injuries to the hands and legs."

Sheriff Larson interrupted, "No identification? At all?"

"That's right. No identification and no sign of a backpack or any gear at all." She paused for a moment. "I want the remains and the surrounding soil taken to my lab for a complete examination. We're gonna need a helicopter to remove it."

"What?" Sheriff Larson's voice rose to the level of a hawk screeching. "We can't afford that."

"Calm down, Richard." Felicia patted her husband on the arm. "The interest in this is going to be much wider than just Wolfe County. The state will have to cover this. Most search and rescue teams operate on volunteer staffs and sponsor donations. Stop worrying about your budget."

Sheriff Larson took a deep breath. "I have good reason to worry. Our new state comptroller has determined that the eastern mountain counties don't need separate funds. He's pooled all the money into one giant pot. I'll have to request and receive approval for every exceptional expense."

"Ouch. That's a shortsighted change." Felicia pressed her lips together. "You'd better start filing requests. This is going to be a complicated case."

Austin pulled out his phone. "I'll call down to the rescue center for their helicopter." He looked up at the sky. "The wind is picking up, but they can be here in a few minutes." He held his phone out front and walked nearer to the edge of the clearing to get the best signal.

"The weather report was for rain this evening, but it could be coming in early." Miranda looked at the site of the bones. "Do you think we should get everything ready now—just in case the helicopter gets here quickly?"

"Good thinking." Barbara dived into her case and pulled out a body bag compressed into a square the size of a package of printer paper. "Felicia, can you help me? Sorry, Miranda. Only officials should be involved. Lawyers and courts being what they are."

Felicia and Barbara spent a good half hour preparing the remains. The wind continued to rise and was playing havoc with the loose debris. With all the soil that Barbara wanted to accompany the bones, it must have weighed several times more than an injured hiker.

Unconsciously everyone surrounded the body bag like pallbearers.

Austin's phone rang. Noting the origin, he put it on speaker. "Hello, Fred. What's the situation?"

Everyone was all ears.

"We can't get up there. In fact, you can't come down at this point. A ripsnorter of a storm is going to hit you guys in about ten minutes. It's big and powerful. Shelter up in that cavern up there. We'll be in touch the first thing in the morning to get the remains."

Austin ended the call. "Did you hear that?"

Silence.

"We have to stay up here all night?" Sheriff Larson said. "We can't do that."

Miranda pointed to her backpack. "Of course, we can. There's a perfectly dry cavern over there, and I have a two-person emergency tent. What do you have Felicia?"

Looking pleased with herself, she said, "I have a three-person emergency tent that I have been dragging around in my pack for years. Not luxurious, of course, but we can manage for the night."

"The first priority is to get dry wood before the storm hits," said Austin. "Everyone spread out and get all sizes. We'll need to keep a fire going all night."

The wind began picking up, and the group moved themselves into the cavern with plenty of firewood. Austin stacked it into the back of the cavern, then started a small fire in a spot that seemed to be perfect.

"This is mostly likely exactly where the Native Americans built their cooking fire. See how the smoke goes up through a few crevasses in the ceiling?"

Sheriff Larson was wearing a frown. "This is not going to be fun."

"Stop being so gloomy," said Felicia.

A bright flash of lighting signaled the start of a noisy downpour. The group stood at the entrance to the cavern and gave up all hope of leaving before morning.

Miranda pulled her pack next to Felicia's. "We'd better take an inventory of what we have to eat. I've got some leftover picnic supplies, a water bottle, and a pint of my lemonade moonshine cocktail. Let's pile everything onto this napkin."

Ranger Morgan pulled two protein bars from his side pockets. He followed that with a tin of mints from his top pocket. Looking at the others, he said, "I talk to the public a lot."

Barbara dug into her enormous purse and pulled out two instant oatmeal packets, a moon pie, a large chocolate bar, and a bag of chips. She sat them down on the napkin.

"Anyone else?"

Sheriff Larson spread his empty hands. "I got nothing."

"You dolt," said Felicia, who pulled out two emergency rations packets from her backpack, a large bag of nuts and raisins, a large bar of chocolate identical to Barbara's, and a bottle of water.

"I had the students leave their lunch baskets. I had a feeling we might be stuck up here for a few hours. I didn't think it would be overnight. We brought a lot of food and

I don't think we can be fussy about leftovers. Let's see what we have."

The picnic baskets contributed only three pieces of partially eaten chicken, five servings of green beans, three servings of the mustard potato salad, two hunks of corn bread, and a lot of pickled cabbage.

Miranda started sorting the food into five piles. "Let's leave the oatmeal and nuts for breakfast. I think we should eat everything else and clean up so that we don't attract critters. It's going to be hard enough to get any sleep without the sound of little scavengers searching for scraps."

Miranda edged closer to Barbara. "Do you know how long the body has been here?"

"Let's say"—she looked up at the sky—"for estimation purposes—you know, to help y'all search through the missing persons databases—somewheres between three and ten years. Why do you want to know?"

Miranda looked at Felicia, then back at Barbara. "My cousin Howard Cable went missing five years ago today."

Chapter 6

Sunday Evening, Battleship Rock

It was a miserable night. They set up both tents with the openings facing the fire for what little reflected warmth it could provide. Everyone agreed to a rotating one-hour shift for tending to the fire.

Miranda, Felicia, and Barbara took the larger tent and the men took the smaller, but getting any sleep was hopeless. It was damp. The ground was hard and smelled like soured modeling clay. The flashes of lightning found their way through tightly closed eyes. The howling winds and the creaking pine tree sounds of the woods fighting the storm kept them on edge. No one could settle, so the sound of rustling bodies was continuous.

Felicia cleared her throat, then whispered, "I have a question for you, Miranda. It's been tickling my mind since you demanded to stay up here. Why are you so sure these bones belong to your cousin?"

Miranda kept her voice low, too. "That's a good question." She paused again for several minutes.

Barbara started to speak but Felicia shouldered her quiet.

"I think," began Miranda, "I think it's a clear memory for me because it was a time of big decisions. I was thinking about how I didn't really fit in up in Dayton. My Appalachian landscape paintings had a small following, but not enough to support even my modest needs. My few artist friends had gone to either Asheville, Santa Fe, or had dropped out altogether and were bartending in the Oregon district near downtown. So—"

"Why bartending?" Barbara interrupted.

"Did you know that you can make more than a thousand dollars on a Friday or Saturday night in as little as six hours?"

"Wow."

"I would have to sell four or five paintings all at once to do that well. Oh, and I spend about forty hours on each one." Miranda's voice sounded wistful, not bitter. "Anyway, I was planning to go big and move to New York City. One of my art buddies was already living up there and she was getting some recognition, so I decided to go."

Felicia shifted in a fruitless effort to get more comfortable. "You haven't answered my question. Why do you think this is Howard?"

"He called me the week before he disappeared."

"Why?"

"My mom and his mom were discussing my situation, and he said he felt drawn to give me some advice."

"What about?"

"He said that he understood how I was feeling about risking everything for a dream. He felt the same when he went to college. He said he was on the brink of another life-changing adventure, but he couldn't share it with me right now. He gave me the confidence to move to New York City. Otherwise, I don't think I would have done it. His encouragement was the tipping point." Miranda paused and lowered her voice. "But he would never leave without letting his mother know."

By the end of the second hour, the men had migrated over into the larger tent. That raised the temperature inside from painfully frigid up to merely bitter cold.

Barbara complained in detail about each discomfort in a running stream of scientific detail. At first, Miranda appeased her by placing her in the coveted spot closest to the fire, giving her a drawing tablet to sit on. Then Miranda even handed over the extra pair of socks she was wearing. She gave up after realizing that nothing stemmed the relentless whining.

It was going to be a long night.

Risking frostbite, but getting relief from Barbara's endless barrage of unpleasantness, Miranda stepped out of the tent and phoned her closest neighbors, Roy and Elsie Kash. She explained the situation and asked them to run over to her farmhouse to feed Sandy. As she expected, they said they would take him in until she got home. Sandy adored Elsie, who was so softhearted that a sad puppy face would be rewarded with a treat—many treats.

Ranger Morgan kept a check-in text chain going with the rescue crew every thirty minutes. Each time they texted, he touched his phone and it would light up the tent and he would step outside to have a few words with the mountain rescue organization. The contact calls stopped when the signal suddenly dropped to zero. "I think the tower is down. It might have been struck by lightning. They know we're up here and waiting for them to take the remains down off the mountain. We just have to wait."

The storm claimed all their attention as it grew in strength and intensity. The lightning flashed across the sky lighting the cave and the faces of the stranded. The tent surrounded them like a mother protecting a frightened child.

At dawn, everyone was huddled in a drowsy pile and the fire had burned down to a few glowing embers. Ranger Morgan carefully untangled himself from the heap and quietly rebuilt the fire. He left the cavern and stood by the gate to assess the weather.

He smiled and turned back to the group. "Hey, guys, the storm has passed and everything's gorgeous. You can tell it was really bad last night from the looks of things up here. Branches have fallen and are hanging from everywhere. Give me a chance to check for widow-makers before we start moving around."

Miranda crawled out of the tent, stood up, and stretched her aching muscles. "Wait. What's a widow-maker? I've never heard that one before."

"Good morning," said Austin. "You have no right to look as if you spent the night at a five-star resort."

Miranda felt a flush bloom in her cheeks. She covered her face with one hand then said softly, "Thank you."

He cleared his throat. "A widow-maker is a large branch that is precariously positioned to drop with the next puff of wind. Like that one." He pointed to a six-foot branch snagged by a twig on a bobbling tree branch. "I'm gonna fix it right now." Austin grabbed the branch and tugged with his body weight. It crashed with a resounding thump. "That could have killed someone."

After rubbing her hands together to warm them up, Miranda pulled out her phone. "Still no signal. We have no idea if they're coming for us. No signal could mean damage to the helicopter."

"They'll be here," said Sheriff Larson. "They have the resources to reach out to other volunteer organizations throughout the state. Don't worry. A stranded group of state officers is a priority matter."

Felicia got up and out of the tent, stretched herself tall, and groaned. "I used to be able to sleep on the ground without even dreaming. Boy, those days are gone." She turned to Sheriff Larson. "Look at that." She pointed to the bank of thick clouds that loomed over the cliff in cotton-like silence. "That's where the rescue should be coming from. We're fogged in and I'll bet the helicopter is grounded. It's that time of year."

"I know," Austin grumped. "I was hoping for a clear day."

"There's no chance of that," said Miranda.

"I agree," said Barbara, crawling out of the tent on all fours. "I want some coffee and I want to go to my lab. I desperately crave a completely boring day." Barbara stood beside Ranger Morgan with her hands on her hips. "I'm certainly glad I prepared the body so well last night. I'll check to make sure it's still safe."

"Hang on a second." Felicia popped up as fresh and bright as a Girl Scout—not as if she'd slept rough on a cold, hard cavern floor. "I'll go with you."

Miranda stretched and rubbed her knuckles into her eyes. "I kept having nightmares about the bones forming an articulated skeleton and chasing me along the cliff edge." She shivered, then put her hands out toward the open fire. "That feels really good. How about I rustle up some sort of breakfast?"

"Breakfast?" Sheriff Larson was all ears. "Do we have anything?"

"A little." Miranda opened the oatmeal packets and put them in one of her mason jars. Then she used the last of the water to make a thin mixture. She sat it onto a rock next to the fire. While it was heating, she passed around the package of trail mix.

Barbara stood stamping her feet and slapping her arms to try to get blood circulating. "I'd kill for a cup of coffee."

Miranda put a bit of the oatmeal gruel in the mason jars and handed them around. "Drink up. It's not coffee but I've saved back an extra pone of corn bread from last night. It's not a lot, but better than nothing. We'll be off this mountain one way or another this morning."

There was no chance that a single morsel of food would be left. Miranda had to admit that her appetite was always better in the outdoors. In fact, she would describe herself as ravenous. That's why she'd packed the extra corn bread.

"Hey," shouted Sheriff Larson. "I've got a signal!"

"So do I." Ranger Morgan quickly dialed the rescue organization. "How's the fog down there?" He walked over to the view of Battleship Rock. "It's beginning to thin out up here as well."

He exchanged a few more comments with the dispatcher and ended the call.

"Good news. The helicopter should be up here in

about thirty minutes. That should give us plenty of time to pack up and make sure the remains are ready for transport."

Miranda grinned. "Wonderful. I wasn't looking forward to the climb down until I wasn't able to climb down. I'll get everything out of the cavern so we can start down the trail as soon as the helicopter takes down the body." She took a few moments to call her neighbors. She confirmed that they had taken Sandy in for the night and were spoiling him rotten.

Barbara took her backpack and forensics case and placed them beside the remains. "I'll be going in the helicopter. I never want to step a foot into these woods ever again."

Given Barbara's complete lack of tolerance for any physical discomfort, Miranda thought that was a fine idea.

The sound of the helicopter reached them long before they could see it approaching from down the cliffside. It rose high above the overlook and hovered for many long minutes before landing neatly on the bald sandstone patch just above the Indian Staircase. The prop wash was impressive, and everyone shut their eyes to avoid the flying sand and dirt. The silence returned with a vengeance as soon as the helicopter shut down its rotor.

Barbara grabbed her gear and walked beside the two rescue volunteers as they strapped the body bag into the litter on the side of the helicopter. It was the first time she wasn't harping. She turned back to Felicia and resumed her professional demeanor as smoothly as she hefted her backpack. "I'll call you with my preliminary findings later this afternoon." Then she got into the helicopter.

The pilots ran through their checks, then started up the

engine, and in a few moments the forest was back to normal. Perhaps a bit more silent as the helicopter disturbance repressed both birds and insect activity.

Looking around to make sure they left the area pristine, the four started down the trail back to the Gladie Learning Center. Sheriff Larson and Coroner Felicia walked ahead discussing a topic that appeared to be an ongoing domestic argument. Austin and Miranda let some distance grow between them.

"Can you give me a ride to Hemlock Lodge? I let my group take my van," asked Miranda.

"Sure. I need to check in there anyway."

"At least I don't have clients today," Miranda told Austin. "I would have had to cancel. I'm exhausted, but when I get home, Sandy will want to run and then play fetch. If I exhaust him, that will be the only way I get a nap. What about you?"

Austin smiled. "One of the advantages of being a ranger is that I get a flexible schedule. Unfortunately, it mostly consists of being on standby twenty-four seven. But, I'm for sure taking the rest of the day off."

The four of them reached the Gladie Learning Center in good time. Before the sheriff and Felicia got in their car, Miranda stopped them. "I know you don't have an identification yet, but if you find out that the remains are my cousin, can you please give me a call? The two of us weren't particularly close, but Aunt Ora has been holding on to her belief that he would return. She will be devastated and I want to be there for her."

"Of course, Miranda," said Felicia. "I'll call as soon as I know anything."

"Thanks."

They turned to leave but Miranda continued, "I have a strong feeling that we've found Howard. I also know it's impossible that my cousin's death was an accident. Howard was an expert woodsman. If this were a case of becoming ill or experiencing an injury, or even the result of a prank, he would have called for help. The missing backpack and identification can't be explained. This has to be foul play."

Chapter 7

The phone started ringing as soon as Miranda stepped into her farmhouse. It was Austin's sister, Tyler, who worked as a crime reporter for the *Lexington Herald-Leader*.

"Hey, I heard that you found bones up at the Indian Staircase cliff. Austin told me, in case you're wondering. I have a weekly call with him every Monday. He spilled the beans, but don't get mad at him. I'm like a terrier when I smell a story. Is it true?"

"One of my clients fell onto the remains while we were sketching the view on our tour. Her name is Jennifer O'Rourke. I uncovered the bones and discovered that they were human."

"Where's she staying?"

Miranda fell silent. She knew that Jennifer's name

would be in the sheriff's report, but maybe where she was staying should remain private.

Tyler broke the silence. "Come on, where is she staying? You know I can call around and find out. Remember, I'm from that area and that people there have known me since I was a baby."

"Perfect." Miranda could hear the tapping on a keyboard at high speed. "You'll have to use your resources, then. I'm protecting my clients."

"Got it." Tyler hung up.

Miranda had never been so delighted to take a long hot shower. It felt wonderful to remove the forest grit. Before this indulgence, she had taken Sandy for a long run and then fed him. She followed her shower with her favorite comfort food, an onion-and-cheese omelet using fresh eggs from her hens. Hunger normally won over cleanliness. But standing in the stream of hot water felt like her just reward for persevering on the mountaintop.

The shower was part of a modern add-on to her late uncle's farmhouse. She had been surprised to inherit it after his death a few months ago. It certainly provided her with an excellent excuse to leave New York City without confronting how she hadn't made much more than a piddling amount of money with her landscape paintings. It still seemed like a gift from the heavens to have this farmhouse and the chance to share her love of the sandstone cliffs and arches with visitors.

After washing the dishes and tidying up in her bedroom at the front of the house, she dialed the receptionist at Hemlock Lodge. Doris Ann Norris was her primary source of information about what was happening with her clients. Everyone knew her and she was lovely to chat with—full of humor and an accumulation of folk wisdom not seen much nowadays.

Given that her clients had returned without her and that she and others had been on the mountaintop overnight, Miranda was sure the news about the bones had spread to the lodge and its best source of information. Before calling Aunt Ora about her suspicions, Miranda wanted to know how much information was circulating.

"Hemlock Lodge reception. This is Doris Ann. How can I help you?"

"Hi, Doris Ann, this is Miranda. Have you heard about my overnight adventure up at the Indian Staircase overlook?"

"Oh, my, yes. It's all over the place. Why, those young whippersnappers you took up the mountain yesterday have been holding court in front of the fireplace in the lobby. I swear, they're telling everyone that passes about finding those bones. Humph! Acting like celebrities."

"It was a shocking experience. One of my clients fell into the bones, and it still makes my teeth tingle to think about it." Miranda shuddered from head to toe. "Have any of them checked out yet?"

"Yes, they're all gone, but I heard tell they rented a private cabin for the rest of the week." Doris Ann tilted her head to the side. "Why?"

"I have a feeling that Sheriff Larson will be needing to speak to them, but he didn't seem interested."

"Well, he probably has his reasons. He is our most popular sheriff in decades for very good reasons. He's honest, careful about spending our tax money, and he gets the job done without creating a political ruckus."

"He seemed a little stressed-out up on the Indian Staircase. Wasn't there was a political ruckus last month?"

"Hmmm." Doris Ann put a hand to her chest. "Oh, I forgot about that. Those idiots in Frankfort must have been sippin' corn likker. They decided that a pay cut would help the sheriff watch his budget closer. What utter nonsense, but that's politicians for you. No horse sense at all."

"Which cabin have they rented?"

"That huge one called Big Rock Cabin."

"I know the one. Thanks, Doris Ann. Give me a call if anything unusual comes up. Okay?"

"Sure, sweetie. See you tomorrow."

Tomorrow? That woke Miranda up. She needed to get things prepared for her next tour tomorrow. Everything was still in a great jumble tossed in the back of the van. She was relieved to prepare for an ordinary Paint & Shine cultural tour. She looked forward to packing up her back-packs with painting supplies, canvases, three brushes, a water cup, and a sketching pencil. Then after arriving at the view to Lover's Leap along the main trail behind Hemlock Lodge, they would paint. Afterward, she would bring them back to the farmhouse for a traditional South-ern meal paired with moonshine. Although her business was only a month old, it was comforting to have a rou-tine.

While she was toweling her hair, the house phone rang.

"Oh, honey. I just heard the news that a body was found up at the Indian Staircase. It's Howard, isn't it?"

"Hi, Mom. I didn't know that the news had gotten out. Austin's sister called me a bit ago. She's at the *Lexington Herald-Leader*."

"Yes, I get both the real-paper and online notifications. It says you spent the night up on the Indian Staircase bluff. What on earth were you thinking? You could have caught pneumonia. What happened to the good sense I taught you?"

"Mom, calm down. I was perfectly safe. For heaven's sake, I was up there with a forest ranger, the sheriff, his wife the coroner, and a forensic anthropologist. I was as safe as a baby in its crib."

"But sleeping out in a storm. You could have gotten hypothermia or bit by a snake or eaten by a bear or—"

"Mom, stop it. You know I'm a seasoned hiker. We took shelter in the cavern at the top of the Indian Staircase. It was dry and we built a fire to stay warm. We had enough food from my event leftovers. We even had two tents. I was fine."

"Have you spoken to Aunt Ora yet?"

"Not yet. They haven't confirmed the identity of the remains. Coroner Felicia has promised I could be with Aunt Ora when they're sure the body is Howard."

Miranda tucked the phone in her shoulder and lifted Sandy into her arms. She walked out the front door into the yard and let him loose for a bathroom break.

"I think I need to be there as well. My sister is going to need all her family around her. In fact, I'm coming down now. She was a big help to me when your dad died. I started packing right after I heard the news. I'm on my way. See you in about an hour."

"Now? But—"

"Yes, now. Love you, honey."

Miranda heard the dial tone. She called Sandy back into the house, replaced the handset into the base and looked down at Sandy, at her feet, looking up and wagging his tail. "Your grandma is coming to visit. We have an hour to get the attic bedroom ready. One hour."

She gathered up her cleaning supplies and went into the dining room to climb the stairs into the attic. It was divided into two rooms. The first one, over the kitchen, was a storage area, and she hadn't had the heart to sort things out. There were trunks, suitcases, boxes, and crates of all types ready for her attention. They were the remains of her family's accumulated trash and treasures. She shuddered at the amount of sorting that needed to be done.

The other room was directly over the living room, and the fireplace flue ran up through here to provide a bit of heat in the winter. She didn't expect that her mother would visit often during the colder months. A large window looked out over the road and had a wide view of the valley across from the farmhouse. Her great-grandfather's ornate iron bed stood against the wall with a bare, worn mattress.

Against the other walls stood a dresser with a large mirror, a wardrobe, and a chest of drawers that had seen better days. Luckily, Miranda had just washed all the bedding and stored it away anticipating a visit from her mother in a few weeks.

She swept and mopped the rough wooden floor. One day she'd have someone sand the floorboards and put down a coat of varnish. The worn wide boards would look wonderful. At the moment, all her money would be spent on building the new distillery in the barn.

Miranda made up the bed, made sure the wardrobe had hangers, and put a vase of wildflowers on the low table in front of the window along with a candle and matches. Power outages were frequent. She folded a quilt for the foot of the bed and, finally, stacked a few books on the bedside table along with a bottle of water.

Satisfied with the coziness of her mother's bedroom,

Miranda gave the rest of the farmhouse a quick cleaning. By then, she and Sandy were more than ready for a relaxing walk along the creek at the back of her property.

On their return, she stopped to inspect the work that was being done in the barn for her new distillery. The inspiration for this massive project originated with Uncle Gene's reputation for distilling the best corn moonshine in eastern Kentucky. His secreted money stash had given her the finances to make this happen. She was determined to re-create his recipes and distribute the product as widely as possible.

The house phone was ringing when they returned. She snatched it up before it rolled over to voice mail. "Hello."

"Hi there, is this Miranda Trent?"

"Yes, sir. How can I help you?"

"Well, Miss Trent, I'm driving for a company called Acme Distillery Equipment over in Louisville. We're trying to deliver a fermenter to you, but our navigation software doesn't recognize the address. Can you give us some help here?"

"Absolutely, I don't know why it doesn't show up, but you're not the first one to have a problem getting here. Where are you?"

"We've pulled off of the Mountain Parkway at exit forty-four and are sitting in the parking lot of the Campton Super Motel."

Miranda knew the motel well. It was the local version of a mostly friendly, mostly clean, and mostly vacant motel used by travelers who needed a good night's sleep at the cheapest rate possible.

"Just turn back west onto the parkway and use exit forty-one. Head back down toward Slade and make the second left onto Hobbs Road. Follow it straight up and around the hill beyond where the pavement ends. I'm the first house on the right. It's painted yellow with turquoise-and-coral trim around the windows. Give me a call if you miss the Hobbs Road turning. It's difficult to see coming from that direction."

"Thanks, Miss Trent. We should be pulling up directly. Bye."

She scooped up Sandy and twirled him around in a circle. He responded to her excitement by trying to lick her and wiggle out at the same time. "We're going to get our fermenter today! We're going to get our fermenter today."

This was the last large piece of equipment she needed installed to start brewing large batches of moonshine. She tucked the wiggling Sandy in a secure hold and stood out on the porch to catch a first view of the delivery truck. The roar of the diesel engine announced the coming arrival long before she saw it approaching down the gravel road.

Sandy began to bark in sheer panic at the behemoth heading toward the farmhouse. Miranda wasn't sure she could contain him, so into his crate he went. She shut the door to her bedroom and was just in time for all the yelling.

"Crazy fool. Can't you make a simple turn?"

Miranda inhaled a panicked breath. The delivery truck driver had misjudged the farmhouse driveway and was now tipping precariously over the drainage ditch that ran along the road in front of her farmhouse. The rig was completely blocking both the road and her driveway.

She ran down her front porch steps and met the passenger, who was yelling, "I don't know why I keep you on the payroll. You're absolutely useless. You hear me—useless."

"Honestly, everyone in this end of the county can hear you," said Miranda. "And none of that yelling is helping." She put her hands on her hips and looked at the canted truck. Her fermenter was securely chained to the flatbed trailer, but the tilted angle would be putting enormous pressure on the fastenings. "You're gonna need a big tow truck. A really big one."

The name on the side of the truck was SHADY STREET DELIVERY & SON. The driver was clearly the "& son" part of the company, and his father was wasting this teaching opportunity by doing nothing but yelling at the red-faced teen.

"Just leave this to me, missy. I've been in worse fixes than this little giddyap." The father got out, walked around the front of the truck, and pulled open the driver's side door of the cab. "Get out of there. I don't believe you learned a thing I taught you about driving this rig. You sure weren't paying attention. Stand over there and guide me off this driveway."

The son slipped out of the cab and stood along the driveway, his eyes wide. Miranda tried to hide her fear that her fermenter would soon be rolling down the hill. She was certain that a punishment would be in his future.

The furious father ground gears putting the truck in reverse, but one of the tires was in the air and two others were slipping on the thinly graveled dirt road. A cloud of dust and diesel smoke rose and fouled the air. He tried many different combinations of wheel-turning, gear-shifting, seat-bouncing contortions, but nothing worked. The truck was stuck.

Miranda could only stand there with her heart sinking. If they upended the fermenter so that it fell off, she would be forced to wait until all the insurance battles cleared before getting another one on order. She had enough money for the current business plan, but not enough to cover a duplicate order.

"You idiot. This is going to cost us more than we're getting to deliver this. I told your mother I didn't think you would be anything but trouble. So far, I've been right." The father pulled out his cell phone and looked around. "No signal." He looked at Miranda as if she were his assistant. "Y'all got a phone?"

Miranda responded in a low, calm voice, "I do have a phone." Then she smiled and waited.

"Well, fine. Can I use it?"

"Absolutely, follow me." She turned to let him into the farmhouse and spied the plume of dust that signaled a car going too fast down the gravel road. She groaned. The only person who knew that road well enough to take it like a NASCAR driver was her mother, Dorothy Trent. Miranda exhaled a long sigh and showed the deliveryman the phone in her front room.

She walked back outside and saw her mom's white Mustang skid to a stop just inches from the jackknifed flatbed. The door flew open and her mom hopped out of the car. "What is this doing here? You can't put up with this? This is a public road!"

Miranda ran across the yard, jumped over the drainage ditch, and wrapped her mother in an enormous hug. Her mother hushed and hugged her back and then started to cry. "Oh, honey. I'm so upset. I can't believe after all this time they've finally found our Howard." Dorothy released Miranda and held her at arm's length. "Oh, sweetie. You look so thin. Are you eating?"

"Yes, yes. I just have a fast metabolism. You know that."

Miranda heard shouting coming from her living room as well as some terrified barking from Sandy. She left her mother in the road and ran back into the front room.

"I need that tow truck now. I'm renting the flatbed and it's an hourly charge. This is costing me big money!"

Miranda couldn't hear the speaker, but she heard Sandy's frantic clawing on the sides of his crate. She rushed into her bedroom. Sandy immediately stopped clawing and sat as innocent as an angel. "Don't play with me, young man. I saw that."

She lifted him up for lots of snuggles. He was still very much a young puppy and still needed comforting when experiencing new things. Men yelling in her farmhouse was definitely a new thing.

She went back to the front room.

"An hour? Is that the best you can do? Well, git on out here!" The deliveryman turned and started to dash out of the house.

Miranda stepped in his path in front of the door. "What's the verdict?"

He skidded to a stop as if she were a strange animal he had never before encountered. "Oh. He's coming out in about an hour. He says he knows this road and should have us to rights in no time."

"Thanks, I feel much better. That's a very expensive piece of equipment. I'm sure your insurance company will be happy that you're doing the right thing."

"Humph!" he called out as he left the house.

Oh my God. I'll bet the man has no insurance. What next?

The US mail truck pulled up behind her mother's Mustang.

Chapter 8

Monday Afternoon, the Farmhouse

"A tow truck is on its way," Miranda told the mail-man. "If you leave the mail here, I'll deliver it to everyone down the road."

"That's mighty nice of you, Miss Trent, but not especially legal. I know a back road down over the ridge. It'll take me a little longer, but I can manage." He backed up the mail truck to a little road that shot off away through the woods across the valley and went along the properties that were adjacent to Miranda's farm.

I really need to get out and explore this area. I have no idea how many people live along this road. I'm glad he didn't take me up on that rash promise.

"Mom, we've got to get your car out of the way. The big tow truck will be here in about thirty minutes. Let's unload your car and I'll drive it down to my neighbors' to park. It's only a short walk."

"Okay, but I brought a lot of food. I don't know just how long I'm going to be here dealing with Howard's death. Aunt Ora is going to be beside herself with grief. She's been holding on to the hope that he had merely left and decided not to contact his family. That happens."

Miranda had her mother pop the trunk of the Mustang. It was loaded for bear. With every square inch filled, her mom was fully prepared for any eventuality. Hands on her hips, Miranda said, "Mom, this looks like you're moving in! There's enough here to feed Washington's army for the entire Revolution."

"Don't fuss, baby. I'm only staying for a few weeks, maximum."

Miranda's eyes widened. "A few weeks? Really?" That was not particularly welcome news. Mom could be interfering and in the past was known to turn cantankerous if things didn't go her way.

The son of the delivery-service owner came over. "I'll help with this." He lifted the largest suitcase and put it on the front porch. Miranda followed his lead. In no time, a big pile of clothes, bedding, and food was out of the car and onto the porch.

"Thanks so much, young man," said Dorothy. "That was very kind of you."

He glanced over at his dad, who had crawled back into the cab and sat fuming while smoking a hand-rolled cigarette. The father looked over at Miranda from the cab. "You better get that car out of the way or I'll charge you wait time if that tow truck doesn't have complete access from the start."

Dorothy stretched to her full five feet one and her eyes narrowed. Miranda had seen that look all her life. She almost felt sorry for the dad—almost.

Pointing a perfectly manicured index finger within an inch of his nose, Dorothy said, "Don't you even think about starting to fuss at me, you crass old bully. If you had the sense the Lord gave a duck, you wouldn't have made your son nervous by yelling at him while making the turn." She turned to look at the son. "That's what he did, didn't he?"

The son bobbed his head forward the tiniest bit possible.

"See," Dorothy continued, "you brought this on yourself. Don't you dare push the fault on anyone else." She put her hands on both hips. "I'm going to get a soda for that youngster. Are you thirsty as well?"

The dad twisted his lips into a frown, but he silently mouthed a yes.

Miranda got her mother's keys and drove the Mustang in reverse all the way to Roy and Elsie's house. She parked it along a little turnout next to their house and went inside to explain the situation and give them the car keys in case it needed to be moved. Their farmhouse was perched on the cliffside and flat ground was at a premium.

She was walking back to her house when a giant tow truck rumbled its way up the hill and started toward her farmhouse, kicking up an enormous cloud of road dirt. It came to a halt behind the jackknifed delivery truck. A young man with a plaid shirt and baseball cap on backward jumped out.

"Howdy! This is completely messed up. Who drove this? How did you miss the turning? You should've backed in. You know that, don't you?" The young man spoke at the staccato pace of a popcorn popper. He left no time for answers.

"Hold on, youngster," said the owner of the delivery truck as he lumbered over to the tow truck, hitching up his britches as he walked. "You just hold on."

The young man stopped talking, smiled broadly, and tilted his head to listen.

"Your job is to get this rig out of the ditch. That's all. No lip—no opinion—no questions. Have I made myself clear?"

"Perfectly." The young man took out a plug of chewing tobacco and with a penknife sliced off a chunk and stuffed it in his mouth. Talking around the chaw, he said, "I'll just need to assess the situation before I commit this rig to the job." He looked the truck owner right in the eyes. "If I hear one more word from you, I'm leaving. Have I made *myself* clear?"

"Wha—" The owner started to protest, but quickly closed his mouth. Miranda thought he must be remembering how difficult it had been to find a large tow truck closer than Lexington.

After circling the precariously situated delivery truck, the tow truck driver opened one of his truck's storage compartments and pulled out a set of enormous chains. He began attaching them to various points on the flatbed. Occasionally, he would spit in the road, but he worked quickly and said not one single word.

Miranda admired the professionalism of the tow truck driver. He pulled the rig a few feet, then reset the chains and pulled the rig again. In less than an hour, he had the delivery cab and the flatbed back on the gravel road positioned so that it was an easy reverse for them to back into the barn and safely unload the fermenter.

The tow truck driver spritely walked over to the older

man with an invoice. "Here's your bill." He turned the bill around on his cap and tipped it. "Pleasure doing business with you. You can pay cash now for a ten percent discount or you can mail in a check for the full amount."

Reaching into his back pocket, the owner peeled off a roll of bills and handed them over. "Mark this here invoice that I've paid in full."

"My pleasure." The tow truck driver wrote on the invoice, signed it with a flourish, tipped his hat again, and in a flash was speeding down the road, radio at full blast with a mournful country ballad and the dirt road cloud of dust trailing behind.

Miranda smiled. She appreciated a well-run business where the owner knew what was what. She palmed her forehead. Was her moonshine distillery cursed? Every single step in the process had so far been plagued with setbacks, disasters, paperwork snafus, and just plain trouble. If she weren't so practical, she might conclude that her uncle's spirit didn't want her to replicate his wonderful brew.

While the delivery truck was righted, Miranda had helped her mother put away all her belongings in the newly cleared and cleaned attic bedroom. Doing that had taken them both about a dozen trips up the narrow stairs. Then they had stuffed Miranda's cupboards and refrigerator with supplies.

"Okay, sweetie. Thanks. I'm gonna give Sandy a long walk, then start a late lunch while you get that thingama-jig of yours put in the barn. I don't think that delivery company knows what they're doing."

"Thanks, Mom."

Miranda walked out back and was just in time to see

the fermenter placed on its waiting concrete pad. It was the final piece of equipment she needed to start making large batch moonshine.

Shady Street Delivery was bolting it down when Miranda finally got into the barn. The equipment looked exactly like she'd imagined when she sketched out her plans. Now, all she needed to do was start brewing with it.

"Okay, Miss Trent. That's it," said the son. He and his dad were looking over at her late uncle's original still she had installed in that part of the barn. The son said, "Say, are you going to be making Gene Buchanan's brew?"

"Yes, I'm surprised that you know about it."

"It's famous among real 'shine experts. How long before you'll have a batch? I'll tell my friends."

"I'll probably start the mash as soon as I clean out the fermenter. Maybe even today."

"If you ever need help—even part-time—I used to help your uncle when he needed it." The son pulled a towing-business card out of his back pocket. "Call this number and ask for Lance Campbell. I'd be willing to intern for no money just to be around Gene Buchanan's distillery."

"Thanks." Miranda took the card.

Lance's dad had no patience for his son's interests. "Come on. We're done. Let's get out of here. I want to forget we were ever here. We lost money on this one thanks to you." Lance's dad tromped out of the barn and got in the passenger's side of the cab. "Do you think you can back this rig out this time without me having to call back that tow truck?"

The son gave Miranda an apologetic half smile. "He's really not as bad as he seems. He crippled up his leg last year so he can't drive. He's in terrible pain and frustrated. He only goes out with me when he can't stand to work in the office anymore."

"You're more understanding than he has a right to expect."

"Maybe." Lance turned to go out to the truck. "He's the only dad I have."

Miranda stood in the doorway of the barn and watched while the son carefully and slowly backed the rig out of her driveway and onto the gravel road. He executed the maneuver perfectly, and she waved as they went down the road.

Miranda tapped the card against her fingers. She was going to need some help and the price was right.

"Miranda!" called her mother. "Lunch is ready. It's a bit late, but come and get it!"

Walking into the back porch and into the kitchen, Miranda was met with the aroma of her favorite meal as a child. Grilled cheese sandwiches with a rustic basil tomato soup. How her mother managed to rustle up everything she needed so quickly, Miranda had no idea, but she made no complaint.

She sat at the kitchen table and tucked in with the eagerness of a child that had been playing outdoors all day.

Her mom sat opposite with a large mug of coffee steaming in her hands. "You handled things very well outside."

Miranda raised her eyebrows but didn't stop eating. Her mother didn't often compliment her. It was better to wait until she could figure out the reason for this ploy before she spoke. Many times in the past she had regretted the commitments she made after a seemingly innocent compliment.

"I mean, it's a side of you I have never seen." Dorothy sipped from her mug. "It's going to take a while to get used to you being an independent businesswoman."

Miranda used the last crust of her grilled cheese sandwich to sop up the dregs of the tomato soup. She leaned back in her chair. "That was wonderful. Exactly what I was craving. Thank you."

"Of course."

Miranda steepled her hands and looked closely at her mother. "I was an independent businesswoman in New York City. This isn't new for me."

"It was different up there. You were working for your art. You created your paintings on your own. You didn't have"—Dorothy waved her hand around the kitchen—"property, staff, large-equipment deliveries. This is different."

Miranda returned a weak smile. "It's different all right."

"And it suits you. You don't look like a scared rabbit not knowing when the farmer was going to trap you for dinner."

"Did I look like that?"

Her mom slowly nodded. "Yes, The whole time you were trying to scratch out a name for yourself up there."

"Okay, maybe I did feel a bit out of my depth. But this feels right. It feels solid. I mean, like this is what I'm supposed to be doing. Right here in Uncle Gene's farmhouse trying to brew up his famous moonshine."

Miranda smiled. It was rare to receive real feedback from her mother. Her mother's usual philosophy was to let Miranda try to make her own way in life.

Dorothy coughed into her hand. "Now about these bones you found up on the Indian Staircase . . ."

Aha, here's where the penny drops.

Dorothy shifted in her seat. "I understand, of course, that you didn't know Howard very well, your interests were so different, but I agree that they're his remains."

"Mom—"

"Now, don't interrupt me." Dorothy put a flat hand out toward Miranda. "I've got what I'm going to say all figured out. Where was I? Oh, yes, I'm convinced that the bones you found belong to Howard. He was a little older than you and he was the first baby in the family of the current generation. We all doted on him."

Dorothy paused and took another sip of her coffee before continuing.

"He was such a charming, chubby, happy baby. It was unsettling to see him grow up into a surly, lanky, unruly teenager. It was hoped that college would straighten him out. He was the first child in our family to even graduate high school, so everyone had high expectations."

"Wait!" Miranda leaned forward. "You didn't graduate from Wolfe County High School? You never told me that."

"Never mind that now," her mother huffed.

Miranda jumped in. "You're not getting away with that. Why didn't you graduate?"

After a disparaging look, Dorothy finally said, "We didn't have enough money. As soon as I was sixteen, I started to work at the drugstore to help out. It was the way of the times. That's not at issue here. What's important is to make sure that you get to the bottom of who killed Howard."

"Me?" Miranda sat back in her chair so quickly, it nearly tipped over. "Why me?"

"Because I want my sister to have the full truth of his death. We can't let Sheriff Larson shirk his duties just because he's being punished for overspending a stupidly tiny budget. It's true he could have been caught off guard up on the mountain, but if Howard didn't die by accident, you have the skills to find out what happened."

Chapter 9

Felicia Larson was on edge. It wasn't a condition that fell upon her often, but it had arrived with a full marching band today. She'd arrived back at work after a quick shower and a nap to await word from her friend Dr. Barbara DuPont.

The two of them had met at the University of Kentucky College of Medicine during long hours in the labs. Then they were both selected for internships at the university's Chandler Medical Center.

Felicia wouldn't say that they were besties in any sense of the word. But they knew each other well and respected each other's professional standards. But Barbara's behavior on the mountain was disconcerting. Everyone tolerated discomfort in different ways, but that was a side of her friend that she hadn't known existed.

Could she be wrong about Barbara's professionalism?

No, they had worked well together many times. Anyway, she knew Barbara would call as soon as she had something to report. Not sooner. Not one moment sooner.

To calm herself, Felicia tackled a clerical job she had been putting off for months. Okay, maybe even years. She needed to empty her filing cabinets of old reports and prepare them for archiving into off-site storage. It was the perfect task to occupy her distracted mind. She had two full document boxes labeled and was halfway through filling up the third when the phone rang.

"Dr. Larson, Wolfe County coroner."

"Hi, Felicia. Are you busy?"

"No. Frankly, I'm packing up archival boxes of paperwork waiting for your call. I'm too distracted to trust myself with anything more taxing. Did I do right by calling you in?"

"That was exactly the right call. These bones are quite the challenge. I needed every advantage that my modern lab gives me. You might have gotten to the same conclusion, but your results might not have been so clearly compelling."

"What's the result? Do you have an identity?"

"Dental records, sparse as they are, have confirmed that the remains are those of Howard Cable, who went missing five years ago."

Felicia sucked in a breath between her teeth. "Oh, no. That's right in our backyard. His mother lives a few miles beyond Campton on Highway 191 in a little village called Trent. It's not much more than a crook in the road these days. Apparently it was named after a Trent ancestor who established a post office in their tiny general store. He originally owned all the land around there, but he died young." Felicia paused. "Anyway, Howard's mother, Ora Cable, has been expecting to hear from him every day since he disappeared. She had hoped that he had taken off to explore the world, but she didn't think that was likely. Miranda did give a fair warning that it could be Howard."

"Apparently, he found himself in a lot of trouble. There are signs that he had injured himself and wouldn't have been able to get off the mountain."

"What? How?" Felicia leaned forward.

"Well, this is preliminary only, but the bones in his right leg were broken. It would certainly have prevented him from climbing down the Indian Staircase, but I don't understand why he didn't attempt the back trail. It doesn't make sense."

"What about a head injury? A concussion?"

"Nope. No evidence of a fractured skull." Barbara sucked a breath between her teeth. "That doesn't mean that he didn't have bruising from a fall or an altercation."

"If he was injured, went into shock with the pain, and then got dehydrated, he might not have been able to think properly."

"As I said, this is very preliminary. I thought you might want to know about the fractured femur."

"Thanks for that. His mother is going to be devastated. I need to get over there before the news gets out."

"I'll send you an official document with the identification. I have a long way to go before I'll be ready for a definitized cause of death."

"I'll tell the sheriff. He's wanting to get this case closed as quickly as possible. He's confusing me with his attitude to this case. Normally, he would be breathing down my neck to support the investigation in any way possible. Hmmm. Maybe there's a political aspect he hasn't told me about. Sorry, I went off on a tangent. I'm good to wait until you finish your investigation."

Sheriff Larson leaned into her office. "What did she say?"

Felicia rolled her eyes. The thin walls of her office meant that there were no secrets in the office. "She identified the victim as Howard Cable."

His shoulders dropped. "Oh, no. I was afraid of that. Dammit."

"Do you want me to break the news to his mother? It might help a bit if it comes from me. You're the sheriff. It's your call."

"I agree it should be you. She's been in denial for the whole five years. It will be better from you." Felicia noticed his resigned tone, yet he seemed to be relieved. "She lives alone in that house now, right?"

"Yes," Felicia replied. "Her younger daughter, Anna Belle, married and moved up to Maysville last year, and her older daughter, Anna Sue, left the year before that. Why?"

"Telling her is going to be rough."

"I'll call Miranda and have her go with me. It will be good for her to have family around when this news comes."

"When was Dr. DuPont going to send over the death certificate?"

"She said she had more investigation to do. She discovered a fractured femur that would have incapacitated him to some extent. There's not a clear cause of death as yet so she'll be continuing with her autopsy. I know Barb, she'll take those bones down to atoms in order to dig out the cause of his death."

"My poor budget. I can't afford her." He shook his head like a dog shedding water. "But now that we know he's one of ours, it doesn't really matter. If I get fired for serving our citizens, then that's the way I want to leave this job. Not for watching pennies from a self-serving politician's campaign promise. I'll not trade my duties for his political schemes."

"Don't worry so much. The university supplements her expenses. She always gets a couple of technical papers out of each of the cases we send her. You're getting a bargain. Most of the time, Mr. Budget Watcher, the university forgets to send you an invoice."

He shook his head. "Yeah, I still like to whine, though."

"And you're pretty good at it. Go to your room." She turned her back to him. "I'm calling Miranda right now. Once Barb files that paperwork, it won't take any time at all for the news to leak. Gossip is a university's bloodstream."

Felicia dialed Miranda's farmhouse.

"Good afternoon. Paint and Shine Cultural Adventures. How can I help you?"

"Hi, Miranda. This is Felicia. Dr. DuPont has identified the remains and you were absolutely right. Barb says the bones belong to your cousin Howard Cable."

There was no answer on the line.

"Miranda? Are you there? Have I lost you?"

"Sorry, I'm here, Felicia. I was expecting this, but I'm surprised to be so sad."

"There's no way to predict how we'll react to a death."

"Even when it's expected?" Miranda's voice was strained.

"It's the end of all hope."

Felicia was silent for a few seconds. "Listen, I'm going to go over to break the news to his mother. Can you meet me there? I'm going to upset her and I would be more comfortable if she had more family with her."

"How did he die?"

"I don't have the final results from Barb. She says that he had a fractured leg but isn't ready to disclose anything else. I won't get the full report until after she finishes her examination. She's incredibly thorough."

"Of course, and I'm glad for that. I'll get right on over to my aunt's house. Give me about twenty minutes. My mom and I will leave in a few minutes. I'll see you there."

"What? Your mom is here? That's wonderful. How did she get here so quick? I thought she lived up in Dayton. That's a three-hour drive."

"Mom made it in two-and-a-half."

Chapter 10

Late Monday Afternoon, Aunt Ora's House

Miranda pulled off the Mountain Parkway at Exit 43 and turned onto the road that led through the small downtown section of Campton and onto Highway 191. Her mother sat in the van beside her, quietly crying into a tissue. "Mom! What's the deal? You're usually so strong. You've got to get yourself under control before we get to Aunt Ora's house. She's gonna need you to lean on."

Dorothy blew her nose and sniffed. She grabbed another tissue, pulled down the van's visor to look into the mirror while she dabbed at her messy mascara. "You're right. She's been so hopeful all these years. Absolutely every conversation I've had with her since he disappeared, she has been convinced he would be home any day now." Dorothy's hand dived back into her purse and she applied some powder and a touch of eye shadow and freshened her lipstick. "Now that he's going to completely break her heart, I almost wish you hadn't found him."

"Mom"—Miranda heard her voice rise in pitch—"it sounds like you're blaming me for finding him. Surely it is better to know?"

Dorothy tilted her head to one side. "She's lost all hope now."

Miranda drove right on through Campton and took the curvy road as fast as a local. She wanted to arrive before Felicia. They pulled into the gravel driveway to her aunt's house. Just as they shut the doors to the van, a slim frail woman pushed open the screen door of the side porch and walked out to the driveway. "Why, laws. Dorothy! I'm surprised to see you. You should have let me know you were coming down. I would have baked my special spice cake."

Dorothy gave her sister a huge hug. Miranda could sense the control her mother was using to keep from bursting into tears.

"Miranda, you come on over here and give me a hug, too. You're just getting too busy with that tourist business of yours. I haven't seen you but once since you moved down here. Come on in and sit a spell."

Just as they turned, a vehicle pulled in right behind Miranda's white van.

Aunt Ora looked at it as if it had landed from the moon. "Now who would be calling on me? I don't get much company now that my girls have moved away."

Felicia walked over and nodded a greeting to Miranda and her mom. Felicia had slipped on a black jacket over her normal jeans and white T-shirt. It gave her a professional air as she looked at the little woman in the doorway.

Aunt Ora put her hand over her mouth and turned a sickly shade of yellow green. "Oh, no. Oh, no. No. No."

"Afternoon, Mrs. Cable," said Felicia, "I'm glad your family is here. I have some bad news. Can we go inside?"

"It's Howard!" Ora shrieked. "It's Howard! He's been dead all this time. Oh, Lord. I can't stand it." All color left her face and her eyelids fluttered.

Mirada stepped into the doorway and caught her aunt as she fainted in her arms.

Chapter 11

Miranda and her mother were sipping hot mugs of cider with cinnamon sticks on the front-porch swing of the farmhouse. They had kept company with Aunt Ora until her younger daughter drove down from Maysville. Anna Belle assured them that she would stay with her mother. Her older sister, Anna Sue, was expected first thing in the morning. They would both stay to take care of their mother and help prepare for Howard's funeral.

"Mom, I didn't realize how much Aunt Ora has aged until I saw the two of you together."

"I know, it's dreadful. She's three years younger than I am, but Howard's disappearance took a terrible toll. He was her only son and quite the favorite. She spoiled him rotten by indulging his every interest and obsession."

"Like what?"

Dorothy inhaled a deep breath. "They changed from

season to season, but the one that stayed constant was his interest in the legends of the lost Jonathan Swift silver mines."

Miranda huffed, "He wasn't the only one who spent time trying to track down the lost silver mines. Almost everybody has had a try."

Sandy had fallen asleep on Dorothy's lap with his nose barely peeking out from underneath a cozy quilt. Miranda felt the peace of the moment and took her mother's hand.

"This will be hard for my sister." Dorothy squeezed Miranda's hand. "But I hope it brings her peace."

They sat a little longer enjoying the coolness of the evening. Miranda inhaled the moist hint of an oncoming storm. After a comfortable silence, she scooched from beneath the quilt, grabbed her mother's mug, and started for the kitchen. "Stay here with Sandy. I need to check things in the barn. I haven't yet taken a good look at my new fermenter."

Miranda washed up the mugs, grabbed a warm jacket, and walked out the back door onto the path that led to the barn. She flipped on the lights and felt a wave of pride. Getting to this point had taken a long list of things to be done. There were plans to be drawn and approved, permits to submit, equipment to order and install, and, finally, supplies to be delivered and stored.

Since she wanted to start her first batch as soon as possible, she walked over to the stall area she had chosen for storing corn, yeast, molasses, and the flavoring ingredients. Although she had ordered a concrete slab for the distillation equipment, the rest of the barn floor was still hard-packed dirt.

Her clients seemed to appreciate the authenticity of an old-fashioned tobacco barn, and realistically, the cost of paving the whole barn made her shiver. The ground was so hard packed after decades of use, she could literally sweep it like a floor between tours. Still, it was on the list for future improvements.

She reached her supply stall and her heart fell. A huge puddle was at the entry to the stall.

Puddle? There must be a leak.

She stepped into the stall. All her dry ingredients were sopping wet.

Ruined.

As she was standing there, a giant drippy stream of rain hit one of the burlap bags of whole corn. She looked up at the ceiling. There was a hole in the roof about a foot square. The storm had found another way to cause her misery.

She poked around the stall and finally gave up hoping to find anything to salvage. The corn, barley, and yeast were a complete loss. She was able to salvage the jars of molasses and blackberry jam.

She went back to the kitchen and got her high-powered flashlight and scanned the ceiling of the barn, inch by inch. As far as she could see, there was only the one breach. Worst case meant that if more holes were found, she would probably need to have the whole roof replaced.

Back in the house, she found her mother in the kitchen whipping up a huge batch of banana-pancake batter in the large yellow mixing bowl. "I felt like breakfast for our late dinner tonight. How about you?"

Miranda smiled. She didn't always get along with her mother, but no one knew Miranda better. "That's just perfect. I need to call around for a handyman. I found a hole in the roof of the barn."

Dorothy stopped stirring the batter. "What! Your uncle just had that roof done not too long ago."

"It was from the storm last night. There's no protection against a microburst of wind. Everything else looks fine. Unfortunately, the leak spoiled all the dry supplies for my first batch of moonshine. I'll have to gather the whole lot again."

"Can't you just reorder?"

"I'm determined to keep this production completely local. So, I've got to pick up everything from the farmers around here. Not a big problem, it's just that I have a busy week with clients and need the van for transportation. Then add the crisis of the discovery of Howard's bones on the mountain, and I'm pretty much thinkin' that brewing Uncle Gene's moonshine will go to the back burner again."

"Is there anything I can do?"

Miranda smiled. "No, but thanks for asking. After I make a few calls, you can keep those pancakes coming."

In her office, which had been her late uncle's bedroom, Miranda sat at her desk and pulled out her planning journal. She phoned Ron Menifee, the handyman the clerk at the post office had recommended last week. That's the way things worked in Wolfe County. You asked people you knew to give you a contact for things that needed to be done.

He answered on the first ring. "Ron, here."

"Hi, Ron, this is Miranda Trent, Gene Buchanan's niece out on Hobbs Road. I'm needing a roof repair on his tobacco barn, and the clerk at the post office in Campton recommended you. My problem is that the roof got damaged in last night's storm. Can you come out anytime soon?"

"Yeah, sure. I've worked on Gene's farm a few times. He had a new roof put up on there a couple of summers ago. Must have been a weak spot that they missed. I can come out tomorrow morning and give it a look-see for you."

"That would be great. How early can you stop by? I have to pick up my clients over at Hemlock Lodge by ten o'clock."

"No problem. I'll see you first thing—around eight o'clock?"

"That's perfect. Thanks so much!"

She made an appointment in both her planner and her electronic calendar then shut down her computer.

"Hello there in the house. I smell something mighty good coming from the kitchen."

Miranda found Austin standing on the front porch with a big smile on his face. "Is your mom making banana pancakes?"

Miranda opened the screen door. "Yes, come on in. She's made a giant stack and we can't possibly eat them all. They don't keep well, you know." She followed him through the front room and into the dining room with its huge round table. It frequently sat eight and could manage ten in a pinch.

As soon as he was in the dining room, Sandy tore through the kitchen door and rolled over to show his belly in front of Austin, accompanying this with puppy whines. Austin knelt and happily complied. "You sure know how to beg for belly scratches."

Holding an enormous platter of fluffy pancakes, Dorothy's eyes twinkled when she saw Austin. "Oh, I'm so glad you're here. I've made a mountain of banana pancakes. We need a big strong man like you to help finish these off. Have a seat. These are best when the butter melts into them." She put the platter on the dining room table and made sure that Miranda sat next to Austin.

Miranda rolled her eyes. Her mother had been trying to make a match for her since she turned sixteen. Using her fork, she got a stack of three cakes, put pats of butter between the two lower pancakes and a final pat on top. Then she took the bottle of real maple syrup from the saucepan of hot water with a pot holder and drizzled a good amount on top of the pancakes and added more around the perimeter of the plate.

Austin followed her lead and took four pancakes and dressed them the same way. He put his fork through the syrup- and butter-soaked stack. After he put the first bite in his mouth, Austin put his fork down and placed each hand flat beside the plate and closed his eyes. "This is exactly the way I remembered them."

Miranda surfaced after her first bite. "Mom's been trying to teach me how she makes them, but I just haven't gotten the trick yet."

"Now, now." Dorothy took two pancakes from the platter. "You know what the secret is—I've told you enough times."

"Right," said Miranda through her second huge bite. "They're made with love."

Dorothy smiled. "My job is done here."

"Whatever you do, don't change anything about these pancakes." Austin cleared his plate and glanced at Dorothy. She waved a go-ahead to him and he grabbed four more pancakes.

After his third stack had disappeared, Austin took a

swallow of the hot cider and leaned back from the table and looked at Miranda. "Your mom cooked, so I'm betting we'll be doing kitchen duty?"

Dorothy grinned at Miranda. "This one knows his manners. I reckon he was brought up that way. The right way."

Miranda laughed. "Bring your dishes. We're on clean-up duty."

Austin stacked up the plates and added the forks and knives. "I'll wash and you dry since you know where everything goes." He walked into the kitchen, put the dishes on the counter, and turned on the hot water.

"That's nonsense. You don't like drying. You're not fooling me."

"Guilty as charged." He squirted soap to one of the two enamel pans in the deep porcelain farm sink and filled both of them with hot water.

Miranda opened one of the kitchen drawers and pulled out a dish towel. "I decided not to install a dishwasher, even though the farmhouse is attached to the city water line. Living for generations with a limited supply of well water means that our deeply entrenched habits still conserve resources. I'm going to apply for a green-business certification through the state."

"Will that help you appeal to more clients?"

"As a matter of fact, yes. This area is beginning to attract tourists from New England, Ohio, Michigan, and even out West. I had two clients from Santa Barbara, California, last week. They had never seen anyone hand-wash dishes before. Amazing, but they have a different lifestyle out there."

"The rock-climbing opportunities down in Red River Gorge have gone international. I heard that there were climbers from Australia, Japan, and India last week. We're becoming known to the world as an area of natural beauty."

"Too bad some of the old-timers still behave like these visitors are outsiders trying to steal their privacy. Some of the old-timers cling to their clannish way of living."

"Things are changing very fast for the old family farmsteads—too fast." Austin said more with his shoulders than anything else. "Tobacco is no longer viable. Hemp is the new cash crop."

"It's so strange for it to be legal in most states, and the final insult seems to be my moonshine distillery. It is out in the open and completely legal."

While Miranda dried the last few dishes and put them away in the cupboards, Austin wiped down the counters, the kitchen table, and the gas stove. He emptied the soapy water first, then washed the dishcloth in the rinse water and dumped that pan as well.

Miranda caught his hand and turned him to face her. "I want to thank you for being there up on the Indian Staircase last night. I'm an experienced woodsman, but you made such a difference to everyone's comfort." She raised up on her toes and kissed him on the cheek.

He swallowed hard, flushed pink to his scalp, and coughed. "Um, my pleasure. It was an experience I'm not likely to forget anytime soon."

Miranda looked down to see that her hand was still in his. It felt good.

At that moment, Sandy ran into the kitchen to sit by his food bowl and let out a little yip. Miranda's eyes went wide. "Oh, my goodness, Sandy. I forgot to get your dinner." She tucked him up into the crook of her neck. "I'm so sorry. It won't take a minute."

She opened a can of wet dog food and plopped a good dollop onto a layer of puppy dry chow. When she lifted the bowl, Sandy was hopping up and down on two feet to try to get to the bowl. "Where are your manners? Sit."

Sandy immediately sat at perfect puppy attention. Miranda put the dish down and filled Sandy's water bowl at the sink.

Austin leaned against the counter with one leg crossed over the other and his arms crossed over his chest. "I heard you had some damage to the barn in the storm last night."

"How did you know that? I only just discovered it myself." She threw back her head. "Oh, Ron has spilled the beans, right? Is he one of those guys that has never experienced an unspoken thought?"

"Yes. He's a real chatterbox." Austin chuckled. "He called to ask if he could borrow my tallest ladder. He seems to have misplaced his at a customer site—but, of course, he doesn't remember which one."

Miranda furrowed her brow. "That's odd."

"He also asked me if I could drive him over to the hardware store in town. It appears that he doesn't have a truck right now."

"What? How can he work without a truck?"

Austin grimaced in frustration. "He's been calling every distant relation who even has a faint family connection. He's apparently one of my third cousins, although I can't verify the connection. I'll help him out, but you might want to find someone else to work on your place."

Miranda frowned. "I heard from the post office clerk about how Ron tackles jobs in a disorganized flurry, but she says that his actual workmanship is excellent. She said he's a bit ditzy, so the cure for that is that I need to be here while he works. I might have to cancel a few of my tours."

"Cancel? That's drastic."

She rubbed her chin. "Maybe reschedule the ones that are flexible. Another idea is to offer an afternoon tour without the meal once or twice a week. I might be able to attract clients who have morning scheduling problems. Right. Maybe I'll do that on Tuesdays and Thursdays. That will give me all day Monday and two mornings to get distillery work done." She tapped Austin on the arm with her fist. "Good idea."

"Right, but I still strongly suggest that you cancel Ron and find someone else. He's bad news."

Miranda stood to her full height and began to walk toward the front of the farmhouse. "That's not happening." She continued to walk out through to the front porch. "This is my business and he will do his best work. I'm perfectly capable of managing him."

Austin followed her out to the porch. "I know that, but—"

"No buts. This is my business. Good evening." She turned and went back inside closing the front door with not quite a slam, but definitely with purpose.

"What was that all about?" Dorothy had added more wood to the stove and sat in one of the rockers with a large quilt in her lap. She was making some repairs with a fine needle. "What did you say?"

Miranda blew out a long breath. "Too much."

Chapter 12

Tuesday Morning, the Farmhouse

Ron, the handyman, knocked on her door at the break of dawn. Sandy growled like a big dog. The warning wasn't needed. Miranda had been up for an hour expecting that Ron would arrive early. She didn't want to face him in her nightclothes. It was tricky for some men to take orders from women. She didn't want their employer/employee relationship to get off to a bad start.

He stood six feet six at the door in bib overalls over a threadbare flannel shirt. Neither he nor his clothes had seen wash water in quite some time. He pointed over to Austin's still-running truck parked in the driveway beside her van. "Hey, missy. I need to unload my tools in the barn. Austin needs to get to work."

Ron had all his tools piled in a jumble in the bed of Austin's truck. They unloaded them smack-dab in the middle of the barn. There would be no client tours showcasing her uncle's original moonshine still until the roof repair was complete. She had assumed that, but in any case, the mess irritated her.

Austin raised his eyebrows and pressed his lips together barely suppressing a smile. "I'll see you on the trail tomorrow. Good luck." He left with a grim look on his face.

Ron leaned the ladder up against the barn to examine the hole. It wasn't far from the edge of the roof, but he climbed up with a measuring tape to estimate the amount of material he would need. He made of bunch of moaning and tsk-tsk noises that did nothing to raise Miranda's confidence.

He came back down the ladder and showed her the measurements he had written in a small spiral notebook. "This is a whole lot bigger hole than it looks like from down below. I'm gonna need quite a bit more material than the roofers left behind. Can you take me to the hardware store now? I don't have any cash money so you'll have to pay for that."

Miranda sighed heavily and rubbed the back of her neck.

Remember, the post office clerk promised me that he does great work, but you know this is going to be a pain.

"I can't go this minute, but I can take you over when I finish with today's event. It's a golden anniversary so I can take you over at about three o'clock. You can start with the material I have. There should be plenty."

"I'm going to need some two-by-fours for replacing the substructure first. I can't really start without that."

Miranda smiled and waved Ron over to the back of the barn. "I have several piles of leftover wood from my uncle. He was so skilled he didn't need anyone." She led

Ron to the tool storage stall and pointed to the neatly stacked building materials. "There are all sorts of offcuts and scrap pieces from everything that's ever been built on the farm. The leftover roofing materials are in here as well. This will have to do until I get finished with my clients. Will that be enough for you to get started?"

He rubbed his chin. "I'm not gonna be sure until I dig in."

She nodded. "I understand you have a going rate of twenty dollars cash per hour, right?"

He tilted his head. "Well, costs are going up you know. I'm charging twenty-five dollars an hour. I'll need today's cash in advance, you know."

"But you can't go anywhere."

"I'm gonna walk down the road to the gas station for my lunch break."

"Fine." Miranda exhaled in a puff. "I'll give you six hours' worth and we'll see where we are after that." *Darn, I'm already losing control.*

She returned to the farmhouse and got the cash, then walked back into the barn. Ron had already taken out all of the scrap wood and stood them up against the walls, stalls, and support columns.

"Oh." She involuntarily shuddered. *Thank goodness he's got a good reputation as a workman or I would send him packing right this minute.*

"You know, it wouldn't take but maybe an hour or so to build you a sturdy set of racks in that stall so you could store your extra material a mite better."

Here he goes already. Trying to start more work before he's finished with the roof repair.

"No. I don't need anything else done. It's the roof that's the critical task. I can't ask you to start anything else since I'm not making enough money to pay for it. That's why I need the roof fixed right now."

He didn't need to know that she had discovered her uncle's hidden stash of moonshine money in the small cave where he had brewed his last batch. It wasn't a lot of money but would keep her from going out of business while she worked on getting the distillery licensed.

Miranda looked at her watch. "I've got to go. Call me if anything urgent comes up. I'll be back soon." She turned to go but turned back. "I almost forgot. My mother is visiting, so if you have any questions, she'll be glad to help."

"Dorothy is here?" His eyes lit up like those of a kid in a candy shop. "That's wonderful."

"She's only here for a few days. Good luck, and, Ron"—she waited until he looked at her—"be careful." She knew that he didn't have a lick of medical insurance or any kind of normal life. He lived completely off the grid and would apparently keep it that way.

She wondered, *Who paid for that cell phone?* It looked like someone's hand-me-down. He certainly wouldn't have it in his name. *Never mind. I don't want to know.*

On this crisp fall morning, Miranda's clients had traveled from nearby Winchester and were all members of the same family. Three generations were on her tour in celebration of the grandparents' fiftieth wedding anniversary. On this sentimental expedition they were painting the view of the limestone arch from the spot where the grandfather, Courtney, had proposed to the grandmother, May. The couple were joined by two grown sons, their wives, and two preteen grandchildren.

They met in the lobby of Hemlock Lodge and hiked the short distance to the first spectacular view of the underside of the Natural Bridge Arch against an incredible azure sky. They were grouped in a little clearing a few feet off the trail right next to one of the resting benches. When she'd scoped out the site, Miranda didn't know how healthy the grandparents were and didn't want to leave their comfort to chance.

It turned out that the couple had wed as teenagers and were in better shape than some of her clients in their thirties.

As a lesson learned, she thought she should add a comment section to her online application form. She could ask that people mention celebrations, special needs, or anything that would enhance their experience. She mentally added that to her list of ongoing website updates she needed to make.

She was a bit concerned about the attention span of both the grandparents and the grandchildren. However, she was pleased that this appeared to be a kind, loving, and close-knit family. The sons and wives kept everyone on task, and the paintings were similar because they were all sharing the experience.

The wives had preordered a cake to be delivered to the farmhouse and had invited local friends and relations to join in the celebration after the paintings were finished. Instead of a sit-down meal, Miranda would be offering finger foods, as well as her newly created moonshine mimosa.

Since it was planned to be a short painting session, Miranda skipped the ranger talk. She had given them a history of the view along with their painting instruction. Austin had taken the news quietly, but she was keenly aware that there was still a disagreement between them. It bothered her that it bothered her, but maybe that was a good realization.

Ron's behavior was at the back of her mind. He was a wild card to her determination to survive the event in perfect calm. This amazing couple deserved a wonderful celebration. She mentally crossed her fingers, eyes, and toes.

Grandmother May kept looking at Miranda. Furrows of thought appeared and disappeared on the matriarch's forehead. "What was your name again, young lady? My hearing isn't as good as it used to be."

"Miranda Trent. I'm the niece of Gene Buchanan, from up on Pine Ridge."

"Oh, that's right. He left you that nice farmhouse, didn't he?"

"Yes, I'm a lucky girl."

"That's not what I'm remembering, though. I've heard about another relation." Her brow furrowed then smoothed out again. "Never mind. It'll come to me directly." She turned back to her painting.

"She's the one that discovered those bones," piped up Grandfather Courtney. "They're cousins. That's what you heard, honey."

"Laws-a-mercy." May turned to Miranda. "That poor hiker that got lost out on the trail. I remember when that happened. Such a sad time for dear Ora Cable. It hit her very hard. I took over my special tuna casserole."

Everyone knows everyone up here. I keep forgetting that.

Grandfather Courtney looked over to the trail just a few yards from their painting site. "He must have gotten lost on one of those false animal trails up there over the Indian Staircase. I've heard that the tribes used to do that to confuse their enemies. I wonder if that's what happened."

"Sir, I doubt that. My cousin regularly hunted deer with a bow and arrow to put meat on my aunt's table. He always took his limit on the first day of hunting season. He couldn't get lost in these woods if he tried. Something else must have happened." Miranda hesitated, thinking that exact details shouldn't be shared.

"Aw, that's wishful thinking," said the grandmother. "But it shows that you have a sweet nature. Ora Cable has always spoken so well about you."

Miranda felt the warmth fill her chest. Nice. Miranda also wondered about those legendary woodsman skills. Maybe she was falling for a family myth about Howard, who had become a better woodsman the longer that he had been missing. It would be a way to keep alive the hope that he would show up someday.

"He wasn't lost."

Chapter 13

Miranda stacked everyone's paintings along the floor-to-ceiling windows at the far end of the lobby. Each client kept the painting backpack as a souvenir. As the last group activity, she liked to take a group picture of the clients displaying their works. One of the advantages was that passersby would see them and ask about her tours. It was a handy way to drum up more business.

She gave the family instructions on how to reach her farmhouse. They were going to change their clothes and then meet her there for their celebration.

"Hey, Miranda," called out the receptionist behind the counter next to the lobby. "What's this I hear about Howard Cable being found up on the bluff above the Indian Staircase? I heard that you were in the middle of all that. Is it true?"

Miranda went over to the counter and received her

bear hug from the plump receptionist. Doris Ann Norris had worked at that desk longer than anyone could remember. It was rumored that Doris Ann's father had been part of the construction crew that rebuilt the lodge in 1962 after a fire destroyed the original.

It had taken Miranda quite a long time to win Doris Ann over to supporting the Paint & Shine cultural adventures. Doris Ann had a deep-seated loathing of alcoholic beverages of any kind. She was still against drink, but not against the painting classes that Miranda held out on the trails.

"I found his bones." Miranda felt her body shiver at the thought. "Ugh! It was awful. If Jennifer hadn't scraped her hand at that spot, no telling how much longer he would have remained up there. I had nightmares about his bones last night."

"That wouldn't have bothered me as much as getting stormbound on that mountain." Doris Ann moved her head slowly from side to side. "I would have been terrified of being struck dead by lightning."

"It wasn't really so bad. We holed up in that cavern. Luckily, Austin had the key since he included the pictograms as part of his lecture to my tour group. We were sheltered from the storm, but it was a long, cold night."

"How is your aunt taking this? I heard that Howard had a broke leg and died of exposure. That just doesn't sound right to me. He should have been able to get back to the main trail and get help. Something isn't right."

"That's a good point. He was a strong, healthy fellow. Why didn't he splint the leg and move away from the tree?" Miranda rubbed the back of her neck. A knot was beginning to form. That usually meant that something was bothering her. Maybe it was the constant comments

from everyone about of his reputation as an expert woodsman. She didn't personally know that. Could it be a family myth? Yep, that's what was bothering her.

Doris Ann began to fiddle with one of the logo pens
that advertised Hemlock Lodge. "He stopped by here on
the day he went missing. I'll never forget that. He was in
a strange mood. Well, not strange as much as he appeared
to be angry about some big deal he was about to lose."

"What kind of deal? He was a college graduate, but I
really don't know very much about his career. I need to
follow up on that with Mom and Aunt Ora."

"It wasn't anything to do with local business. I know
that. I still remember him turning purple and yelling at
someone on his cell phone. It was almost bad enough for
me to think about asking him to leave. But he calmed
down and he told the man on the line that they were going
to fix things later."

"Fix what?"

"He didn't say."

"Did you tell anyone about the argument after he disappeared?"

"I did." Doris Ann sat a little taller in her chair. "I tole
that new deputy that the sheriff hired that year for traffic
patrol. He swore that he would tell the sheriff. It looks
like he didn't. Sheriff Larson fired him at about the same
time. He was an awful deputy, even worse than our current one."

Doris Ann saw a family coming down the hall dragging their luggage ready to check out. "Stop back later. I
have more to tell you about that group you took up to
paint the view of Battleship Rock."

Miranda left but didn't know why on earth Doris Ann
was holding back. She appeared to like to pass on infor-

mation to Miranda, but this seemed urgent. She rubbed the back of her neck—still worried about something. She had an event to manage and it wouldn't organize itself.

When she arrived at the farmhouse, she could see that Ron was on the roof with a crowbar prying up shingles. The patch of stripped roof had grown to an enormous size—at least half the roofing on that side of the barn.

She groaned. "I hope he's not featherbedding this." She didn't have time to talk to him until after the golden wedding anniversary party finished. Miranda walked into the farmhouse and was relieved to see that the cake had been delivered. It was in the center of her dining table surrounded by stacks of dessert plates and an arrangement of the hodgepodge of forks that she had partly borrowed and also found at the nearest charity shop.

She was determined to keep her business as true to the spirit of a past country life as possible. No plastics. No wipes. Cloth napkins. No single-use items that weren't compostable. It had not been easy to increase her inventory for her usual eight to ten guests to serve a crowd of fifty. But she had done it.

Her two cooks, sisters Lily and Iris, were in the kitchen making all kinds of traditional dishes that they had modified to serve as finger food. Only the cake would require forks. Just coming out of the oven were little squares her mother had called Cheesy Bits on sourdough toast. They were also serving traditionally fried chicken wings, squares of cheddar cheese on wooden skewers, and oodles of deviled eggs.

Lily removed the hot cheesy squares onto a serving platter and had another tray ready for the oven. Iris was also loading a tray with the eggs.

Miranda lined up the fifty four-ounce mason jars on the buffet in the dining room and put two cubes of ice in each along with her new moonshine cocktail made with equal portions of Cherry Ale-8, prosecco, and a pure corn moonshine she'd bought from her friend at the Limestone Distillery in Lexington. The mixture was a light pink. It matched the cake, which had been decorated with Grandmother May's favorite pink roses.

Miranda's mother came downstairs dressed in a pink floral tea-length dress.

"Mom, what's up with the dress?"

"I'm an invited guest and everyone is wearing their Sunday best in Grandmother May's signature color, pink. I've known those two forever, you know. They only moved away last year to be closer to their sons. It's not easy to manage being old way out here in the sticks. I am so happy that they've come back to Wolfe County for their golden anniversary."

Miranda felt a bit underdressed in her tour guide uniform, but she didn't have either an appropriate dress or the time to change.

"Hey, Mom. Did you know that Howard Cable was having some sort of business problems on the day that he went missing? Doris Ann says she overheard him on the phone having a loud argument."

"Oh, that." Dorothy frowned. "I've heard that from my sister since then, but I never really paid much attention to it. I mean, she had to say something to support her thinking that he had left and would eventually return. He couldn't have been happy and done that to her."

"Right. Also, I heard from the coroner that he had a broken leg. Would you have thought that it would have been so debilitating that he would have just stayed under a tree and not found a way to get back to the trail?"

"Not in a million years. He would have had a first aid kit in his backpack and a good knife in his pocket. He would have made a splint to tie up the fracture, and he would have crafted a set of crutches made of branches and vines to get himself back to the trail. He wouldn't have just sat there."

"Without a backpack, knife, or even identification, this is all wrong. My suspicion is that his death was planned beforehand." Miranda involuntarily shivered at the thought.

Dorothy sighed her great frustration. "I agree. Now, what are you doing about it?"

"Do you remember what he studied in college and where he worked? Doris Ann thinks he was about to make a deal of some sort, but something was going wrong. She wants to talk to me after the party."

"My sister must not have known. She's never said anything about his work, but then again, I didn't ask her."

"Why are you making me drag this out of you. What did he study in college?"

"I'm sorry. My brain doesn't seem to be working right. I'm more upset than I thought. Let me think." Dorothy bowed her head and put a hand on her forehead. "Right! It was geology. He got interested after one of the cows stepped on his foot and wrecked his ankle. Howard blew it off for a few days."

Miranda wrinkled her brow. "Wow, apparently he has an extremely high threshold for pain."

"That's what the doctor said when my sister finally dragged him into the clinic. That foot had to be wrapped and elevated for nearly a week. So, while he was in bed, he began reading some of the old histories about mining.

He was particularly interested in the lost Swift silver mines."

"That makes sense."

"After he got his degree, he worked for one of the local oil companies as a location scout. He was very good at the job."

"So, not moving from the tree seems improbable give his high pain tolerance. Something prevented him."

Chapter 14

Tuesday Afternoon, the Farmhouse

The section of roof to be repaired had grown in size again by the time the last guest left the party. Miranda trotted around to the barn and stood below the tall ladder.

"Ron! What are you doing? I don't need the whole roof patched."

It took a moment, but Ron peered down to her from the edge of the roof. "These are all loose. They would go in the next big wind, and you get a lot of big wind up here in Pine Ridge."

Miranda cupped her hands around her mouth. "You can add more nails instead of stripping them off, right? That roofing is fairly new. A little wind shouldn't have damaged everything up there. You need to only replace what is completely damaged."

Ron raised his eyebrows. "Well, I guess I could, but—"

"I don't have the money for that. Stop ripping off shingles!"

"As you say. When can we go to the hardware store? I'm out of shingles and undercoating."

Miranda clasped a hand over her mouth to keep from cursing a blue streak. "I'll be ready in about an hour. No more demolition. Do you hear me?"

Ron nodded.

Miranda returned to the kitchen and found Lily and Iris doing the washing up. Lily looked up. "You know he'll keep tearing things up until you stop him?"

"I know that. I gave him strict orders not to do anything but the hole, but, of course, we were busy with the party. It's my own fault. I'm going to have to do something different."

Iris was drying the dessert plates with a dish towel and putting them away one by one. "Do you have anyone who could keep an eye on him? He's really good, but needs constant watching."

"I'll give that some thought." Miranda would have asked Austin to keep Ron focused, but their disagreement caused her to hesitate.

"What about your mom?" asked Iris. "It would give her something to do."

"And also make her feel useful," added Lily.

After Lily and Iris left, Miranda gave Sandy a good long walk to calm herself before she dealt with Ron. Before she stood in front of the barn, she heard the nail gun snugging down any loose shingles. That was good.

She had met men like him all her life. They didn't take direction from women very well. It was a bit strange because strong women were thick on the ground in Wolfe

County. The first woman postmaster in the state had run her post office here for more than a decade in the sixties. No one batted an eye.

The elected office of Wolfe County clerk had been held by a woman since right after World War II. It was a powerful position, and again no one batted an eye. Maybe it was Miranda herself. Was her attitude too demanding without being compassionate? Her introverted nature fought against social interactions. She could work on being more kind, more patient, more friendly. That wouldn't hurt in any situation.

As she looked back at her actions, her decision to move to New York City seemed both brave and reckless. She had dreamed of sharing her unique style of highland mountain paintings with the elite but hadn't expected the complicated, insular, narrow-minded politics. Skating through art classes at Savannah College of Art and Design was thin preparation for the sophistication of the coldly polite rejections that her work met in the city.

Living there had been a constant penny-pinching struggle, but at the same time a delight to be in an epicenter of power, diversity, culture, and liberation.

Returning to her family's roots highlighted the ways that she had changed. She loved being a modern woman, but she also admired the old-fashioned ways of her country family.

It took about two hours to drive Ron down to the hardware store, pick up the supplies he needed, pay for them, load them into the van, and unload them into the barn.

Dorothy appeared just as the last of the supplies were unloaded. "Hi, Ron. I haven't seen you in years."

Ron turned to face Dorothy and whipped the hat off

his head, "Howdy, Dorothy. I've never met anyone as pretty as you."

Miranda was surprised to watch her mom blush at the compliment. Did they have a history?

"You're a sweetie, Ron. You've always had a lovely way with words." Dorothy turned to Miranda. "I'll set another place for supper." She headed back toward the house.

Ron stood there for a moment, then put his hat back on. "You don't mind if I doss down here in the barn, do you? It would save me a lot of hassle getting a ride back out here. I can do that, of course, but it would be better if I could stay right here."

Miranda had a feeling this request was coming. She had noticed the rolled-up sleeping bag and mat when he unloaded his tools. "That's fine. The loft has some fresh hay that would make a great mattress. I don't know about rats. There hasn't been a barn cat around for several years, and Sandy isn't old enough to root them out, either."

"I'll be fine. I'm used to sleeping rough."

"Suit yourself. Come in for supper in about a half an hour."

Miranda and her mother had just finished cooking pork chops, collard greens, scalloped potatoes, and corn bread when a truck pulled into the driveway.

"Anyone home?" called out Austin as he bounded up the steps. "It smells wonderful out here. What's cooking?"

Dorothy hollered from the kitchen, "Pork chops and all the fixings. Come on in."

Miranda whispered, "Mom, we're not speaking at the moment. You can't invite him for supper."

Dorothy whispered back, "Oh, yes, I can." Then in a normal voice: "Come on back, Austin. We're about to sit down. Miranda, call out back for Ron. I'm sure he hasn't had anything decent to eat for days."

Miranda huffed. How did mothers do that? Completely take over a house that didn't even belong to them. They must get the charm installed as soon as the first child is born. She escaped out the back door before she had to speak to Austin. "Ron," she yelled, "supper's ready. Come and get it."

No answer.

"Ron," she yelled even louder. "It's time for supper. Come on down."

Still silence.

She walked back into the pasture beside the barn so that she could see the roof. He wasn't up there. "Ron! Where are you?"

He might be using the rustic outhouse, so she circled around the barn to check. It was empty, but she made a mental note to give it a good clean in the morning and supply it with more toilet paper. She was on her way into the barn when she heard the groan.

"Uhm."

"Ron!" Miranda rushed over to find Ron on the ground in the middle of the open barn doors. He was sitting up squeezing his ankle. She knelt on the dirt floor beside him. "Ron! What happened?"

"Ow. I fell through a spot that looked solid. I was trying to drag myself to the house." He panted like a racehorse. "It was gonna take a long time."

"Where's that harness? It should have caught you."

"I don't like 'em. They get in the way." He groaned again. "I think my leg is broken."

"I'll get help." She pushed a stack of burlap sacks behind him so he could lie back a little, then sprinted for the back door of the house.

"Mom! Austin! Ron's fallen off the roof. He might a broke his leg. I'm calling for an ambulance to take him to Lexington."

"Where's your first aid kit?" Austin asked. "In your uncle's bedroom?"

"Yes." Miranda grabbed the phone from its charger on the kitchen counter and dialed 911.

"Nine one one. What is your emergency?"

"My workman has fallen from the roof of the barn and I think he has broken his leg. He needs to go to the hospital. He might also have internal injuries. It was a long fall."

"I'll contact your nearest emergency services and have them make a run out there."

Miranda gave the dispatcher directions to the farmhouse and was told that it would be between fifteen and thirty minutes before someone could arrive.

She hung up and turned to her mom, who had an old quilt in her arms and was rummaging in the kitchen drawers for dish towels. Miranda grabbed the jar of moonshine from the counter. They both ran out the back of the house. Austin was kneeling beside Ron and had cut off the leg of Ron's overalls to expose the injury.

Austin looked up at Miranda. "Good. He needs a good wallop of your moonshine. He's gonna need to take the edge off before the paramedics get here. Whatever they do is going to hurt."

"I've got it right here." Miranda twisted open the lid and handed Ron the new jar.

Ron reached for it but groaned again and dropped his

arms. Miranda positioned the jar so that Ron could drink a few swigs. He coughed, collapsed back on the burlap sacks, then passed out.

Dorothy covered him with the old quilt and sat back on her heels. She looked up at Austin. "That's all we can do for now. How's his leg?"

"It's probably fractured, but the bone feels at least intact. I can't believe he dragged himself all the way out here." Austin pointed to a section of Ron's leg that was scraped up. "It's probably right there. The real danger is internal bleeding."

Miranda stood and made tight fists. "I can't believe he wouldn't use the harness. He was wearing it when I left this morning."

Austin pressed his lips into a tight line. "These old-timers are set in their ways and just don't care what the rules are."

"I'm going to get a flashlight and help signal the paramedics," said Dorothy.

"Good idea, Mom." Miranda watched her leave and then turned to Austin. "Look how far he dragged himself. It's got to be over thirty feet from the opening in the roof."

"Amazing, really." Austin's voice was low as if he didn't want to wake Ron.

"That means that my cousin should have been able to drag himself over to the trail. He was way more fit than Ron is."

"You're assuming he was conscious."

"Good point. I was thinking that, well, surely Howard didn't fall against that tree and break his leg. He was either placed there or maybe even held there. That's the part that just doesn't make sense to me. I mean, given a decent pain tolerance, he could have dragged himself over to the tree and that's as far as he could go? After all, he might have been in shock and misread his strength."

"I expect that Barbara will have some idea what happened," said Austin.

"I hope she's as good as her reputation. I have so many questions, like could the position of his bones lend credibility to the idea that he was tied up? If a person passes out sitting up, do they tip over to the side eventually? Would the position of the bones show that? But if Howard's body decomposed while tied up, his skull would do what? Roll forward to his feet? I have no idea."

Stop. Please, stop." Austin inhaled and looked into her eyes. "Can we agree to disagree on this? I think you are right to have so many questions. But if you're not savvy about it, you won't get the cooperation you want. Be patient and your friends and family will support you with the answers."

A silence built between them.

"Will you support me?" Miranda said quietly, then held her breath. His backing meant more to her than she knew before this conversation. If he said no, she knew that their friendship would end. She was also hoping for a future that included more than a friendship.

"Yes, I support you. I think there's more to Howard's death than meets the eye. I'm in the camp that does not believe he died by accident. There's a lot that won't pass muster. Why was he there at all? Alone? Why not tell someone or make a cell phone call? Where are his belongings? There are enough suspicious items to choose from to make the case that it needs to be investigated."

Miranda smiled and relaxed. That had been a close one.

"They're coming," her mother yelled. "I hear them from the highway. Only five more minutes."

Dorothy guided the rescue vehicle down the dark driveway to the barn with her flashlight. The headlight beams from the ambulance shone on the unconscious Ron. It blinded Miranda and Austin, who threw up their hands to fend off the glare.

The doors opened and the driver walked over with a big black case in his hand, "Hey, Austin. What have you got there?"

Miranda was annoyed. Why did people always speak to whatever man was handy? This was her farmhouse, not Austin's. She pushed down her irritation. This wasn't New York. The man knew Austin, so of course he would speak to him first.

"Hi, Andrew," Austin said, then nodded to the second responder. "Hi, Scott. It's a bad fall. I'm here having supper with Miranda Trent and her mother. You know Ron Menifee, don't you? He's been doing handyman jobs around here for decades."

"He worked on my granny's old cabin last year," said Andrew Perry. "He did a great job in between drinking bouts. She started withholding money until he completed his jobs. That worked out better for both of them."

Kneeling beside Ron, Scott Caldwell opened his case and pulled out a stethoscope. He moved the old quilt to the side, listened to Ron's heartbeat, then draped the stethoscope around his neck. He took out a blood pressure cuff and took that reading as well. "Heartbeat's strong and steady. Blood pressure is textbook. Let's see what we can see for breaks."

Scott felt all Ron's limbs and then looked up at Miranda. "The main injury seems to be his left ankle. He doesn't appear to have any fractures, but he needs to get that confirmed with an X-ray. Everything else seems stable. Let's get him in the vehicle and take him over to Doc Watson's clinic over in Campton. The doc put in two extra rooms at the back of his house specifically for this kind of case."

Andrew piped up, "Ron can't afford a hospital stay over in Lexington. He doesn't have any insurance, and he isn't old enough for Medicare. Help me get him on the gurney."

They loaded Ron up, and as they were putting the gurney in the back of the vehicle, Ron woke with a start. "Hey! What's going on here? Where are you taking me?"

Andrew leaned over and spoke slow and clearly. "Don't you worry, Ron. We're taking you over to Doc Watson's little clinic. You can work out your medical bills in trade."

Ron held up a hand toward Miranda. "Don't you worry, little missy. I'll be back on my feet in no time. This is just a little setback. I'm sure you won't get anyone better to fix that roof."

Miranda, her mother, and Austin watched the taillights of the rescue vehicle disappear down the gravel road.

Dorothy broke the silence. "I'll go reheat our supper. It'll only take about ten minutes. Why don't you two give Sandy a nice little walk? The moon is out and the evening is gorgeous." She held the screen door open for one last order. "Don't waste that moon."

Miranda got Sandy's leash, and in moments they were walking down the moonlit road. "Let's agree that the circumstances around the discovery of Howard's bones are not what you would expect from a simple lost hiker."

"Possibly," said Austin. "You must have heard of the case of the missing hiker on the Appalachian Trail. After two years, she was found less than two miles from the trail. She had survived for almost thirty days. She was very experienced."

"Right, but they found a written record of her experience along with the body. They also found all her equipment and identification. None of Howard's equipment has been found. If he moved himself, he wouldn't have left it behind."

"That does make it different if by that you suspect that he was moved by his attacker." Austin stood while Sandy sniffed at a pile of rabbit scat. "He should have been able to get over to the trail. But that means there has to be something else in play. Mainly, it points to some sort of restraint that prevented him from rescuing himself."

"I agree that we need to investigate further, but I don't expect we'll get any help from the sheriff. He seemed annoyed that Felicia hired her friend."

"I'm confused by that. Something must be happening politically." Austin picked up Sandy and tucked him into his arm. "I'm not sure he'll support any additional expenses now that the body has been identified. I'm throwing in with you on further investigation is needed. Besides, this happened in my park. If worst comes to worst, the Park Service will pay for any extraordinary expenses associated with Howard's death investigation."

Miranda smiled. "Yes, that will make my mother and Aunt Ora happy. And you?"

"I might get to experience the kind of budget-focused grief that the sheriff is receiving, but it still must be done."

Chapter 15

Tuesday Night, the Farmhouse

After dinner and dishes, Miranda took Austin into her uncle's bedroom, now turned into her business office, to use the internet. She logged in and brought up a search page. "I'm starting a new murder notebook and I want you to help me search for information about Howard and his past."

She opened a brand-new black-and-white composition notebook, the same kind she had used during their last investigation. She set it up the same way.

"Let's start with his high school record. He went to Wolfe County High School and graduated I'd say about twelve or thirteen years ago."

"Sure." Austin tapped the keys and went to the WCHS alumni website. "Here he is." Austin pointed to Howard's senior year picture. Austin wrinkled his brow and looked at Miranda. "He doesn't look anything like you. Are you sure you're related?"

"According to my mother, he takes after his dad's family. I take after my mother. Have you met Aunt Ora?"

"I don't think I've met her formally, but I know who she is when I see her around. Anyway, it says here that he belonged to the following clubs: Rock Climbing, Young Geologists, Track and Field, and the Chess Club. He sounds like a pretty smart guy from that." Austin swiveled around the chair and looked at her. "You know where we can find the yearbook, don't you?"

"Yes, at the Historical Museum in downtown Campton. They have every single WCHS yearbook ever printed. Too bad their hours are so limited. It conflicts with the times that I'm conducting tours."

Austin smiled. "My schedule is a little more flexible. I'll drop by tomorrow and copy the pages where he appears."

"Great. Now let's look up his college record. He went to—let me think—the University of West Virginia. There was such a to-do over him being the first relation to go to college. Everyone was so excited. When I went?" She turned her head from side to side. "'What a waste of money. You're only going to get married and waste all that money.'"

"Ouch!"

"Mom stood up for me, of course. She knew how much I wanted to be an artist." Miranda paused. "But she also insisted that I minor in business administration."

"Clever woman."

Miranda smiled and leaned over Austin to look at the screen. He had clicked over to the UWV alumni site. "You say he graduated about eight years ago?"

"Yep."

A few more clicks and Austin found Howard Cable's profile. He had gotten a full-ride scholarship and graduated magna cum laude with a degree in geology. His scholarship was granted for his track-and-field abilities.

"He was a first-rate athlete and became captain of UWV's track-and-field team." Austin clicked a few more links. "They won their division his first year and then won the nationals each of the next three years. Several of his team members went on to the Olympics. I wonder why he didn't."

"I didn't know he was that good." Austin looked back at her. "Keep going," said Miranda. "We're only scratching the surface."

He had been an active member of the Rock Climbing Club, the Chess Club, the Debate Team, and the Adventurers Club.

"Wait. Something in what you just said feels familiar." Miranda felt her brow crunch. Something was trying to come to the front of her thoughts. It felt like a memory, but it wasn't. "Rats, I can't remember the details, but there was a scandal during his last weeks of college about the admissions policy." She was silent for a moment then huffed. "Whatever it was went away. Keep going."

The next few searches displayed that Howard had been recruited by Giant Oil Company and selected for their Emerging Manager Program to prepare him for future promotions to the highest circles of influence in the company.

"He really had everything going for him." Austin sat back in the chair.

"I know. In my family, he was the golden child. Everything he put his mind to just bloomed into opportunity after opportunity. I was too young to hang around with him. He seemed aloof and driven to my mind. I don't know that his mother will ever recover from this loss."

Austin bent over the screen again. "Here's a social media reference to an adventurers club that he established in college. It's called Risky Business Adventurers. It's a closed club and you can only get an invitation from an existing member." Austin clicked a series of search links. "It looks like some of the members are from his graduating year."

"Risky Business Adventurers is the name of the group I took up to Indian Staircase. But if my aunt didn't mention it, then I wouldn't have known. I was struggling my way through school. I had a skimpy scholarship and survived mainly on cheese grits and ramen noodles. I remember thinking it was odd that he didn't show up for Christmas."

"Let me search for any mention of his disappearance." Austin leaned back after a few moments of key tapping. "There's an article that calls for information. It looks like your aunt got suspicious and reported him missing. Did you know he was with that closed group?"

"No one mentioned it to me." She raised her eyebrows. "But, like I said, I was deep in survival mode with only a few months to go before I dropped out."

It was Austin's turn to wrinkle his brow. "Wait. Here's an article in the *Lexington Herald-Leader* interviewing one of the members of the Risky Business Adventurers group. It says that they started up the group when they were at UWV and that Howard had continued to be the leader even after graduation."

"Oh, my stars! That's what I was trying to remember. Look at the name of the group member."

"It's Jennifer O'Rourke making the statement. Remember, she was the one who scraped her hand on his bones up above the Indian Staircase."

"That's a huge coincidence. Howard was part of the same Risky Business Adventurers club? They were there when he disappeared and no one mentioned it after the bones were discovered? Unbelievable! Does it say who else was in the club?"

Austin used his finger to scan down the screen. "Here's where the reporter lists the members: Alfred Whittaker, Ben DeBerg, Kevin Burkart, Jennifer O'Rourke, Howard Cable, Kurt Smith, and Stephanie Brinkley."

"Oh, my goodness! It's the complete list of Risky Business Adventurers clients that I took up to the Indian Staircase. This is too much of a coincidence for it to be unplanned. We have to let the sheriff know right away."

"Are there any quotes from them? What did they say about the disappearance?"

Miranda pointed to a section of the article. "Hmm. They reported that they saw him at the final dinner as usual, but he had already gone the next morning when everyone checked out of Hemlock Lodge and went their separate ways."

"Curious."

Miranda continued reading aloud: "'Alfred Whittaker, the leader of the group, stated that it wasn't unusual for Howard to get an emergency call from his company and simply leave. He usually left a note, but not always.'" She leaned back in her chair. "Telling, don't you think?"

Austin stood. "I agree. I did notice another helpful tidbit about the article."

"What?"

"The byline. It was written by my sister."

Miranda sat taller in her chair. "That's wonderful. I'll call Sheriff Larson and then you call your sister. Ask her what she remembers about it. Even better, have her send us the *Lexington Herald-Leader* archives associated with Howard's disappearance. Not even the sheriff is looking at this angle—just us."

Miranda phoned Sheriff Larson's office and left a long message about what they had found. Then, since cell phones didn't work at her farmhouse, she turned the handset over for Austin to dial his sister.

"Hi, Tyler. . . . Yes, I know it's late, but Miranda and I have found an unusual connection to the bones that we discovered up above the Indian Staircase. Are you interested?"

As he related the story to his sister, Miranda motioned that she was going to make some tea, so she left and was surprised to see her mother sitting at the kitchen table in her favorite floral bathrobe and fluffy pink slippers. "Mom, I thought you were asleep long ago."

"I couldn't sleep. So I called Doc Watson's clinic. Ron is fine. He'll stay there overnight, but he'll be back here tomorrow. I think I'll be fine with some chamomile tea. I've made a huge pot that's strong enough to do the job. Do you want some?"

"That's why I came in here." Miranda got a tray and two mugs from the cupboards. "Austin and I have done a ton of internet research about Howard. I didn't know he was so athletic."

"That's one reason it hit Aunt Ora so hard. He turned down a chance to compete in the Olympics. The Olympics, because he knew he needed to make money to support his mother and sisters. He couldn't afford to train at that level and still hold down a high-powered job. She thinks he would be alive today if she had forced him into trying out for the team."

"But her daughter went away to college anyway. How?"

"Partly sports scholarships, but mostly because their dad had made some early technology investments, and before he disappeared, Howard signed over his shares to her. He was young when their dad died, but he took his role as man of the family seriously."

"I would never have thought of that at his age."

"It's why Aunt Ora is still living in her house. She lives frugally to be sure, but I think that is just habit. The house is paid for. Now that his death is confirmed, she'll get a life insurance payout from his company. She'll be okay financially, but that side of the family have always been resourceful. She would never have starved."

"Howard was much more complicated than I thought."

Dorothy got up from the table and scuffed her way over to the sink to rinse out her mug and put it in the dish drainer. "I'm surprised you didn't notice. He was very ambitious." She kissed Miranda on the cheek. "You two were alike in many ways."

Miranda finished off with the tea tray by adding some leftover cake from the golden anniversary party. She carried it out of the kitchen and poked her head into her office. "I've got some tea and cake. Come on, we'll have it in front of the fire in the front room. We need to come up with a plan for tomorrow."

"Sure." Austin followed her and they ended up on the comfortable couch, full of tea and cake with a sleepy puppy between them.

Chapter 16

Wednesday Morning, the Farmhouse

Miranda woke at dawn to the sound of a nail gun accompanied by bouncing yips from Sandy. She threw her robe on over her pajamas, shoved her bare feet into her hiking boots, and ran out the back of the house. Sandy was close on her heels, trying to play fight her flying shoelaces. She'd made it to the ladder propped against the damaged side of the barn when Sandy caught a lace and pulled her off-balance.

She and Sandy tumbled in the dewy grass, missing the ladder by inches. "Sandy! You little scamp. Sit." Sandy obeyed instantly with his big puppy eyes looking innocent. "Who's up there?" she yelled up the ladder.

"It's me." Austin stood at the edge of the roof with Ron's heavy-duty nail gun hanging from one hand. "Sorry to wake you, but I thought you might want the place to be watertight. It's going to rain today."

"My goodness, Austin. You didn't have to do that. I planned to call around today for another handyman."

"It's what neighbors do. I'll only be a few more minutes."

Miranda smiled. "Come in after you're done and have breakfast with us. I can be neighborly, too. Be careful." She turned away and soon heard more rat-a-tats from the roof. She took Sandy on his morning walk and then went back in through the farmhouse front door.

"Good morning, sweetie," Dorothy said as she was coming down the stairs into the dining room. She moved one step at a time, hanging on to the banister with one hand and rubbing her eyes with the other. "What time is it? Who's making all that racket?"

Miranda waited at the bottom of the stairs and gave her mother a great big hug. "It's Austin. He's nailing a tarp over the giant hole Ron made in the barn roof. He says it's going to rain, but it's as clear as a bell outside. I think he wanted to be useful. That's sweet."

Dorothy put the tips of her fingers on both temples and rubbed gently in small circles. "It feels like rain to me. He might know more about the weather than either of us since he spends so much time outdoors. Have you started the coffee?"

"Just getting ready to. How does that predicting-the-weather talent feel? Is it passed down to certain people? Austin predicted there would be a storm coming when we were up the Indian Staircase. I don't feel anything."

Her mom followed her into the kitchen. "I'm starving and I'm sure Austin hasn't eaten yet, either." Dorothy rummaged in the refrigerator and took out a carton of eggs and a package of thick bacon slices. "Feeling the approaching weather isn't fun. It's either a gift or curse de-

pending on how it takes you. For me, I get a sharp headache right behind my eyes. Then I know rain is due in less
than an hour. For some people, their old injuries ache.
I've also heard that some people feel light-headed."

"It sounds terrible. I'm glad I don't have it."

"Is an onion-and-bacon scramble good for you and
Austin?"

Miranda beamed. "I love those. I'm sure Austin will,
too." She turned to focus on making the coffee. Miranda
put spring water in the kettle and measured out coffee into
her largest French press. As soon as the water reached the
boil, she poured it in the press, gave it a quick stir, and set
it on the kitchen table to steep.

Moments after Dorothy pulled the iron skillet out of
the oven and placed it on the kitchen table, Austin came
in through the back door. "Wow, that looks fantastic and
smells even better." Miranda tried to thank him. He just
waved a hand at her and tucked into his breakfast.

Dorothy tried to put another helping on Austin's plate,
but he put a hand over his empty plate and pushed his
chair away from the kitchen table. "That was delicious,
but I can't eat another bite." He stood. "I need to get in to
work. There's a work order about a section of trail that
eroded the night of the big storm. It's not a popular trail
so it didn't get reported until late yesterday."

Miranda stood as well. "I've got a little time before I
lead today's tour. I think I'm going to do a little doodling
around in my murder notebook. We gathered quite a bit
of information last night. I don't want to forget any of it."

"I'll clean up the kitchen before the Hobb girls arrive
and then I'm going to go over to my sister's place for the
day," said Dorothy. "I think her other daughter is due to
arrive today, but I can't remember which one. I told her at

the time that naming them Anna Belle and Anna Sue would cause confusion. Anyway, I'll stay with Ora until whichever one of them gets there. You go on and get your sketchbook going."

Miranda went into her office and pulled out the composition notebook she'd started last night. On the first page, she sketched an image of Howard Cable from the portrait in the Wolfe County High School yearbook. She looked at it for a long time. It was an excellent sketch, but instead of showing the shining promise of a bright future, she had sketched him with an expression of resigned disappointment. That felt right to her.

She turned to the first page and wrote "Suspects" at the top and listed the names of the members of the Risky Business Adventurers club:

Alfred Whittaker	Client #1—a freelance reporter
Ben DeBerg	Client #2—a criminal defense lawyer
Jennifer O'Rourke	Client #3—a jewelry artist
Kevin Burkart	Client #4—owner of a financial services business
Kurt Smith	Client #5—a cosmetic surgeon
Stephanie Brinkley	Client #6—a licensed pharmacist

Then she added his closest relations:

Ora Cable	Howard's mother
Anna Belle Cable	Howard's younger sister
Anna Sue Cable	Howard's older sister

Finally, casting her net even wider, she made a list about anyone else who might be a suspect:

A high school rival?
A university enemy?
A lover or past romance?
A boss at the oil company?
A coworker at the oil company?

That was a long list, but she had long ago figured out that when you were in brainstorming mode, you wrote down every little thing that occurred to you while the thoughts came rushing into your brain. This free-associative technique had led to emotionally powerful paintings by opening her creativity to its fullest.

Then she flipped to the next page in the notebook and wrote "Alfred Whittaker" at the top of the page and drew his portrait in seconds. Sometimes those quick drawings could reveal personality traits that would later become important.

On the next page, she did the same to Ben DeBerg, then continued to create a page for everyone on her suspect list up through Anna Sue Cable.

After all that, she felt absolutely drained. She had sketched quickly without a rest between people, trying to capture their essential characters. Maybe one of them was telling her something subliminally. She didn't doubt it, but when flipping through the pages again, none of them felt as if they were the cause of her unease.

She closed the sketchbook and prepared for her cultural tour. It was a relatively light workday. She had only four clients, and they had signed up for her most popular offering, the view of Lover's Leap and a traditional venison-chili dinner back at the farmhouse. She could conduct this tour with her eyes closed.

She called out, "Mom, don't forget that Sandy needs to be in his cage before you leave."

Miranda had her hand on the front door when the phone rang. She checked her watch; still a few minutes early, so she answered it.

The call was from Felicia Larson. "Morning, Miranda. Have you got a minute?"

"Only a couple. I've got a group to collect at the Hemlock Lodge."

"Okay. My friend Barbara has found something curious among the remains of your cousin. I'm hoping you can help us with some details about its origin."

"What is it?"

"It's a silver bracelet with a thistle charm attached. It looks handcrafted, so anything you can tell me would be helpful."

"Well, the Scottish thistle is a family symbol. It goes all the way back to our first Scotch-Irish ancestors. It's a popular decorative theme in almost everything that my family creates. Did you want to bring it over or should I stop by the sheriff's office?"

"Please come by the office. Barbara also found a map that is too fragile to handle without damaging it further. I'd like for you to tell me what you can about the notations on it. It looks like some sort of code or maybe it's a language I don't know."

"No problem. I'll see you right after my tour this afternoon."

"Fine. Try to stay dry. It's going to rain this afternoon."

Miranda looked up at the clear blue sky and exhaled. Some of the tension she had been carrying slipped away. At last she felt some hope that she was on the right track to solving Howard's death. "We'll see."

Chapter 17

Miranda arrived at the sheriff's office and walked right in. Felicia, apparently expecting her, stepped outside her office and waved her inside. After the door closed, Felicia placed a small silver bracelet into Miranda's hands. It was beautifully crafted. The links were delicate but sturdy. The fastening was an old-fashioned spring ring clasp, and a single charm hung from the center link of the bracelet.

"This looks like the work of my late grandfather Buchanan. He worked silver in his spare time to supplement the family income." Miranda held the bracelet up to the light. "There should be a maker's mark on it someplace. I don't remember where he hid them."

"I didn't know your grandfather was a silversmith." Felicia tilted her head a bit.

"It's not widely known, but my mother has a bracelet

very similar to this. Do you have a flashlight? I know there's a mark."

"Hang on a second. Richard, are you here?" Sheriff Larson appeared at the door to her office. She used a soft voice the polar opposite of her professional tone. "Honey, I need a flashlight. Do you have one handy?"

"Sure, baby." Sheriff Larson went back to his office, apparently rummaged in a desk drawer, and returned with a huge flashlight. "Will this do? I use it on night patrol."

"That's enormous. Really? That's all you have?"

"Beggars can't be choosers." He splayed his hands out palms up, then stood waiting for what was next.

Felicia rolled her eyes but flashed him a flirty smile. She flicked on the flashlight and it lit up the bracelet like a Broadway spotlight. She carefully examined every nook and cranny in a focused state of mind Miranda recognized.

That same altered state sometimes took over Miranda when she was painting something intense. Each of those paintings sold in a heartbeat when she was working in New York City. The trouble was that she didn't experience it often enough, and her ordinary paintings were just that—ordinary. Miranda shifted her weight. She needed to get her art studio set up in the barn before she lost all incentive to ever paint again.

"I found it." Felicia looked up at both Miranda and Sheriff Larson. "Your grandfather was a clever fellow. This is masterful." She shone the light onto the clasp. "See this little flat space on the clasp? He stamped a tiny mark here. There's a tiny lowercase *b*."

The sheriff bent over to see the stamp. "Right, but what does this tell us? Why would Howard be carrying a family heirloom?" He turned to Miranda.

"Grandpa Buchanan worked on his silversmithing mostly in the winter when the demands of the farm were a little lighter." Miranda folded her arms. "I wonder how he got the silver. They had no cash money at all. The garden fed the family and the cow. He raised at least two pigs and they had chickens. His cash crop was tobacco, but that went for taxes and shoes."

"That wasn't unusual even as recently as ten years ago," said Felicia. "It's more difficult now with cell phones, cable TV, the internet. Those services need real money. They can't be paid for in trade goods or services."

Sheriff Larson tilted his head in thought. "It's possible he found a silver mine that was too small for anything but making his bits of jewelry. I'll ask around. Some of his old cronies still hang around the Senior Center. Do you want to stop in and get them to talk about the old days?"

"Perhaps, but what about the map?" asked Miranda.

"Oh, sorry, it nearly slipped my mind." Felicia handed the flashlight back to the sheriff and waved her arms to shoo him out of her office.

As he was leaving, he tossed out. "Are you two cooking up something that will get us all in trouble?"

"Of course not. These are personal artifacts. I want Miranda's opinion before I have to speak to Howard's mother about them. Ora seems on the verge of an emotional breakdown. I don't want to push her over the edge with mealy-mouthed questions that produce no helpful answers. Now scoot." Sheriff Larson left.

Felicia led Miranda to a table at the other end of her office. A discolored map was resting on an archival-quality backing board. It was covered with an overlay of tissue paper. Felicia lifted the tissue paper. "What do you make of this?" She handed Miranda a large magnifying glass.

Miranda bent over the table and examined the map. From the symbology, it was clearly a topographical map, but it was tattered and horribly discolored. In a flash of understanding, Miranda realized why it was in such bad shape—it had been with her cousin as his body decomposed.

Miranda straightened up and felt her stomach roil.

Felicia stepped close and grabbed Miranda by the upper arms. "I know what you're thinking. Take some really deep breaths. Try to put that aside."

Miranda pressed a hand on her belly and took breaths until the sick wave passed. She looked over at Felicia. "Thanks for that. It's gone now."

"Good." Felicia pointed to the edge of the fragile map. "We need to know if these words mean anything to you. Are they some sort of code?"

Miranda examined the faint lettering. It looked familiar, but she couldn't remember why. "I've been clearing out the farmhouse attic. This looks like some of the letters I've been sorting through and turning over to the Campton Historical Museum. Can I take some pictures?"

"Oh, sure. I've already exhausted my limited language knowledge."

Miranda snapped about twenty shots of the map with the high-quality camera on her smartphone. "I'll let you know if I can match any words. Some of those old letters go back a long way."

"Perfect. I'm packing it up to send over to a language specialist at the University of Kentucky. It will take him a few weeks to get back to me. That's assuming he can decipher anything at all. I'm betting that you'll have better luck."

"May I have the language expert's number? I may want to see the original again."

"No problem." Felicia looked him up in her phone contacts and read off the number.

There was a tentative knock on the door. Felicia didn't even look up. "We're still talking about the case."

The sheriff poked his head in from the outer room and blurted, "You're not giving her evidence, are you?" Sheriff Larson noted the look of irritation on his wife's face and backpedaled, using a softer voice. "Are you?"

"No," Felicia answered in her professional voice—not her wife voice. "I'm consulting her about the writing around the edge of the map that Howard Cable had with him. It's an old one and I think it may be a shorthand dialect of Scots-Irish. I remember listening to my relatives speak it to some of the old-timers at family reunions. I haven't heard anyone speak like that lately. I'm sending it over for the University of Kentucky specialists to drool over."

"How do you think that affects the case? Howard Cable mostly likely died of exposure after breaking his leg."

Felicia pressed her lips together in a tight line.

Miranda noticed the amount of self-control she used to maintain an even-tempered discussion with her husband-sheriff.

Felicia glanced at the sheriff. "I'm tending to agree with Miranda that this is more than just a case of disoriented hiker. We still don't have a full report from the autopsy, and I want to get this document in the hands of the experts before you pull the plug."

Sheriff Larson stood silent. He dropped his head a few inches. "Fair enough." He turned on his heel and returned to his office.

"One for the coroner." Felicia grinned. "Anyway, I'll send this along and tell them that you might want to examine it again."

"Thanks, Felicia. I'm off to talk to the clients that were up on the Indian Staircase on Sunday."

"Why?"

"I want to know why they didn't tell me that Howard was a member of the Risky Business Adventurers."

Felicia squinted her eyes into a questioning look. "But you didn't fess up to thinking it was Howard until your group was already packed up and heading down the trail. I don't know if any of them heard you say you needed to stay to represent the family."

"Rats, that's right. Let me think." Miranda closed her eyes and massaged her temples. "I don't remember any of them being close enough to hear me. I certainly didn't tell them."

"This will need follow-up. I think you're best suited for getting that information out of the Risky Business Adventurers members."

"You mean you think Sheriff Larson will provoke them into silence?"

Felicia smiled. "The sheriff is sharp-sighted, but not particularly subtle."

Miranda scratched the back of her head. "I see what you mean. I'll stop by their cabin and see what I can gather. I've got some drawings to return."

Chapter 18

With the charcoal sketches stacked on the seat beside her, Miranda drove over to the bed-and-breakfast where the Risky Business Adventurers were staying. The Big Rock Cabin wasn't far from the most popular natural attractions in the area. It was run by an antiquarian-book dealer who owned a rare bookstore, Glover's Bookery, in Lexington. His wife worked as an electrical engineer with Lexmark. They had built Big Rock Cabin as a week-end and holiday sanity retreat. After it was finished, they couldn't let Big Rock Cabin sit empty for most of the year, so they decided to rent it out to their families and friends. Word spread about its charms, and they expanded their offering to the online rental sites.

Miranda parked the van and spied Alfred Whittaker standing on the porch that ran the full length of the cabin. He had a mug of coffee cupped in both hands and a plate of shortbread nearby on a small table between two comfortable-looking rocking chairs.

"Miranda, how nice to see you." His eyebrows raised. "You've brought our drawings? Great. I was afraid they would be lost or forgotten."

"No, I would never forget a customer's artwork." Miranda went farther down the porch to a family-size dining table and arranged a display of the drawings.

Alfred opened the screen door that led to the great room and yelled into the cabin, "Hey, guys. Our drawings from the Indian Staircase are here. Come on out. They look great."

"Wonderful," said Ben as he came out to the porch and stood in front of the impromptu exhibition Miranda had created. "We should really have some sort of exhibit. These are great."

"That's a great idea. I could talk to the Hemlock Lodge manager if you're willing to let me keep them for a while," said Miranda. "I'm stealing that idea as a promotional ploy for my upcoming tours."

Jennifer followed Ben and looked at the drawings. "These are fantastic," said Jennifer. "It looks like we responded well to your instruction."

Jennifer bent over to peer at the signatures. "It's hard to tell us apart. Awesome! Did you say you wanted to arrange for a showing?"

"I did." Miranda continued to scan the drawings. "Don't you think they're fantastic?"

"Well . . ." Jennifer pointed out. "Drawing isn't my best medium. But, if everyone else agrees to exhibit, I'll go along."

Kurt walked out onto the porch followed by Kevin and Stephanie. "What's going on?"

Miranda waited until everyone was looking at her. "I brought your drawings over. They've been treated with a fixative and I slipped them into archival mats for you to take home. However, Ben"—she pointed at him—"has suggested that they're good enough for a showing. I agree, so, if you're all in favor, I'll start making the arrangements. It might take a while, but it would benefit both Hemlock Lodge and my Paint & Shine business."

Stephanie folded her arms across her chest. "Wonderful. It would be nice to support both the arts and a local business. We could dedicate the exhibit to that volunteer rescue organization. That would be a fitting charity, don't you think? We could come back to the cabin, couldn't we? I love this place even more each time we return."

"Return?" asked Miranda. "You've been here before?"

"This is our second adventure tour in this area," said Alfred. "Yeah. I think I still have a map for that in the Risky Business Adventurers scrapbook. Hang on just a second, I'll get it."

Kevin picked up one of his drawings and compared it to the others by propping it next to each drawing. He muttered, "We've been doing this since college. At least one adventure a year. I haven't missed a single one—not like some of our members." He turned his head and stared at Stephanie.

She flushed a light rose color from her throat to her hairline. "Some of us have jobs that require a lot of advanced notice for time off. The hospital is frequently short-staffed. You own your own business. It's easier for you."

"I'll give you that, but you?" He pointed to Jennifer. "Jewelry doesn't have hours."

She snapped back, "I have a set schedule and a limited number of festivals that I attend. If I'm not there, I lose my table location for the following year. I can't afford to be assigned the terrible locations. Festivals are more political than you think. I've spent years now positioning myself to get the best locations at each show."

"For me, I can't predict how long it might be or what kind of trial I'll get," Ben joined in. "But I put my times in the court calendar way in advance. That helps a bit, but I've still missed a few."

"I just block out my surgical dates." Kurt smirked. "If my client numbers drop too low—I just raise my prices. Fortunately, I'm so good, I can set any fee and clients still clamor for my time."

He apparently didn't know how arrogant he sounded. Miranda didn't think she would want him to give her for a manicure. What an ego. But then, each of them appeared to be self-centered in different ways. What on earth did they have in common?

"It's unusual for a group to have such a strong bond. I'm curious, how did y'all meet?"

As one, they all looked at Stephanie. "Right, I'm the unofficial official keeper of the oral history of the group. We get asked this question all the time."

"Why?"

"We also show up at extreme sports competitions like triathlons, mud runs, cave diving, bungee jumping, and snowboarding. Basically, a laundry list of extreme sports. Anything that takes athletic skill and endurance. We met in our freshman year at the University of West Virginia. We were all on the same floor of a student residence building."

Ben continued, "We were all hyperathletic, and so our food choices were quite different from the normal pizza-and-beer cuisine. It wasn't long before we started cooking together. That was superefficient and saved us tons of money and time."

"So much that we agreed to share a house together," said Kurt. "Some of us stayed longer to finish up our medical degrees. But we've kept in touch."

"In some ways," said Stephanie, "I think it is because we're all a little introverted. Making new friends is so much harder for me than it is to hang on to ones who already know about me and my quirks."

Kevin raised his eyebrows. "That's exactly why we've been together all this time. Interesting that you figured it out first, but you have the most knowledge. I don't have the head for dates and times like you."

"Maybe not first," said Jennifer. "She's the first to say it out loud. I've always known we weren't like the other college groups. I mean, we haven't included a single new member since the beginning. Even after—"

Kevin cleared his throat and glared at Jennifer.

"After what?" asked Miranda.

"Oh, nothing. We're happy as we are. No new members."

Alfred returned and handed Miranda a map of the Indian Staircase and Battleship Rock area. It was in great condition, and the trail was clearly marked. "Here you go." He scanned the group. "Of course, no new members. If we were going to do that, we would have chosen one after we lost Howard."

Silence fell upon the group like a foot of snow. There

were nervous glances at Kevin, and Albert finally noticed the odd reaction.

"What?" Albert shrugged his shoulders. "Everyone knows that Howard is why we're here."

Kevin glared daggers at Alfred. "No, that's not true. No outsiders knew until you had to go and spill the beans."

Everyone stood breathless like children about to be punished and all wishing they were somewhere else.

Miranda broke the spell. "I already knew that. Howard Cable was my cousin. I knew he was a member of an adventurer group. I wasn't aware that it was your Risky Business Adventurers.

"Oh, no. I am so sorry," said Stephanie. She looked around at the group. "I had no idea you were related to Howard."

Stephanie tilted her head and glared at Alfred. He finally caught the message. "Oh, yes, of course. Our deepest sympathies on the loss of your cousin."

Miranda blinked several times. "Thank you. That's kind. But I don't know why you have come back. Is it for some kind of group anniversary?"

More silence, followed by Alfred shuffling his weight from foot to foot. He then put a hand over his mouth, but it didn't settle him, so he dropped his hands to his sides.

"Yes," said Alfred. "That's why we're here. We've come back for the five-year anniversary."

'Our first adventure up here was five years ago," said Ben. "Alfred's map is from the racing challenge we arranged for ourselves."

Kevin splayed his palms up. "We found it more and more difficult to participate in the large races. There was just so much interaction with other competitors that it became too much. We felt like we were losing the closeness that was the purpose for starting the group in the first place. So, we started creating events and challenges of our own."

"Your tour is our first attempt at something artistic rather than strictly athletic. Jennifer is the one who insisted that we start balancing out our trips."

Jennifer folded her arms across her chest.

Miranda repeated, "Five years ago? That's when Howard Cable disappeared." She looked at the whole group. "He disappeared during your private extreme adventure."

As a group, they all said, "Yes."

Stephanie continued in her historical role, "We wanted to commemorate his disappearance with a memorial. Jennifer made a little concrete plaque to put in the spot where we were all together for the last time. We were going to do that while we were painting. It seemed like a good idea at the time."

"Of course, at the time, we didn't know that we would actually find his remains," said Alfred.

Stephanie looked around at the group. "We were also going to visit his mother and share some of our adventure pictures with her. I don't think he ever told her about us. I collected an album for her."

"Most of us haven't told anyone about that trip," said Ben. "I didn't want to do this. I knew it would be trouble."

"Does anyone else know that Howard was part of your group?" asked Miranda.

Everyone looked at each other, shaking their heads.

"Why didn't you call his mother?" Miranda's voice rose and held a sharp edge. "How could you be so cruel?"

The group looked at one another in turn with looking at the ground.

Miranda put her hands on her hips. "You didn't think of it? Really!"

Silence followed this question. Miranda's closed her eyes at such selfishness. It seemed to pervade the group in a fatal-attraction kind of way.

"I'm going to call Sheriff Larson." Another thick blanket of silence fell on the group.

Chapter 19

Wednesday Afternoon, the Farmhouse

Miranda drove straight home, walked into her front room, and found her mother and Sandy fast asleep on the couch under a quilt. She tiptoed into the kitchen, filled the teakettle with water, and put it on to boil.

The information that Howard had been a member of the Risky Business Adventurers had shaken her. What selfishness for the group members to keep that information from Howard's family. Maybe he could have been found in time.

She started to pick up the phone to dial Sheriff Larson, but the sound of a nail gun stopped her.

She ran out the back of the kitchen. "Austin, you can't take over Ron's job!"

Instead of a protest from Austin, Ron's voice boomed out instead. "I'm fine. The doc released me this afternoon for what he called light duty. Our great buddy right here"—

Ron patted Austin on the back—"dropped me off so I could get back to work. I'm lucky nothing got broken. My ankle got all stove up, but Doc Watson taped it up."

"But you were supposed to take it easy for a few days."

"Yeah, sure. But—"

Austin's voice lowered. "I heard Doc Watson tell you to rest with your leg elevated. I was right there."

"Look, I don't need to do that. You know I'm tough and I sorely need the money." Ron pointed to his properly worn safety harness. "I'm all hooked up. I won't forget again. I swear." He returned his attention to the roof and started to whistle. He seemed genuinely happy to be back to work.

"Be careful," Miranda yelled up to him.

Ron waved a hand and turned back to his repair work.

Miranda dared to hope that her roof would be finished by the end of the week. She could possibly be starting her first brew on Saturday. But not if she didn't get fresh supplies. She would call in her order after she talked to Sheriff Larson.

She returned to the kitchen and picked up the phone handset. It took her no more than five minutes to tell him that Howard was a member of the Risky Business Adventurers. It took longer for her to give Sheriff Larson all the background information she had gleaned from Tyler Morgan and also her visit to the rental cabin.

"I hope this raises your doubts about Howard's death. You can't deny that his belonging to their group wasn't disclosed. There have been plenty of opportunities to reveal that."

"No, I don't deny that. But it's also true that I didn't

connect this group with the investigation five years ago. That's my mistake. Just a second. Hang on."

He put his phone on mute for a second. Then he returned to the line. "Well, both you and Felicia are now officially right. The autopsy has revealed information that means Howard's case is a suspicious death."

"What did she find?"

"Miranda, you know I can't tell you."

"But I just handed you a bunch of new suspects. You can't leave me out."

Miranda heard a voice in the background. It belonged to Felicia. Again, the phone went mute. Miranda waited for more than a minute, then Sheriff Larson returned.

"I need a statement from you and Ora Cable regarding Howard's background with this group. Can you meet me at her house later this evening?"

"Absolutely. I'll bring my mother as well. She's very good with Aunt Ora."

"Fine." Sheriff Larson hesitated before continuing. "But make sure she understands the seriousness of the visit. This isn't a social call. We'll be examining Howard's background in painful detail. Everyone should be prepared to answer difficult questions."

"That's where Mom will help. She knows as much as her sister. They've always been incredibly close." Miranda hoped she sounded way more confident than she felt.

"Great. Shall we say seven o'clock sharp?"

"Yes, we'll be there."

Miranda hung up and prepared two mugs of strong ginseng tea and then added a great dollop of local honey to give it an energy burst. She took the mugs out to the front room and whispered softly, "Mom."

Sandy woke first with a yip and struggled out of his quilt cave to lick Miranda's hand. His tail began a windshield-wiper dance that threatened to tumble him to the floor.

Dorothy hummed a soft sigh and stretched out like a cat. "I didn't mean to nap, but I couldn't hold out any longer." She sat up and reached for a mug. "Mmm, that smells good. Did you get the ginseng from the boys down in Laurel Valley?"

"Of course. I wouldn't think of getting wild roots from anyone else. They find the best."

Dorothy took a deep draft of the tea. "They've been cultivating their secret spots for generations." She looked up at Miranda. "You look tired. What's happened?"

Miranda scooped up Sandy in her free arm and sat in one of the rockers. "I talked to the clients who were up at the Indian Staircase when I found Howard's body. Howard had been a member of their group. It started when he was at the University of West Virginia."

"I didn't know that!"

"Did Aunt Ora?"

"I don't think so, why?"

"It was in the papers."

Dorothy tilted her head. "Which one?"

"The *Lexington Herald-Leader*."

"She doesn't read that one. She only takes *The Wolfe County News*. It's a weekly paper. If it wasn't in there, she wouldn't know. Why?"

"We're going over to her house at seven o'clock. Now that there is more information from Howard's autopsy, the sheriff wants to ask her questions. He's agreed that you and I can be there."

"Isn't that unusual?"

"Yep, but this is an unusual case."

They enjoyed their tea until Sandy wiggled out of | Miranda's arms and sat in front of the screen door. "I'm taking Sandy for a little walk. I need to decide where to create a temporary gift shop. I'm missing out on sales be- cause of the construction."

"What about the woodshed?"

"It's full of wood?" Miranda tilted her head slightly.

"You haven't looked in there yet, have you?"

"No, I've been buried in work to get everything else running. It's off a little distance from the farmhouse and I don't think about it. Besides, Uncle Gene told me to stay out of there because of the snakes."

Dorothy laughed. "He had a good reason. Trust me, it is perfect for a temporary gift shop. You must have the key around somewhere. I'm gonna fix us a cold supper before we see my sister. Check out the woodshed."

Feeling as if she were splitting herself into too many pieces, Miranda grabbed the bunch of keys that hung on a peg in her office. Concentrating on tasks that supported her business appeared to keep her mind from obsessing on the grim reality of her cousin's death. Just because she didn't know him well was apparently no escape from being unnerved by his death.

She took Sandy for a walk down her gravel road to- ward the woodshed. He sniffed and piddled on every blade of grass and tuft of weeds along the way. After only a few guesses, she unlocked the metal hasp on the wood- shed door and pulled it open.

About a cord of wood was neatly stacked against the back wall, but the front part of the shed was completely empty—almost. About a dozen sturdy shelves were along the side walls. It only took a moment for Miranda to figure out why her uncle had built them.

This is where he sold his moonshine. This would be a perfect temporary gift shop. Yep, moms know everything. It wouldn't take but a few minutes to move her stock into the woodshed. She glanced at her watch. She had time to at least get a start and maybe sell of few of her items to tomorrow's tour group.

She whistled for Sandy to follow her and went down to the barn. She could use the wheelbarrow to transport her wares. She met Ron coming toward the house on the path down to the barn. His black boot didn't appear to make any difference to his mobility at all. Of course, it might signify that he wasn't particularly concerned with a little wobbling in his balance. Maybe he was used to it.

"I'm finished for the day," said Ron. "Do you mind if I have a bit of a washup?"

"Oh, sure. We're about to have a cold supper. You're welcome to join us."

"Yes, ma'am. I should be finished with the roof tomorrow. Thanks for letting me crash in the loft. I'll be ready to start work as soon as it gets light."

"No problem. I'll be in for my supper in a few minutes."

She walked into the barn and felt like ripping Ron from limb to limb. Tools and scraps of wood, tar paper, and shingles were everywhere. Not a single foot of the barn was free of his mess.

"Oh, no," she groaned. He had set up his chop saw in the middle of her gift shop. It looked as if it had been hit by a sawdust tornado. She should have moved her stock before Ron started his repairs. Now, everything would have to be thoroughly cleaned before she could offer anything for sale.

Ron was lucky that the quality of his work was so good because the magnitude of his mess was epic. She grabbed a wheelbarrow and filled it full of jams made by Lily and Iris. She could at least get them out of danger and safely on the shelves in the woodshed. All the clothing, T-shirts, and custom aprons would have to be washed.

She could feel an important source of income dwindling away. Sometimes her business seemed more like a janitor's job of endless cleanups.

Chapter 20

Wednesday Evening, the Farmhouse

Miranda managed to get through a frosty supper without losing her temper and firing Ron. Was he really her only choice? she wondered. It would be difficult to find someone else at the last minute, but maybe not impossible.

Another complication was that she felt it would upset her mom, who hadn't looked this happy in years. Ron and her mom were reliving their teen years with tales of yesteryear and lots of silly jokes and giggles.

I need to calm down and manage the repair with a kinder attitude.

Her problems were simple compared to Aunt Ora's. The shock and grief over the death of an only son must be overwhelming.

After helping her mother clear the kitchen, Miranda loaded up the wheelbarrow with another batch of her gift shop items. She stood back and admired the selection of local foods. No matter what else happened tomorrow, she at least had something to sell.

Tourists were happy to buy locally prepared foods and genuine craft items, not that mass manufactured stuff from China. The steadily growing profits from selling local crafts from her little gift shop in the barn were vital to the health of her business. She thought it might expand into a local co-op for the small farmers near her. She was beginning to attract some traffic, which reminded her that she needed to address the parking problem. With only a small driveway, she was limited because there wasn't a lot of flat land around the farmhouse.

She tucked Sandy up in her bedroom and drove her mother over to Aunt Ora's house. They arrived early at a quarter to seven but the sheriff's car was already there.

Miranda frowned at her mother. "He told me seven. I'll bet he has upset Aunt Ora to the brink of hysterics."

They walked up onto the front porch. Miranda could hear her aunt's high trembling voice through the screen door. "Oh, no. You are completely wrong. Howard would never worry me with foolishness like that. He was a very careful boy. He never wanted me to worry."

They were too late. The interview had begun.

"Aunt Ora," said Miranda as they walked into the front room. "What's wrong?"

Her aunt looked right through her to see that Dorothy was following right behind. "Oh, Big Sissy," said Aunt Ora. "They're saying that Howard was murdered. How can that be? Who would murder my Howard?"

Aunt Ora looked an ugly crying mess. Her nose was red and her eyes were puffy. Tears were streaming down her face. She gripped two floral cotton handkerchiefs, one in each hand. She sat in her favorite overstuffed rocker by the front window. Her knitting had been thrown in a tangle into a large wicker basket beside her footstool.

"Oh, Little Sissy," said Dorothy as she hurried over to give her sister a smothering hug. "What they have told you is true. You must have thought that Howard might have come to harm. I'm sorry this has upset you. I was supposed to be here when they told you."

Aunt Ora looked over at Sheriff Larson and Coroner Larson. Each was sitting forward at the edge of the floral couch looking stunned at such a powerful surge of emotion from Aunt Ora.

Miranda power-whispered to Felicia, "Why didn't you wait? This is going to be hopeless. She'll never calm down, at least not tonight. I told you."

Felicia rolled her eyes at the sheriff and whispered back, "Some of us have no patience with the emotional side of the job."

Miranda stood in front of her aunt. "Where are Anna Belle and Anna Sue?"

Aunt Ora pressed her handkerchief to her eyes. "They're down at Porter and Sons Funeral Directors picking out a casket for Howard. I couldn't face it."

"Of course not." Miranda patted her hand. "Would you like some fresh hot tea, Aunt Ora? I know you have chamomile. Wouldn't that be nice?"

Her aunt pulled another flowered handkerchief from the deep crease in the left side of her chair. She blew her nose, automatically stuffed the two used handkerchiefs into the opposite chair crease, then looked up at Miranda. "Oh, sweetie, you are so thoughtful." Aunt Ora coughed

and spoke in a clearer voice. "I don't know what has happened to my manners. That would be very nice. Make a
very large pot, please."

Sheriff Larson had a look on his face that betrayed his
irritation. He frowned, fumed, and fidgeted like a toddler
during church prayers.

Aunt Ora sniffed loudly. "There's also a plate of fresh
gingerbread cookies in the pie safe. Everyone will want
some. Right?" She began to recover her senses by way of
habit—she had hostess duties—as Miranda had hoped;
long-held traditions were strong patterns of behavior.

Sheriff Larson sat back on the couch and eyed Miranda.
He tipped his head toward the kitchen as a signal for her
to get the tea served so that he could continue with the
interview. He did not look happy.

Miranda sighed. *Does everyone feel the need to tell me
what to do?*

Dorothy had brought in a straight-backed chair from
the eat-in kitchen and placed it right beside her sister.
Dorothy sat down and took one of Aunt Ora's hands in
both of hers and rubbed it to bring back some warmth.

Felicia struggled to get out of the deep soft couch.
When she finally freed herself of its smothering softness,
she told Miranda, "I'll help."

They went into the kitchen. Miranda opened the door
to the pie safe and grabbed a cookie for each of them
from the yellow cookie jar. That jar had magically always
held cookies. Miranda didn't remember seeing aunt actually bake the cookies. As a small child, Miranda assumed
that cookies refilled the jar every night. It was a special
memory.

"I'll find the tea. You start the water." Miranda had

never rummaged through her aunt's cupboards, but she knew the typical pattern for most of her women relations. The dishes would be in a china cabinet and the tea would be in a cupboard near the stove.

Felicia spoke while filling up the huge stainless-steel teakettle at the sink. "All this upset wasn't necessary. I'm so sorry. I knew we should have waited until you had prepared your aunt, but patience isn't one of the sheriff's virtues." She put the filled kettle on the stove. "That helps his investigations most of the time."

Miranda found a serving tray and started loading it with her aunt's company-best cups and saucers. "She'll be fine. By the time we're serving tea using her bone china, she'll snap out of it. This set only comes out during the holidays."

Felicia smiled. "Clever. What a beautiful pattern. Is there a matching teapot?"

"Of course." Miranda found it along with silver spoons and a fancy plate for the gingerbread. The final effect would have looked perfectly at home in the latest issue of *Tea-Time* magazine.

They returned to the front room to find a calmer Aunt Ora still being comforted by her sister. Sheriff Larson had settled back on the couch and seemed resigned to let this interview progress much slower than he had intended.

Aunt Ora sat up straight when she saw the lovely tea tray. "Oh, Miranda, how sweet. You're gotten out my company-best china." Her mood changed from helpless victim to charming hostess at the first sight of her treasures. Aunt Ora beamed and directed the serving of the refreshments like a pastor's wife.

After everyone had been served to her Southern-lady

satisfaction, Aunt Ora sat up straight and said in a clear voice, "Now that we've had a bite, Sheriff, did you have some questions for me about my poor Howard?"

"Yes." He glanced over to Felicia and mouthed a thank-you. "We've been searching through Howard's past, his college years in particular., We want to know if you knew that he was a member of a group that calls itself the Risky Business Adventurers. And if so, what do you know about them?"

Aunt Ora lowered her head. "I've been trying to re-member back to those days. It was a painful time that first year that he was gone. While he was in college, he only came home during Christmas and Easter. His sports scholarship was generous in support of his classes and books, but he really only had whatever pocket money I could send him. His spare time was taken up by class-work. Then there were all the practice sessions. Then, of course, the team played so many out-of-town games." She looked from Sheriff Larson to Felicia and back to the sheriff. "You understand that all that meant that he couldn't hold a job."

Aunt Ora stopped for a moment, but no one spoke. "That first Christmas visit was a big shock. He had changed so much from the gangly teenager that went off to college that fall. He returned as a mature, fit, focused athlete—a growed-up man, I hardly knew him."

Another pause. "But he seemed happy. He said he had made friends with a group that shared his love for sports. They were planning to rent a house together for their sophomore year. All freshmen have to stay in the dormi-tories for their first year, you know."

Sheriff Larson leaned forward. "Did he mention their names?"

"Not at first. He would occasionally let a name drop when he was telling me funny stories. I'm sorry, I don't remember more. I was just so happy that he had found friends. He didn't make friends easily."

The sheriff continued, "What about after graduation? Did he keep in touch with them?"

"Not that I remember. He stayed here at home for a few weeks. He had a small break before he started work."

"We'll be checking with them about his vacation time," said Sheriff Larson. "They will probably contact you now that his death is confirmed. Please refer them to my office."

"That company of his'n wasn't very helpful when Howard disappeared. They told me that they had stopped his employment because he hadn't called in sick by the third day. Really? What a terrible people. They called several times after that. It upset me something awful."

Sheriff Larson glanced at his wife. "Go ahead. Show her."

Felicia nodded slightly and pulled a small evidence pouch from her large black bag. "Mrs. Cable, we found this among the remains. Do you recognize it?" She opened the pouch, poured the bracelet into her palm. Felicia struggled out of the couch, even slower this time holding the bracelet. She placed the silver jewelry into Aunt Ora's outstretched hand.

Aunt Ora's left hand dipped into the side crease of her chair and pulled out a pair of bright red reading glasses. She put them on and caressed the delicate bracelet. "I haven't seen one of these in years. I have no idea where Howard got this. I thought they were all accounted for within the family."

She looked up and there was a distant look in her eyes.

Dorothy started patting Aunt Ora's hand again. "Concentrate, Little Sissy. Tell the sheriff what this means."

Aunt Ora continued, "This was made by my father. I would recognize this anywhere. He didn't make very many."

"Do you know why Howard would have carried that up the Indian Staircase with him?" Felicia asked.

Aunt Ora continued to caress the bracelet as if she could summon her father by rubbing it in the right spot. "By tradition, these bracelets have been given to young women as a pre-engagement gift. It was a signal that an understanding had been reached, but there was still a bit of negotiation yet to be agreed on before the formal engagement was announced."

Tears again started rolling down her florid cheeks. "My late husband somehow convinced my father to make one. He presented it to me on my sixteenth birthday."

"Where did your father get the silver? He was a farmer, right?" asked Sheriff Larson.

"Let me answer, Little Sissy," said Dorothy. She patted Aunt Ora's hand again and looked directly at Sheriff Larson with cold, calm eyes. "Our father was a frequent forager in the surrounding hills. He searched for coal to burn, dug ginseng roots to sell, trapped small game for the table, and collected the wild berries that my mother used for jellies, jams, and pies. He was intimately familiar with the land. He also found enough silver to make small gifts."

"If he found silver, why didn't he sell that?"

"He didn't find enough to do more than make these bracelets. He loved silversmithing, and if he had found a good vein, he would have certainly sold the silver to help out with the family. As it turned out, my sister is right, he only made a few bracelets."

"Where is that bracelet now?" Felicia asked.

Aunt Ora wiped her eyes and pointed the soggy handkerchief at Miranda. "Sweetie, go into my bedroom, and under the bed on the left furthest from the door, bring me a small wooden box." She made a shooing motion with the handkerchief. "Hurry, now. Everyone is waiting."

Miranda leaped up and rushed into Aunt Ora's bedroom. She stood at the door and let her hand search for the light switch. After her eyes adjusted to the darkness, she found it much lower than normal. She blew out a frustrated puff. *Old houses.* Flipping the light switch, an overhead fixture lit up the profoundly floral-dominated room. The room was small, so although it only contained a bed, a dresser, a chest of drawers, and two nightstands, there was barely enough room to squeeze around to the far side of the bed.

Miranda wasn't sure how her aunt managed to move around in here. Pushing aside the images of her aunt's delicate frame moving in this overcrowded space, Miranda lifted the dust ruffle and reached under the bed. She encountered a neat but compact horde of shoes, boxes, gift bags, and rolls of wrapping paper. Determined to find the wooden box without having to go back out for a flashlight, Miranda reached and stretched her way through a series of stacked boxes of greeting cards to land her hand on it.

"I found it!" she yelled, mostly as a reward to herself, but also as a way to relieve her aunt's anxiety over letting someone, even though she was family, search underneath her bed. Miranda brought the box out to the front room and placed it in aunt's lap.

"Thank you, sweetie."

Aunt Ora carefully opened the small wooden box. "I haven't been into this for a long, long time." She held up a small velvet pouch, opened the string tie, and looked inside. The florid pink in her cheeks turned to ash. "It's missing. My bracelet is gone." She pointed to Felicia. "That's got to be my bracelet. I don't understand why Howard took it. He had to know I would have let him have it for his sweetheart."

"If a reason comes to you later, and that's often the case, just give me a call. Anyway, that brings me to my last question," said Sheriff Larson. "Did Howard have a will?"

Aunt Ora sighed and hung her head down for a moment. She grabbed another handkerchief from an apparently endless supply tucked into the crease of her chair and wiped away the flowing stream of tears.

"He did," she sniffed. "We didn't understand it, but it hasn't been to probate yet. He has been known to be missing, not deceased. But he did have a will. That's quite unusual for such a young man. He left everything to his girlfriend, Jennifer O'Rourke."

Chapter 21

Miranda felt her lack of sleep. She was restless and on edge after the visit to Aunt Ora's last night. She had so many questions that it was going on 3:00 a.m. before she dropped off. Relaxing on the front-porch swing with her mother and a hot cup of fresh ginger tea seemed the perfect reward for such a nice day.

For once, the tour had been routine and completely uneventful. Her clients each produced a great painting of Lover's Leap. They enjoyed both the traditionally Southern meal as well as the moonshine cocktails paired with each course. They even purchased most of the items she had displayed in her temporary gift shop.

"Mom, do you know why Howard chose to study geology in college? It seems to me that it's an odd choice. I would have thought that maybe sports medicine would have been a better fit. Or given our farming background, agricultural studies. Why geology?"

Dorothy took another sip of the hot tea. Then she inhaled a long breath. "That's a good question. Your aunt Ora was confused by his choice as well. Something inspired him that summer before he went off to college. I don't know what happened, but he changed his major from sports medicine to geology right away."

"With the bracelet turning up with him, it seems like there should be a reason that he took it from his mother. Do you think he was going to make a copy to give to Jennifer? Or maybe he thought there might be silver somewhere and this bracelet was proof?"

"I think both ideas are very good possibilities. You should put that information in your murder notebook."

"I will. But first, I need to check on Ron. He's been far too quiet out in the barn. I'm betting he's still sleeping off a hangover. What do you think?"

"Fine, but don't forget."

Miranda ran through a mental list of things on her mind. Howard's murder was at the top. Her nonrelationship with Austin was next. The possibility that her mother's visit might be permanent. Her business could stall without the addition of the distillery. Sandy was misbehaving and needed consistent training.

Added to that was the actual work involved in the cultural tours. She needed fresh and traditional cooking ingredients that were not always available. Her cooks were excellent but young. Her painting supplies were running low. Her tour backlog never built up to more than three days.

She sighed. *That's a lot.*

When she walked into the barn, a feeling of cool calm washed over her as it always did as soon as she passed through its door. As far back as she could remember, she associated the smell of stale hay, wormy wood, fresh sawdust, and cold dirt with Uncle Gene in the barn, whistling something tuneless while he worked. He had been born in the farmhouse and took over when his parents died. But she associated him with the barn—his true home.

Miranda heard a strange noise. She looked up to the ceiling and saw a blue tarp snaking its way down to the dirt floor through a hole in the roof. The flapping sound turned into a crinkly plop on top of her ruined moonshine ingredients. She had forgotten to unload them onto her garden compost pile. She could add that to Ron's list, but wouldn't say anything until he had the roof done.

"Hey, Ron. Watch what you're doing up there. You could have dropped that on my head."

A tussled shock of hair preceded a tanned face that appeared in the opening. "Sorry, I didn't know anyone was down there. Are you okay?"

"Sure. How's the repair going?"

"Good." Ron's head disappeared and she was left staring up at the sky through the hole.

"Ron?"

No answer.

"Ron, I need to know how much longer it will take to complete the repair."

Still no answer.

"I'm going to the bank and need to know how much cash to get."

That got his attention. Ron's head popped into view. "I should be done by the end of today."

"Are you sure? There's still a lot of cleanup to do."

"The patch will be done today. All the clearing up will take most of tomorrow."

"That's fine. I'll get enough for your time until noon tomorrow, and when I give that to you tonight, we can take another estimate. Okay?"

"When will you be back with the cash?"

"Not until after five."

"The bank closes at five." His voice sounded high-pitched and raspy.

"I'll be back soon."

Ron's head disappeared, then she heard the staccato of the nail gun again. Miranda was convinced that he was dragging out this project, but the quality of his work was superb and a good roof was critical to her distillery. Uncle Gene had told her that a good manager didn't blame her tools—she brought out the best in them. Ron was certainly testing her fledgling management skills.

Miranda returned to the farmhouse and called the company where she had ordered her distillery equipment. She had added consultation fees to the purchase order. She knew the basics about brewing moonshine, but she needed a crash course to get all the permits and licenses she would need to sell her product.

She had an advantage over most new distillers. She had her uncle's famous secret recipes. He had been known far and wide as the best source of dew in the area. She was determined to continue his legacy.

Taking a leap of faith, she scheduled her training to begin on Monday and continue through to the end of the week. If she started her mash tomorrow, everything would be ready for the training.

As soon as she placed the phone back in its cradle, it rang. She picked it up.

"Miranda. It's Aunt Ora."

"Hi. Do you want to talk to Mom? Hang on. I'll get her."

"No, it's you I want. Sheriff Larson called me and said that Dr. DuPont found some new information about Howard's injuries. I think I have the gist of it, but I want you to make sure that I understood what he said."

"Sure, Aunt Ora. Anything."

"He said that the an—, anthr—, you know, that expert over in Lexington, said that Howard's broken leg had begun to heal before he died."

Miranda frowned and the phone slipped out of her hand. She grabbed it up. "I'm so sorry. I didn't mean to do that."

"Do you know what that means? I was too embarrassed to ask."

"I'm sad to say that it means Howard was alive long enough after the injury for his bones to begin to repair themselves. In time, they will know how long."

"Sheriff Larson said that it meant that the case now indicated foul play." Miranda heard her aunt break down and begin to sob. "I'm so confused. Will you and Austin please get to the bottom of this for me? I need your help to see that Howard's killer is brought to justice."

"But, Aunt Ora, I'm not a law officer or even a private investigator."

"No, but you've got a good head on your shoulders. You and Austin have already solved one mysterious death. You can do it again."

"Of course, I'd be pleased to look into the case for

you, but I'll need to ask Austin about joining me. He's off duty in order to attend a training session with the local Fire and Rescue organization. It was something about rappelling down cliffs with an injured hiker."

"He's quite a busy young man. Do you need his help?"

Miranda raised her eyebrows. She considered it to be an unusual question given her aunt's strict Southern background.

"I don't particularly need his assistance, but I think it would be a good move to include him because the death happened in his jurisdiction. We'll do what we can, I promise."

"Thank you. I trust you. The word of a Trent is an honorable promise."

Miranda ended the call and dialed Austin. She told him the new development in Howard's case, and he said he'd be right over.

"Oops, I've got to get to the bank and pick up some groceries for tomorrow's tour. Can you stop by for dinner instead? Mom's making her famous chicken and dumplings."

"I'd walk five miles for that," said Austin. "See you around six?"

"Six is great."

Miranda hustled into Campton's Farmers and Traders Bank and withdrew Ron's cash. Her next stop was Halsey's Country Store for a quart of buttermilk. Tomorrow's meal was more country-fried chicken, and that was a key ingredient for the coating. She also picked up a couple of garden-grown beefsteak tomatoes.

When she returned to the farmhouse, she dropped off the groceries and took Sandy with her out the back door to pay Ron.

He hobbled up to her with a huge grin, reminding her of an overfriendly Labrador retriever. The black boot barely slowed him down. "Payday! I love getting paid."

She turned over the bank envelope. "This pays for your hours up through noon. Do you think you can finish by then? I'd really like to show the barn to my tour tomorrow."

Ron slipped the packet into his back pocket. "Sure. No problem." He smiled wide and went back to the barn.

Miranda watched with a deep furrow in her brow. She had a bad feeling, but she ignored it, then went into the kitchen. She pulled out the ingredients and mixed one of her newest cocktails, which she called A Cola Moon. It would pair up nicely with the classic chicken-and-dumplings meal that her mother was preparing.

Her mom took the cast-iron Dutch oven from the oven. The biscuits on top were browned to perfection. "Let's eat in the dining room. Do you mind if I invite Ron in or should I take out a basket?"

"Make him a basket. Austin and I are going to discuss our strategy for investigating Howard's death. We need some privacy."

"Do you want me to eat in the kitchen?"

"Nope. You're going to help us plan."

Her mother raised an eyebrow in a sign of misgiving.

Chapter 22

Thursday Evening, Aunt Ora's House

Miranda and Austin were on the road to Aunt Ora's farm. They had discussed the disturbing discovery of Howard's leg injury through dinner. They disagreed on how to proceed.

"She needs to know what happened." Miranda took the curve at top speed. "I can't imagine not wanting to know."

Austin touched the dashboard as a subtle hint for Miranda to pay more attention to her driving. She noticed and slowed down.

He sighed. "You haven't lived here full-time until these last few months. Your aunt is fragile. This could plunge her into a deep depression. It took months for her to even go out onto the front porch after Howard disappeared. Months of isolation. She wouldn't open the blinds, get dressed, fix meals. Nothing but bleak depression."

"I didn't know. I didn't see any of that reaction. How did she come out of it?"

Austin shifted the large bowl of chicken and dumplings to rest closer to his knees. Dorothy had packed up supper for her sister. It was piping hot, and the heat was radiating through the kitchen towel that was supposed to protect him.

"All her friends gathered and simply took charge. They barged into her house. Spring-cleaned it from top to bottom. Gave her a bath, shampoo, manicure, and dressed her in a Sunday dress. They refused to leave until she was sitting on the porch with a clean house, a full refrigerator, and a smile on her face. They took turns for months keeping her on track. It worked." He shifted the bowl again.

"Wow . . . I'm impressed."

"Small communities look after themselves." He finally lifted the bowl off his lap altogether. They were only a few twisting turns away from Aunt Ora's house.

They pulled into the driveway and were greeted by Aunt Ora, wearing a floral housedress and twisting her apron in her nervous hands. "Thank you for coming. I've got some cocoa on the stove and I've made some shortbread. Come on in and sit a spell."

They presented her with the still-steaming bowl of chicken and dumplings. "My sister is a great cook. She knows this is my favorite." Aunt Ora looked down at the dish and then back up at Miranda. "This news must be bad."

After helping her aunt put away the bowl and refusing any refreshment, Miranda made sure her aunt was settled into her favorite chair before Miranda said a word about Howard. Austin sat on the soft couch with his elbows planted on his knees, looking dreadful.

Miranda looked into her aunt's eyes and spoke low and carefully. "Aunt Ora, the injury that Howard suffered up on the bluff above the Indian Staircase indicates that he lived for some period of time afterwards. It means that he was alive for at least several days."

Aunt Ora inhaled a deep breath. "Oh, no!" She covered her eyes with her hands. "Oh, dear Lord, no." She began to weep. "He was all alone." She dug out a handkerchief and dabbed her eyes, then her eyes crinkled into a questioning look. "Why didn't he call out? Someone must have passed by in that time."

"That's the same question that Austin and I have, too. If he couldn't move his injured leg, why couldn't he yell?"

Austin cleared his throat. "As we're here and trying to make sense of this, I want to add a few explanations. One is that he could have been completely unconscious during the few days after his injury. Healing would have started, but he couldn't move or call out."

Miranda grabbed her aunt's hand. "The worst-case scenario is that he was restrained in some way so that he couldn't speak or move in order to attract attention." Miranda glanced at Austin, and he gave her a slight nod. "We think it is more likely that a man as fit as Howard was probably restrained. It answers all our questions."

Aunt Ora threw her head back and released a keening howl. Both Miranda and Austin leaned back and looked at each other not knowing what to do.

The single burst of grief swept through quickly and left behind a look of cold steel in Aunt Ora's eyes. "This monster must be caught." She reached out and grabbed both Miranda's and Austin's hands in each of hers. "You must find out what happened. I will not rest until I know that this foul beast has been caught and made to pay for my baby boy's suffering." She took in a full breath. "Promise me."

They both sat silent.

"Promise me on the bones of my baby boy."

Miranda swallowed hard. Her throat threatened to close up. The words "my baby boy" punched her in the gut. "I promise." She looked over to Austin.

He nodded. "I promise."

The drive back to Miranda's seemed both long and short. Austin took his turn driving, and she didn't feel like protesting. Every little thing wasn't about power. They arrived so late that her mother had already retreated to the attic. Sandy was ready for his last visit outside.

Miranda stood next to Austin in the front yard. They watched the frisky puppy piddle on every leaf, blade of grass, and twig. She could feel the tension in Austin's posture and see his clenched jaw by the light of the front-porch light.

"We need to go back up the Indian Staircase and look at the area," he said. "When will you have time? You see things that no one else picks out."

She twisted her lip and rubbed the back of her neck. "I've been thinking about that." She picked Sandy up and snuggled him into the crook of her neck. "I haven't told tomorrow's class where we'll be painting. I can take them up the Indian Staircase. They're members of a home-schooling co-op over in Jackson. They asked for a physical challenge as well as a way to fulfill their liberal arts credits. I think they'll be delighted."

"I can lecture on the history of the Daniel Boone National Forest and also the basic geology of the Red River Gorge."

"That should make their counselor happy."

"What about lunch?" asked Austin.

"It's too late to change that. I've got a nonalcoholic meal all planned out for them. I'll tell Lily and Iris that it will be later than normal. I'll pack a lot of snacks to tide them over."

Austin gave Sandy a good scratching behind his ears. "I'll see you up on the bluff tomorrow." He leaned in and gave her a tender kiss on the cheek. "Be careful. Wait until I get there before you take them up."

She smiled. "I certainly will. The first step in safety is to respect the danger of the woods."

Chapter 23

Friday Morning, the Farmhouse

Miranda was up and about earlier than normal and trying to be quiet. Her mother had come back downstairs after Austin had gone. Miranda and her mother had talked late into the night about Aunt Ora, Howard's partially healed injury, and that Jennifer O'Rourke was his sole beneficiary. Miranda told her mom about the change in the tour plans.

Miranda was packing her supplies into the van when her mom appeared on the front porch still in her nightgown and robe. "I still don't understand why Jennifer didn't tell anyone. Howard had a mother and sisters to support. He should have told them."

"Maybe he wanted to make sure Jennifer wanted to marry him before he risked the information on his mother. Then, of course, he didn't get a chance. Don't worry about things here. I'll handle everything."

Miranda hugged and kissed her mother. "Thanks. You're being such a great help."

Dorothy grinned. "I love working with Lily and Iris, they're such good girls. Ron is coming along very nicely, too. I think you've misjudged him, but you need to handle Ron all on your own."

"He doesn't like women in charge. I've met quite a few like him, and he's not changing. He certainly responds well to simple orders repeated often." Miranda looked over to the barn. "I didn't check up on him last night after I handed over the cash. Could you check in and see that he's at least attempting to finish the roof today? Please?"

"Sure. I'll take him a plate of buckwheat pancakes with real maple syrup as a peace offering."

"Thanks, Mom. I appreciate the help."

On the drive to Hemlock Lodge, Miranda wondered if having her mom stay would be such a bad thing. It certainly helped to have her in the kitchen making sure that Lily and Iris kept their cooking authentic. It was nice to have someone around to help with Sandy and picking up organic foods from the nearby farms. Her mom was better at knowing who grew the best tomatoes and who had just shot a deer.

She walked into Hemlock Lodge and was greeted by Doris Ann Norris. "Hi, Miranda. You're a mite early. Your group isn't down yet."

"I wanted to have a few words with you first. My clients have been keeping me so busy, I haven't had a chance to say more than two words to you. What did you want to tell me about the group I took to draw Battleship Rock?"

Doris Ann rested her forehead in her palm. "Now,

what was it I wanted to tell you?" She paused for a moment. "I got it. That Ben lawyer fellow was here the week your cousin disappeared. I thought you ought to know that."

"Thanks. I'm not sure how that helps, but thanks. What is the local gossip about Howard's discovery?"

"Most folks have been trying to figure out how he didn't rescue himself. He had been wandering these hills searching for oil fields and silver mines for a long time."

"You knew he was searching for silver?"

"He didn't come right out and say so, but he was interested in the legends and family stories about the lost Jonathan Swift mines."

The myth of the lost silver mines had been a tale told around evening fires for years in the area. Miranda remembered the first time Uncle Gene told her about them; she was probably only about four. They inspired a life-long interest in lost treasure. She read any book with treasure as a theme.

"*Mines?* I thought it was only one." Miranda frowned.

"No. They say that Swift found more than a dozen silver mines in this area alone. Secrecy was an absolute fixation, and he rarely excavated ore from just a single mine in any trip. He was obsessed with leaving dozens of false trails. Otherwise, I think the mines should have been discovered by now." Doris Ann's eyes softened into a gentle look. "If Howard was on the track of the mines, maybe he had uncovered the meaning to some of the pictograms while he was searching for silver. If he was about to make a breakthrough about the mystery of the images up there above the Indian Staircase, he could have tried to hide it."

"Hmm." Miranda noticed that a group of youngsters had gathered in front of the stone fireplace in the lobby.

"There's my group. Keep on the lookout for anything unusual, will you? Austin and I have promised Aunt Ora that we would see that Howard's killer is caught."

Doris Ann pursed her lips in a thinly disguised attempt at looking shocked. "I figured you would get pulled into this. Your aunt is nobody's fool. I'll keep an ear out for you."

Miranda thanked her and went to work. Her tour group today were all tall, lanky, clean-cut athletes, including their coach. She handed them each a pack that contained water, snacks, and sketching supplies. They set off at a brisk pace down the trail and in no time were standing at the bottom of the carved steps.

Austin was waiting for them with a broad grin and a quick lecture about the origin of the carved footholds. He demonstrated the most efficient way to ascend and sent Miranda to the top so that they were both in the best location to help anyone who got into trouble.

Given her last experience, Miranda had both lightened and rebalanced her pack. By concentrating carefully, she was soon up the cliff and waiting to assist her clients to climb safely to the top.

The view was even more beautiful on this cool autumn morning. The red maples had turned crimson, and each one seemed to have a bright yellow poplar neighbor. She seated her clients in a semicircle for their lesson and they began sketching.

Austin took over and presented his geology spiel. Miranda felt a smile play on her lips. She enjoyed this ranger talk no matter how many times she heard it. Her clients, however, were that youthful combination of intelligence, exuberance, and curiosity. They were going to ask him some interesting questions.

She quietly backed away and took herself over to the tree where Howard's bones had lain for the past five years. First, she slowly circled the area looking beyond the disturbance that had been caused by the removal of Howard's remains. She didn't pick up on anything unusual.

Then Miranda scanned the bark of the pine tree looking for slight discolorations, abrasions, or damage. She squinted to blur her vision to further narrow her focus on color and texture. A tiny strip of bark on the back side seemed to have been disturbed at some point. The growth was thicker, as if it had suffered a wound.

She pulled out the magnifier she had stowed in her pocket, stooped over, and examined the area. A tiny crease no wider than a phone charger cord circled the trunk at about eighteen inches from the forest floor. Something caused that injury to the bark, but it had recovered and left this mark.

Miranda stood and looked over to Austin. She waved a hand for him to join her. He was by her side in a flash. "What is it? What have you found?"

"Look." She pointed to the tiny crease. "What could have caused this?"

He squatted and held out his hand for her magnifier. He studied the crease for a few seconds and stood up. "A rope or cord has damaged the bark in the past. It was organic or we would see a raised weal where the bark grew over it. Whatever it was, rotted away and did relatively little damage."

"Would you say that a natural handmade rope of, let's say, hemp could have caused that?" Miranda's voice dropped. "Howard could have been tied to the tree."

Austin rubbed his eyes with both hands. "Yes, that

would explain the crease, and it would have rotted away pretty fast."

"It also explains why he couldn't drag himself over to the main trail. But it doesn't solve the question of why he didn't call out for help." She looked down at the area around the base of the tree. "I can't figure that one out. Even if he were gagged, he would have made some noise."

"A drug of some sort?" Austin said. "Or maybe he was unconscious."

"Argh! We keep trying to interpret this as a natural injury but keep coming back to an act of foul play." Miranda pressed her lips tight. "I'm going to call Sheriff Larson. We need an arborist to examine the crease in this tree."

"He's going to hate that."

Miranda agreed.

Chapter 24

Friday Afternoon, the Farmhouse

Miranda returned from dropping off her clients to Hemlock Lodge. The leader praised her cultural tour for its educational content. He promised to leave a five-star review with the leading tourist-review site. She was thrilled. Reviews were hard to get but were vital to attracting clients.

She stood next to Austin on the front porch when he called Sheriff Larson to report their discovery of the crease in the tree where Howard had died. She didn't think the sheriff yelled at Austin, but Miranda watched Austin repeatedly clench and unclench his fist. When he finally ended the call, he gave her a wave and left.

The screen door opened and a scrabbling flash of puppy ran down the steps, followed by her mother. "Sandy missed you this morning. He seemed restless and kept searching for you." Dorothy's words were clipped and her brow knotted. "I don't know what's wrong."

Miranda scooped Sandy up to get puppy licks. "Oh, yes, my little puppy wupkins. What's wrong, buddy?" She looked up at her mother. "Do you think he senses our feelings? It has been pretty emotional around here."

Her mom splayed out her hands and lifted her shoulders. "Things have been routine around here. Even Ron hasn't had a calamity. I sent Lily and Iris home after they finished cleaning up the kitchen. Then I reset the dining room table for tomorrow's tour. Was that all right?"

That was one more thing that her mother was taking over. "If you're trying to make a case for how much it would help me to have you move back here—you already win. Have you thought about it?"

Dorothy crossed her arms and shifted her hip. "I'm not saying anything until everything with Howard is resolved." She threw a stern look over her shoulder on the way back into the farmhouse. "You might want to go back and check on Ron. He did promise to be finished today."

"I've been dreading that." Miranda snuggled Sandy and kept him in the crook of her arm. "Is that what you've been sensing?" The mess in the barn could certainly cause anyone on the property an injury. They walked in through the open large barn doors. "Ron. . . . Ron. . . . Where are you?"

"I'm out here. Come around to the back."

Miranda frowned. Why was he in the back? Her stomach tightened. What kind of trouble could he cause out there? As soon as she walked out the back, she found out.

Ron was standing over a crumpled satellite dish device about ten feet from the barn. It was her high-speed internet receiver. It had cost a pretty penny.

"What! You broke my internet receiver?" Sandy whimpered and Miranda could tell that her voice sounded shrill. She cleared her throat, then swallowed hard to lower her tone. "How did that happen?"

"I don't know. I guess it got in the way when I was clearing off the damaged roofing. I swear I didn't see it."

Miranda walked over to the damaged receiver. It was mangled beyond repair. Sandy wriggled in her arms in an attempt to run through the grass, but she held him tight.

"You are very lucky I have a spare antenna, very lucky. I'll have to order another one right away so that I have a spare. I need the extra boost to run my business out here." She paused to emphasize her disappointment. "You're going to have to work off the cost of the replacement. You're also going to install the replacement antenna at no cost. Right?"

Ron looked embarrassed for a moment, then his face turned bright and eager. "It won't take me long, but I'll need to stay another day to finish with cleaning everything up. That's okay, right?"

Although Miranda didn't want Ron hanging around yet another day, it did seem to be the quickest way to move forward. "Fine, but I won't be paying you to fix your mistakes. I expect you to get the spare receiver working before sunset."

Ron glanced at the afternoon sun, calculating the daylight left. "Sure, I can do that."

"Fine. Get the ladder while I fetch the new antenna."

Miranda stomped back into the house and went into her late uncle's bedroom. She had turned it into an efficient office and storage space. She found the new antenna and gave it to Ron, who was waiting by the back door. He was upwind and mighty fragrant. She felt like a Dickens miser for not offering some decent hospitality.

"Since you're staying another night, why don't you take a shower after supper? There's plenty of hot water and extra towels."

Ron grinned and left.

She didn't know if he was embarrassed or grateful. Whatever. She thought it was the right thing to do. Miranda sighed.

She went inside and prepared the touring backpacks for the next day's event. She planned to take her clients to the most popular site, the overlook to Lover's Leap. The stunning view was an easy hike and Austin's ranger talk would be a big hit. His beaming face broadcast how much he enjoyed them. Miranda could recite it word for word, and she had done that the few times he was busy with other duties.

She called her promotional vendor and ordered another seventy-five custom-embroidered backpacks to tide her over for the rest of the month. A quick inventory of her painting supplies resulted in a small order from the art shop in Jackson. By now, the local vendors were giving her a little deeper discount. As she had hoped, her touring business was spreading the wealth to other members of the small business community.

She heard a tap on the screen door and walked out into the dining room. Austin had walked over from his house and brought over a large bouquet of wildflowers plucked from the roadside ditches.

"Hello? Who's out there?" her mom called from the kitchen.

"I've got it, Mom. It's Austin." She headed out toward the front room. "Hi, there." She took in his hazel eyes and still-damp hair. His smile was brighter than the autumn flowers that he held out to her. "Thanks. You picked these for me?"

His lips quirked in a half smile. "Just for you."

Miranda noticed the soft look around his eyes. "Local wildflowers are my favorite. Come on in. Mom's about got supper on the kitchen table. I'll get a container for these."

In the kitchen, her mom closed the lid on a picnic basket. "I'm joining Ron out back. You two enjoy yourselves. I know I'm going to."

After a filling meal of thickly sliced ham with raisin sauce, scalloped potatoes, and glazed carrots, she and Austin went into her office to work with her murder notebook.

Miranda sat at the desk and Austin took the side chair. "I think we should figure out if we can eliminate anyone at all. Let's start with Alfred Whittaker." She pulled a tour application sheet out of a folder on her desk. "I've got the basic information he filled out for the tour. He also introduced himself as a freelance reporter with the *Lexington Herald-Leader*. He lives over on the north side of Lexington near the Blue Grass Airport."

"I remember that he took the role as leader of the group."

"Right. He made the initial group reservation and made sure I contacted him for any questions. A little timid to my mind, but he's very organized. You need someone who is willing to coordinate the information for a group of unique individuals. I wonder why he's the leader instead of Kevin, who appears to have the final say-so on everything." She scribbled that question in her murder notebook. "Do you think your sister could give us some help here?"

Austin grabbed the handset from Miranda's desk. "My thoughts exactly. Tyler might know him." He dialed, set the handset down, and pressed the speaker button.

"Hi, Austin. What's up?"

"Are you on deadline?"

"Already submitted my piece for tomorrow's paper."

"Perfect. There was a guy on one of the hiking trails on Sunday, and he introduced himself as a freelance reporter. His name is Alfred Whittaker. I was wondering if you might know him. Oh, I'm at Miranda's farmhouse and I've put you on speaker."

"Hi, Miranda. Are you working with Austin on another case?"

Austin looked over at Miranda. "It feels more like I'm working for her at the moment, but this whole situation is in my territory."

Miranda nodded in agreement. "You know we told you about the hiker that had been missing for five years that was found up above the Indian Staircase?"

"Of course, you gave me an exclusive. The boss thinks it will make a great investigative piece on wilderness safety. I'm researching missing hikers all over the US and Canada. No one has made a comprehensive report. This could be big—maybe Pulitzer Prize material. I turned in the first in the series a few minutes ago."

"Congratulations. Do you have time to help us get more information about Alfred?" asked Miranda.

"Firstly, the title of freelance reporter doesn't really mean much. He could be an out-of-work journalist or he could be a regular contributor. The name does seem a bit familiar. Hang on a second, I'll check his byline."

They heard a rapid clicking of keys and Tyler muttered, "Not much help, I'm afraid. He was really prolific about five to six years ago, but his work suddenly thins out right after that. Maybe he got another reporting job or something else and his freelance work fell away."

"Can you do a bit of research and find out what happened?"

"Absolutely. It is a bit strange. I mean, the paper was strong and healthy back then. Not like it is now with staff reductions happening all the time."

"Really?" said Austin. "You're not in danger, are you?"

"Print publications are under extreme pressure to change their business models right now. Paper is under threat with tax and import duties that have resulted in price hikes. We compete with everything electronic. Most young people get their news over their phones—not a delivered broadsheet."

Austin's eyes got wide. "I should have known that. What are you doing to keep yourself employed at the *Herald*?"

"I'm looking ahead to see what others have done."

"What's that?" asked Miranda.

"The most successful ex-journalists I know have started writing novels based on their past experiences. Apparently, publishers appreciate the built-in skill set. We're used to writing on deadline, creating clear descriptions, and have a great sense of story. I've already started a thriller series about a crime reporter who helps her forest ranger brother and his artist girlfriend solve crimes."

Austin's mouth dropped open. "You're what?"

"You don't have a problem with that, do you?" Tyler sounded shocked.

Chapter 25

Friday Evening, the Farmhouse

Austin and Miranda took Sandy for a long walk down the dirt road toward the highway. Sandy's energy level was growing as fast as he was. While the humans strolled casually, Sandy ran ahead at top speed for about twenty yards, screeched to a stop, turned, then ran back beyond them for another twenty yards or so. Then he did it again. And again. And again.

As soon as they got to the cattle gate turnaround in the highest part of the road, Austin's cell phone rang. "It's Tyler." He put the phone on speaker.

"Austin, I've got some dirt on Alfred Whittaker."

"Dirt?" said Miranda and Austin at the same time.

"Where are you? I called your cell because the house phone went to voice mail."

"I'm out on the road in one of those rare places where

I get a good signal. Never mind that. You know what it's like out here. What dirt?" Austin prompted.

"I looked back into the paper's archives, and our Alfred was a rising star. He was a golden boy plucked right straight from the University of West Virginia's journalism program. They set him on a fast track for promotion to the editorial staff."

Miranda raised her eyebrows. "I'm sorry, I don't know what you mean."

"Sure. The staff at that point were mostly old-timers, and the *Herald* wanted some young blood, but naturally they wanted the benefits really quick. So, Alfred was one of several new grads that were recruited to appeal to younger readers. It was a great strategy. Too bad it didn't work."

"That's a management scheme. How is that dirt?" asked Austin.

"Hang on, baby brother. Let me finish."

"Okay, okay, quit beating round the bushes."

Miranda smiled. Did all siblings have a pecking order that defined their interactions? It seemed that Austin had a history of prodding his older sister to finish her stories faster than she wanted to tell them. He hadn't done that to her, but then Miranda tended to be terse. Sometimes too terse.

"Fine. Apparently after a couple of years, the competition for top dog had narrowed down to two rising stars. Alfred was one of them, and the owner's nephew was the other. Then something happened to ruin things for Alfred." She paused.

"Come on, Tyler. Don't draw this out." Austin didn't sound irritated. It appeared to be another stage of the ongoing game between them.

"There was a joint project that Alfred and the nephew worked on as a team. It was an undercover investigation into a secret scandal in Lexington. Although I can't verify it, the undocumented gossip is that it was about the police involvement in narcotics in the seventies. They turned in their work and it appeared to be journalism at its finest. There was even talk of Pulitzers for both of them. Then it all went horribly wrong and Alfred was fired in disgrace."

"What did he do?"

Tyler's voice softened. "That's the thing, he might not have done anything. The official issue was plagiarism."

"Oh, boy," said Austin. "That's fatal."

"It is." Tyler lowered her voice. "Another famous journalist was involved and she got wind of their work while she was in the final stages of crafting what became a bestseller. The paper was embarrassed. It had to print a full retraction, and then after things died down a bit, Alfred was laid off."

"Alfred wasn't fired outright. Why not?" Austin sounded skeptical.

"That's what I thought, but since it was a joint project, I don't think the owner wanted his nephew's career derailed as well. So, they both were given counseling, and Alfred was shuffled out at the next group layoff. I don't think the editorial room has quite recovered."

"What's the nephew's name?" asked Miranda.

"Um, wait. I've got it here somewhere." They could hear flipping pages. "It's John Latchy. His uncle is the owner of the California-based company that owns a ton of newspapers."

"Thanks, Tyler. Did you find a connection between Latchy and Howard Cable?"

"Not that I could find in the archives. Do you want me to keep looking?"

"Yes, please, that would be great."

Austin ended the call and stowed his cell. "Interesting."

"Unexpected," said Miranda. "Alfred doesn't seem like someone who would take that path in his work. Even a rumor of such dealings is a career killer. If the nephew was guilty of the plagiarism, that might explain why Alfred now works freelance on his own. I would be shy of team reporting after getting fired for someone else's dirty dealing."

"I don't see a motive for Alfred at all."

Miranda scooped up Sandy, who had finally done enough running to plop down on her shoes panting like a steam engine. "One way that works for me is if Howard somehow got verifiable proof that it was Alfred who was guilty of plagiarism rather than the nephew. Howard might have been threatening to take the evidence to the *Lexington Herald-Leader*."

"Thin, but that would exonerate the owner's nephew and not particularly hurt Alfred. I mean, he had already been let go."

"But proof might threaten Alfred's future freelancing opportunities. Let's search for his bylines."

They returned to the farmhouse and went straight to Miranda's office. She logged on and executed a search for Alfred Whittaker's byline. She didn't know why she hadn't thought to do this before. Lapse of critical thinking, she thought.

The results of the search indicated a huge quantity of material right after he joined the *Lexington Herald-Leader*, a several-year gap, and then he had a large backlog of published work.

"What a strange pattern," said Austin. "But it neither

proves nor disproves the possibility that Alfred had a motive."

Miranda leaned back in her office chair. "Not a dead
end, but Alfred goes to the bottom of the list right now."
She picked up her murder notebook. "I'll write this up
and we should go on to someone else."

"Who's next?"

Miranda turned the page. "Ben DeBerg, the criminal
defense lawyer."

"We had better be careful. We don't want to get on his
bad side. Even when he was supposed to be relaxing at
the view of Battleship Rock, he seemed tense. Like he
was on a high alert of some kind."

Miranda typed *Ben DeBerg attorney* into the search
engine and sat back in her chair. The screen displayed
thirty-eight thousand results in 0.82 seconds for lawyer
Benjamin George DeBerg, Washington, DC, co-owner of
DeBerg & DeBerg Law Firm.

"Wow, look at these glowing remarks." Miranda pointed
to different lines on the screen. "Top criminal defense attorney, law firm holds over twenty-five years' experience
in general practice, hardworking attorneys, accessible
and compassionate." She looked over to Austin. "Look at
this one. 'Attorney DeBerg commanded the courtroom
from start to finish, presenting the case with very evident
knowledge and confidence.'"

"That's from one of his clients?"

"Yes, they wrote reviews about his services—just like
he was a refrigerator."

"Personal recommendations mean—" Miranda was
interrupted by a shotgun blast, followed by a long loud
high-pitched cry from her chickens. She stood. "Something's attacking the chickens."

Chapter 26

Friday Evening, the Farmhouse

Miranda and Austin ran out back to the brand-new chicken coop. Beside the gate to the outer run stood Ron, who was looking out over the field behind the barn. He snapped his shotgun up to his shoulder and fired another round at a glimpse of a reddish fluffy tail.

"Damn, missed him." Ron broke down the shotgun, flipped out the two spent cartridges, then got two more from his pocket. He slammed them home, snapped the gun closed, and was ready to fire again in mere seconds.

"A fox," said Miranda. "Do you think you got him?"

"I got close." Ron puffed up and stood as tall as his bare feet would allow. Seeing him without a shirt or shoes, wearing only a pair of running shorts, Miranda was surprised at how fit he was and how he owned a rugged handsomeness.

"Where's your ankle boot? You shouldn't be walking

around without it, let alone hunting." Miranda felt the irritation creep into her voice so she softened her tone.
"You need to be careful not to stress that injured foot."

"I jes' forgot. I wanted to get that varmint."

"You missed by a mile," said Austin. "Which is lucky
for you. Hunting season for red fox doesn't start until
Monday."

"But I was protecting the chickens." Ron frowned.
"You wouldn't have me just stand by and let her chickens
get took?"

"What's going on out here? What idiot fired a shotgun
this close to the house?" Dorothy stormed out of the
house and stood in front of Ron with her hands on her
hips. "You know better than to try and shoot at a fox.
They're too smart."

"I'm glad you missed," said Miranda. "She might have
a litter of kits to feed."

"Right, but if they were born this spring, they should
be independent by now." Austin looked at the fencing
around the coop. "This is a well-built coop, but you can
use another deterrent."

"What?" said both Dorothy and Miranda.

"Let Sandy piss back here. Nothing is better than a
strong dog scent to cause a fox to search for easier prey. It
works for bobcats as well."

Sandy immediately demonstrated his willingness to
protect the chickens by lifting his little leg against the
fence.

Miranda scooped up the little puppy and handed him
to her mother. "Okay. Show's over. Austin and I need to
get back to our web searches."

Austin started off for the house in a sprint. "My turn to

drive." Miranda chased after him but wasn't able to get in front in time. He plopped into the computer chair in triumph as if he had won an Olympic race.

"Funny." Miranda made a face at him. "But actually, a good idea. No two people word their searches exactly alike. We'll get a broader set of results by taking turns."

"You're just making up excuses for not beating me."

She smiled. "Type. You won the opportunity to type."

He wiggled in the chair a bit and began a new search string. "I'm going to try for Benjamin George DeBerg." He typed using his two forefingers for the keys and his right thumb for the space bar.

"You can't type." Miranda covered her mouth and laughed behind her hand.

"Yes, I can. I just don't use all my fingers. I'm pretty fast."

Miranda watched him tap the information into the search engine with dogged deliberateness. "Sorry, I didn't mean to criticize. I learned how to type as soon as the classes were offered in high school. My mother wanted me to become an executive secretary. She was convinced that was the best job in the world."

Austin tapped the Enter key with a flourish and they peered at the results. "It confirms that he lives in Washington, DC, all right."

Miranda pointed to another entry farther down the screen. "Also, that the co-owner is his mother, Margaret DeBerg."

They both leaned back and looked at each other.

"That must be weird to work for your mother." Miranda looked up at the ceiling where her mother had gone up to turn in for the night. "I'm not sure if I could do that." She inhaled quickly. "I'm hoping I don't find out."

"Why? What's up?"

Miranda waved the thought away. "Nothing. Probably overthinking things."

"Oh, I get it. You're worried that she might stay."

"Bingo." Miranda looked back at the screen. "It looks like he specialized in criminal cases involving the LGBTQ-plus community."

Austin sat up straight. "That's a surprise. He didn't strike me as being particularly tolerant to diversity." He turned to Miranda. "You?"

"I didn't think about it. We didn't talk much during the hike, and then, of course, Jennifer scraped her hand on Howard's bones not too long after we started sketching." Miranda rubbed the back of her neck. "I wonder if there's more to his specialty than a niche business decision."

Austin frowned. "You mean he might have personal experience?"

"Right." She pointed to another search result. "Look at this. Ben's highest-profile case involved a transgender employee who was fired from a famous Fifth Avenue luxury retail store. The clerk says she was belittled by coworkers, forced to use the men's room, and repeatedly referred to by the pronouns *he* and *him* before being fired."

Austin pointed to another search result. "Here's another case involving a funeral home who fired an employee from her position as a funeral director two weeks after she disclosed plans to return from her vacation as a woman."

"Let me try one more search." Miranda tapped the keys in a flurry. "This settles it. Most of his cases involve issues around LGBTQ-plus issues."

Austin leaned in to read the screen. "Most of them are transgender lawsuits."

"Do you think there's a more personal reason?"

Austin leaned back and put his hands behind his head. "It could be that these cases are in the news right now and he's taking advantage of the publicity."

"This is a well-established firm that his mother started years ago. It doesn't seem like they need a lot of publicity."

"What if Ben is transgender, but not out in public?"

"Give me the murder book. Let me have a go at his sketch." Miranda took the notebook and grabbed an eraser along with a drawing pencil. She rubbed out a few lines and modified Ben's features with a few deft strokes. "Look."

Austin took the notebook and shook his head. "That's amazing. He looks like a lovely woman. How do you think this relates to Howard?"

"Five years ago, a transgender lawyer would have great difficulty attracting clients. It isn't such a rare occurrence now. But the DC area has always been hyper-critical. A firm with a transgender partner would suffer."

"Maybe Howard knew from college that Ben might be trans and then used that information to get Ben to give him leverage with the legislature for his oil company. That sounds ridiculous." Austin put his hands on his thighs and stood. "I'm out of ideas. We should get some rest."

"Good idea." Miranda suppressed a yawn. "I'm going to finish making some jelly-sandwich cookies for Doris Ann. She will definitely have an opinion about the Risky Business Adventurers that are from this area." Miranda got up from the desk chair and stretched her back. "Look, let's pick this up tomorrow. If I get any more ideas, I'll let you know out on the trail."

She walked Austin out to the front porch. "See you tomorrow."

He leaned in, kissed her on the cheek, then disappeared into the darkness.

Miranda stood completely still, letting the warmth wash over her.

Chapter 27

Saturday Morning, Hemlock Lodge

Miranda arrived early at Hemlock Lodge holding a pottery jar full of her jelly cookies. She held the jar in front of her and caught the eye of Doris Ann, who was sketching lines on a map for a guest. As soon as she was free, Doris Ann said, "Is that for me?"

"Who else?"

"What kind are they? Gingerbread?"

"No."

"Lemon squares?"

"Nope."

"Potato pinwheels?"

"Guess again."

"Jelly cookies?"

"Yes." Miranda placed the jar on Doris Ann's desk. "Mom made the cookies and I helped with the assembly."

Doris Ann opened the jar and took out a cookie and

popped it into her mouth. She leaned back her head in joy. "Just as good as ever. Your mama is an amazing cook."

"It's good to have her here."

"Do you think she's gonna stay?" Doris Ann gobbled up another cookie and put the jar in her desk drawer.

Miranda squinted. "I don't really know. It's clear she's going to support Aunt Ora until Howard's death is cleared up and he's had his funeral. Anything beyond—I just don't know."

"I'm sure she's a big help right now."

"Yes. By the way, I've got a list here of that group that was with me up above the Indian Staircase on Sunday. Do you know any of them?" Miranda showed Doris Ann the list from her murder notebook.

Doris Ann squinted her eyes but refused to get out her reading glasses. "I remember them pretty well. They were a high-voltage kind of group. Remind me who they are. I should be able to recognize their names."

"Alfred Whittaker, Ben DeBerg, Kevin Burkart, Jennifer O'Rourke, Kurt Smith, and Stephanie Brinkley."

"That's them all right; two of them are from Stanton. That's Jennifer and Kevin. Jennifer has a gift for jewelry design. She makes her pieces from local silver. When she went off to university, we didn't really expect her back. She's famous, you know."

"Really? Tell me how."

"She was so talented that she got her master's in fine arts in record time and had employment offers from some famous jewelry designers like Tiffany's, Cartier, and even Chanel. But she's a real country girl, and there's even a tale that she turned down a marriage proposal because she wanted to stay near her large family over in Stanton."

"What about Kevin Burkart?"

"Oh, that's a different kettle of fish." Doris Ann shifted in her office chair. "He's always been a bit of a bad boy. Grew up in Stanton same as Jennifer, but quite a different type."

"What do you mean?"

"Oh, definitely not what you could call settled. He moved down to Florida to start a financial business managing other people's money. He comes back to hunt and fish here quite a lot but doesn't stay with family."

"That's unusual. My family would be highly insulted if I didn't stay with them. It's a given. That's what you do."

"No idea why that has happened. I haven't heard anything, which might not mean anything at all."

Miranda noticed a group had gathered in front of the tall fireplace in the lobby. "Okay. It looks like my clients have arrived. If you think of anything else, give me a call." She turned to join today's adventurers.

When she had them settled into painting the view at Lover's Leap, she spied Austin coming up the trail. His lecture was as entertaining as usual. After he finished, he and Miranda retreated to chat behind the students just out of their hearing.

Austin folded his arms and spoke in low tones. "I caught up with Doris Ann on what she told you about Jennifer O'Rourke and Kevin Burkart. I'm a stranger in Stanton, so I didn't know either of them. By the way, those cookies are incredible. I had to beg; she's like a hoarder with them. You should package them up and sell them in the gift shop."

Miranda whispered, "Thanks, I'll tell Mom."

"I did have a few minutes to look into Kevin's business down in Florida. It seems he's always had a gift for making money make money. He moved down there right after graduation and started small with a lucky set of customers. He has been successful enough to buy a historic home to use as his office complex. He also owns a luxurious waterfront home in an exclusive neighborhood. His kids attend an expensive private school, and he posts pictures of his African big-game trips. Quite the character."

"He's not that guy that shot the famous lion, is he?" Miranda scanned her group. Everyone was happily making good progress on their paintings.

"No, that was a dentist, but I think he would be capable of it." Austin looked at his watch. "I've got to get back to headquarters for a meeting. By the way, Kevin bought a small ranch in central Florida near Ocala that boards horses almost exactly five years ago. They're a huge expense, but he would have contacts in Lexington for expertise. He's also been returning to the Daniel Boone National Forest to hunt turkey, deer, and elk for his trophy wall."

Miranda shook her head from side to side. "None of this sounds suspicious. He seems like an average businessman from Kentucky who has had a great run of financial luck." She crinkled her brow. "Unless all that apparent wealth is a front. He could be in serious debt. His financial genius might not work for him."

"I'll ask some of the other rangers about him at the meeting. If he's been hunting around here for years, one or more of them must know him. My patch isn't the best area for bagging your limits."

He waved and took off down the trail.

Miranda sighed and watched him until he disappeared around the first bend. So far, they hadn't even made enough progress to tell the sheriff. She felt frustrated and disappointed. Maybe she should leave this to the professionals.

Chapter 28

Late Saturday Morning, Hemlock Lodge

Miranda said goodbye to her tour clients in the lobby. They had signed up for a mountain-view painting class only. She turned to make her way back to her van.

"Miranda," called out Doris Ann from her reception desk. "Miranda, there's something that I've remembered."

"Remembered?" Miranda turned back and stood in front of Doris Ann's desk.

"Yes, you were asking about the time that Howard Cable disappeared. I've remembered that Jennifer O'Rourke and Howard were spending quite a bit of time together. They had been skulking around for a few months. I think they were getting close to announcing their engagement."

"Why were they being secretive?"

"Howard was your aunt's only son and she absolutely doted on him. She also constantly referred to him as 'the man of the house.' He must have been dreading her reaction to the announcement of such a big change."

Miranda rubbed the back of her neck. "I can see where that might be a problem, but Jennifer appears to be a lovely, compassionate woman. Why wouldn't she have told my aunt about their relationship? I mean, did they even know each other?"

"It's funny that everybody thinks we know everyone else. We might know *of* someone. Like you for instance. Everyone knows you as Dorothy's daughter—the one that spent her summers on the Buchanan farm. But not everyone knows you to speak to. That's a good question for sure." Doris Ann turned back to her computer. "You should look into that. It might lead to something."

Miranda smiled. "Thanks, Doris Ann." Miranda went back to her van and thought about that during her drive back to the farmhouse.

Instead of taking the turnoff down to her farmhouse, she drove on to her aunt's place. When she pulled into the driveway, one of her cousins held open the screen door to the back porch. Anna Belle was a pale, thinner shadow of her mother. She wore light denim jeans and a white T-shirt with one of her mother's old-fashioned aprons wrapped and tied in the front. She looked like a little girl playing house.

"Hi, Miranda. I haven't seen you since you left for New York City. Anna Sue's at Doc Watson's clinic to get more nerve pills for Mom. I hope they come up with a type that actually gives her some rest instead of hives. Mom can be quite a handful, and her sensitivity to new medications is not helping."

Miranda stepped through to the screened-in back porch. She was hit by memories of earlier times when she and her mother would help Aunt Ora with the fall canning. There was a large enamel sink; a sturdy wooden table with a two-burner gas cooktop was placed on the left-hand side. It was used for boiling huge vats of water for sterilizing all the canning jars, bands, lids, and rubber gaskets. Everything was still in its place although it hadn't been used in donkey's years.

"I have a couple of questions for your mom. Is she here?"

Anna Belle put her finger up to her lips. "She's down for a nap. I would appreciate it if you wouldn't disturb her. Her sleep has been fitful."

"Okay, maybe you can help me."

"Sure, if I can. We'll stay out here if you don't mind. If we keep our voices low, I don't think she can hear us from the other side of the house."

"Fine." Miranda looked around, but there was nowhere to sit. She folded her arms and leaned against the canning table. "Did you know that Howard was about to ask Jennifer O'Rourke to marry him?"

"What! Mom didn't tell us that." Anna Belle glanced at the room where her mother was napping. "Why didn't she say something after he went missing? Are you sure?"

"Yes, we found your mom's silver promise bracelet that was made by our grandfather near Howard's remains. Do you know if he had spoken to anyone in the family about it?"

"I'll ask Mom when she wakes up. This may put her back into a horrible state."

"I know. It's probably best that you ask her rather than Sheriff Larson. She'll feel more comfortable."

Anna Belle folded her bony arms in front of her chest. "Our grandfather made that bracelet?"

"Your mom says it looks just like her missing bracelet. It has his silver mark struck into the clasp." Miranda stood straight and pulled the van keys from her front pocket. "Call me if she remembers something else. In fact, call me if she didn't know anything about it. That's information, too."

Miranda left the house, then started the van.

"Wait." Anna Belle hunched her shoulders and clasped both hands over her mouth. She walked over to the driver's side. "If he took his mother's bracelet without her knowing, perhaps he wasn't sure that she would say yes."

"So he expected to tell her afterwards? Strange."

Miranda pulled into her farmhouse driveway wondering what calamity Ron would spring on her. It was getting a bit ridiculous, but she wasn't sure how she would behave if her only source of cash was for day labor.

Her mom opened the door, and Sandy bolted down the steps and met Miranda with whimpers and a windmilling tail that wiggled his entire body. She picked him up for puppy licks and gave him a thorough scratching behind his ears.

She unlocked the back door of the panel van and took inventory of her art supplies. For once, everything was in good supply. Although it was another story for Sunday's tour. She needed the supplies that she had ordered. She automatically pulled out her phone to check for a tracking notification from the post office.

Duh! My cell doesn't work here. I'll log in to my desktop for that.

"Ron said he wanted to talk to you as soon as you got

back." Dorothy ducked back into the house like a turtle retreating into its shell.

This can't be good.

Miranda walked down the double-track path to the barn. She stood in the center of the open barn door and looked up at the roof. It was completely repaired. She stepped farther into the barn and looked into the stall where her ingredients had been ruined by the leak. The space was immaculate. The floor swept and—miracle of miracles—Ron had built some racks out of her scrap woodpile. They were the right height and the right depth for the ingredients she needed on hand.

She put her hands on her hips. "I am stunned. Ron," she hollered. "Where are you, Ron?"

Ron poked his head around the rear barn door. "Do you like that?"

Miranda smiled. "This is wonderful." Then she frowned. "But I didn't ask you to do this. I can't pay you for work I haven't agreed to."

"Come on out and look at the roof." Ron waved her out to the back of the barn. He walked out into the back field and pointed to the repairs. "There's a little difference in color, but that doesn't hurt at all."

Miranda let her eyes drift over the expanse of the roof. It was perfectly repaired. Ron was right: if there wasn't that tiny color difference, you couldn't tell that anything had happened at all. She turned her head and smiled up at him. "This is wonderful. What a great job."

"I'm glad you're happy because I want to make a trade."

"Trade?" Miranda thought about what he could have to trade. He was homeless, jobless, and hardly ever sober. "Trade what?"

"I would like to trade my skills for letting me live up in the barn loft."

"What? It's a hayloft. It's all right for camping out up there for a few days, but it's not a permanent lodging. There's no water, no bathroom. Heck, there aren't any walls. I don't know what you're thinking."

Ron put his hands out palms up. "Let me explain. Once you get this distillery up and running, you're gonna need some on-site security. I can build out the loft to be a studio apartment with a full bathroom. I won't charge you a cent. I need a permanent place to live."

Miranda just blinked. Was this a true offer that she needed to consider?

"There's a couple of things that are concerning me, Ron. I'm not going to answer you right now, so I'll think about my concerns and we'll talk about them tomorrow."

"Whatever they are, I can fix them."

"Maybe not. I certainly can't have someone as on-site security who is a confirmed alcoholic. That just doesn't make any sense at all."

Ron began to wring his hands at a rapid pace. So fast that Miranda was sure that his hands must be getting warm. "I've fixed that. I joined the local AA group and my sponsor takes me to a meeting every day. He's going to help me stay sober."

Miranda looked at Ron closely. He did seem a little less scruffy after he had gotten a bath. "Let me think about this."

He didn't say anything, just nodded and disappeared.

As soon as Miranda walked back into the house, the phone rang and it was Anna Belle. "Hi, Miranda. I talked to Mom and it appears that she wasn't sure about when

Howard was going to propose to Jennifer, if at all. It was still such a fragile relationship. She didn't think she should complicate matters for Howard by telling me and my sister. Mom is also wondering why Jennifer didn't confide in her that they were getting closer to an engagement. It makes no sense. I'm not sure if she's remembering it as it happened or as she thought it should happen."

"Makes no sense to me, either. Thanks for getting back to me."

Miranda's mom was standing there not even pretending that she hadn't been listening in. "What's that about? Why has Anna Belle called?"

"It's something that I found out from Doris Ann up at Hemlock Lodge. She says that she was sure that Howard and Jennifer O'Rourke were about to announce their engagement. That's why he had that bracelet on him."

"So, my sister didn't know?"

"That's what she says."

Dorothy pursed her lips. "Your aunt sometimes misremembers."

"Argh," Miranda groaned. "Not helping!"

Her mother opened her arms and Miranda walked into a warm hug, "You know it's going to be difficult to untangle Howard's life. He was a strange duck."

"Yeah, but there are so many secrets." Miranda pressed her hands over her eyes and swung her head from side to side. "I've got to stop thinking about this for right now and get ready for tomorrow's tour. Austin is coming back to do some more research on our motley gang of suspects. He's invited himself over for supper. He's beginning to look forward to your cooking."

"Smart young man."

"Yeah, I think he is. Oh, by the way . . ." Miranda hesitated. "Could you make up a plate for Ron? He's going to be doing some odd jobs over the next few days."

"Really? I thought you couldn't wait to get rid of him."

"I thought so, too, but things change."

Miranda thought about that for a second. That phrase seemed to tickle something in the back of her head. When she concentrated—it disappeared.

"I need to take another plate of treats up to Doris Ann tomorrow. Any ideas?"

"There's loads of dried apples up in the other end of the attic. They need to be used up before the next batch is stored away over the winter. What about a dried-apple pie?"

"Perfect! She'll love that. After bringing her treats to loosen her tongue, I've figured out that the more snacks I bring, the more she shares them out with the guests, and the more they inquire about my tours."

Chapter 29

Sunday Morning, Hemlock Lodge

Miranda had baked her dried-apple pie in a cooking tray with a lip so that she could cut it into squares and wrap them individually. In line with her marketing goals, she put a Paint & Shine sticker on the bottom of each snack. Doris Ann loved giving the treats to the guests.

"What have you brought me today?" Doris Ann eyed the platter.

"These are square pieces of pie made from last year's dried apples. They're from Uncle Gene's crop last fall. I forgot about them until I cleared out the attic for my mom's visit."

"It's nice to have her back. We're going to meet for lunch next week and catch up on old times." Doris Ann grabbed a snack, unwrapped it, then took a bite almost before the platter hit the top of her desk. "Mmm. You're getting to be quite a good old-fashioned cook."

Miranda smiled at how much that comment pleased her. She was determined to keep these old-timey cultural dishes alive. "Have you seen my clients?"

"They're still having breakfast. They're a pokey bunch, so they'll be late. Nice and polite for such a large family."

Miranda's clients today consisted of a single family with eight children. It had taken quite a lot of serious convincing for the mother to guarantee Miranda that they would be well-behaved and attentive to her tour. She was filled with doubt. She didn't think the odds were good with only three adults to supervise eight children.

"The mother told me that if I didn't approve of their behavior within the first ten minutes, we could turn back and she wouldn't ask for a refund."

"That's mighty fair."

Miranda looked down the corridor to watch for the family. Kevin Burkart was standing in the entryway to the dining room with a pudgy man in shorts and a T-shirt. They shook hands and Kevin walked up to Miranda and Doris Ann. He was wearing expensive loafers, with khaki trousers and a white button-down oxford shirt. He carried a slim leather laptop case over his shoulder. He leaned over and gave Doris Ann a smooch on the cheek.

"How's my prettiest client?"

Doris Ann's face flushed to a light rose. "Stop that, Kevin. People will talk."

"I hope so." He sat on the corner of Doris Ann's desk and took a snack. "You've been helping me get clients up here. That was another new one. I appreciate it."

Doris Ann flushed to a deep rose. "That's not true."

Kevin turned to Miranda. "Good morning. Are you running another tour?"

"Every day but Monday. It looks like you've been benefiting from Doris Ann's influence as well."

"Oh, sure. Doris Ann is a client, of course, and people trust her. I think I've gotten, what, maybe eight or ten new customers directly from her recommendation?"

"My pleasure." Doris Ann was practically purring.

He smiled brightly. "I also keep a giant ad in the Wolfe County newspaper. I like to support the local businesses." He dipped a hand into his pocket, pulled out a business card case, then gave Miranda one of his embossed cards. "Here, just in case you need some financial advice after your launch." He leaned over to give Doris Ann another smooch. "Sorry, I've got another appointment over in Stanton."

Miranda watched him stride through the front doors like a man in charge of the world. She turned back to Doris Ann. "He's your financial adviser?"

"Oh, yes. He has a few local customers so he can travel up here on expenses. My uncle left me a nice little inheritance, and Kevin is helping me make it grow. I need something set aside for my retirement."

"Oh." Miranda was a little hesitant to put Doris Ann on the spot with more questions but knew that there was no way Doris Ann would say something she wasn't comfortable telling. In fact, you couldn't force her.

"How long has he been working for you?"

"Only about three years, but in that time, my nest egg has more than doubled. He's a real comfort to me. Being all alone in your elder years is not for the weak of heart."

Miranda spied her family coming out of the dining room, filling the hallway with happy chatter. "I've got to go now, but one last question. Do you trust him?"

"Absolutely, he's the salt of the earth, a good old country boy."

The Wilson family were indeed as well-behaved as their mother had promised. The oldest child was sixteen and the youngest one was seven. Each older child paired up with a younger one as a buddy, and they hiked up to Lover's Leap hand in hand without so much as a single incident.

The setup for the paintings started off well.

"No, no, no!" yelled the mother, and she grabbed the hand of the youngest child before he put the paintbrush in his mouth. "That's not ketchup, sweetie." She picked up his palette and handed it to Miranda. "Can you give him another one with no red? It's one of the things that we have to watch. He is obsessed with ketchup. It drives us all crazy." The mother smiled. "I'm sorry, but otherwise, his autism is very well managed."

"Can I use a deep orange instead?" Miranda asked. The mother hesitated. "It's so he can paint the fall colors, and we have so many red maples this year."

"Oh, yes, that will work just fine."

Miranda quickly mixed up a reddish orange and set up another palette. She handed it to Mrs. Wilson, who knelt down before her son and, at eye level, carefully explained that paint was not food.

Austin met the group and delivered his ranger talk about the history of Lover's Leap. The younger one hung on every word as Austin explained the multiple legends that surrounded the formation.

Miranda and Austin moved back to stand behind the family while they completed their paintings.

"I talked to Doris Ann this morning," said Miranda in a low voice. "Kevin Burkart is her financial adviser. Can you believe that?"

"That is a surprise. I knew she received an unexpected inheritance, but I didn't know it was enough to need a financial adviser."

"Well, she's very pleased with his efforts and recommends his services whenever she gets the chance."

"Well, there really couldn't be a better character recommendation." They agreed to eliminate Kevin as a suspect and continue their online research on the remaining Risky Business Adventurers.

Chapter 30

Sunday, Big Rock Cabin

Miranda called the number she had gotten from Doris Ann for the Risky Business Adventurers' cabin and then convinced her mother to tag along. Her mom would lend a feeling of comfort and safety while she spoke to Jennifer O'Rourke. They pulled up, and Jennifer was waiting for them on the long porch, furnished with about a dozen traditional rocking chairs.

Jennifer had an earthenware pitcher of hot cider and a stack of mugs on a serving table. "Please help yourself. I find the breeze a little chilly this time of year." She pulled her denim jacket closed and snapped it up.

Dorothy poured two mugs and handed one over to Miranda. They sat in the rockers on either side of Jennifer.

Miranda cleared her throat. "Thanks for seeing us. I understand that Howard's discovery has been rather shocking for you."

"It's a shock for us all."

"Right," agreed Miranda. "But one of the things we're curious about is why you were keeping your relationship with Howard a secret. Now that he's no longer missing, can you tell me?"

Jennifer frowned. "Why should I do that? You're not the sheriff."

"I'm investigating Howard's death at the request of my aunt. She doesn't trust that Sheriff Larson will get to the bottom of his murder."

Dorothy took Jennifer's hand in both of hers and patted it with genuine concern. "Sweetie, my sister is not always as kind as she was brought up to be. She was very possessive of Howard. Is that why you kept your relationship from her?"

"Who told you?" Jennifer pulled her hand away, then clasped her hands so tightly in her lap that her knuckles turned red. "I want to know who knew."

"It was Doris Ann," said Miranda. "She hadn't told anyone because, along with everyone else, she thought he had simply run away from his responsibilities."

Jennifer began to cry. "That part is true." She buried her face in her hands and sobbed with the abandon of a small child.

Dorothy took a packet of tissues from her handbag and gave several to Jennifer. "I'm so sorry, honey. Did he leave right after you told him about the baby?"

"How did you know?" Jennifer's eyes held fear and began to fill with tears.

Miranda put her hand on her mother's arm and leaned in with an unspoken accusation in her eyes.

Dorothy shook off the hand. "That's usually why young

men run off. They're not ready for the responsibility of having a family."

"Yes." Jennifer blew her nose and sniffed. She continued to hiccup through her words. "I had just told him the night before he disappeared. I assumed that was the reason. He was horribly upset—unreasonably upset—irrationally upset, but I didn't think he was so shallow to just leave me."

Miranda looked over at her mother, who was now crying herself. Miranda took a deep breath and said what wasn't being said. "You lost the baby, didn't you? You had a miscarriage."

Jennifer bowed her head. "After he had been gone for a week. I was a mess. But he didn't leave me. He would have been a wonderful husband and father."

Dorothy stood and brought Jennifer up into her arms, stroking her hair and making soothing noises.

Miranda sank her head in her hands and let her mother give Jennifer what she needed most—unstinting sympathy.

After several minutes, Jennifer stepped out of Dorothy's arms and stood for a few moments waiting for her sobs to calm. "I haven't been able to tell anyone. It all got lost in the alarm that Howard had run off."

"Why was there an alarm?" asked Miranda.

"He was expected at a board meeting with the oil company. He was presenting his analysis for new drill sites in this area. When he didn't show up, his boss called everyone who knew him to find out why he had missed such an important meeting. It was totally out of character."

"When did you accept that he was gone?"

"We had a date that evening. He said he had important news, but that it was a surprise and he couldn't let anyone know what was going to happen because of his geological study. He seemed to think it would cause a lot of trouble."

"Was he still upset about your condition?" asked Dorothy.

"He seemed calmer and apologized over and over and over again." Unconsciously, Jennifer put one hand on her tummy as if protecting herself again. "I never heard from him again. I honestly thought he couldn't face marriage, fatherhood, a house. You know, the whole settling-down stage."

"You couldn't know that he was planning to propose," said Miranda. "That was part of his good news."

"Propose?"

"Next to Howard's remains, they found a silver bracelet fashioned by my grandfather. It's family tradition. When an engagement is soon to be announced, the prospective groom gifts the bride with a handmade silver bracelet. I believe it was for you."

"Oh." Jennifer collapsed into her rocker. "He loved me, after all."

"Do you believe her?" Miranda asked her mother on the way back to the farmhouse. "She seemed a mess of reactions, and I wasn't quite sure how to interpret Howard's behavior."

"He seemed all over the place. He reacted badly to Jennifer's news. He missed that important meeting."

"And yet, he also had that bracelet with him. That's a complete contradiction to not wanting to marry Jennifer. I'm very confused."

Miranda pulled into her driveway and saw Ron standing on the front porch with Sandy in his arms. "Now
what?"

"He's fine," Ron hollered as soon as they got out of the
van. "He somehow managed to open your bedroom door,
and I found him out by the chicken coop. It looked like he
was about ready to track the fox."

Miranda took Sandy from Ron and suffered an enthusiastic licking along with apology whimpers. "What were
you doing, little one? You aren't big enough to track
game."

"He doesn't know that. They're born to track." Ron
shifted from one foot to the other. "Um, have you decided
if I can work here?"

"Not yet." Miranda cringed inside. She had meant to
think about the situation seriously today, but she hadn't
had a quiet moment to herself yet. "I'll give you an answer tomorrow. I promise."

"Sure, no problem. I'm getting on with making the loft
more comfortable. I found an old iron bed frame behind
some wooden planks. This would really work well as a
vacation rental, too."

Miranda and her mother looked at each other with the
same wheels spinning.

"Vacation rental?" Miranda tilted her head to one side.
"Would that be a feasible way to make a little more income?"

"He's got a good point." Dorothy moved her hands together in a handwashing motion. "You could rent it out as
an opportunity to sleep over the moonshine distillery. I'll
bet plenty of tourists would be thrilled to claim that as an
experience."

"It really wouldn't take that much effort." Miranda twisted her lips to one side. "This is a lovely quiet road and it would be great to have another income stream. It doesn't look like I'm ever going to get the distillery up and running."

They both laughed and went inside.

"I think there's still something that Jennifer is hiding from us," Dorothy said, heading for the kitchen.

"She was surprised about the bracelet, but it was something else."

"Did you notice how she held her hand on her tummy?"

"No," said Miranda. "I didn't catch that."

"Do you think she lost the baby because he hit her."

"Mom! That's an awful thought."

Dorothy rubbed her eyes and frowned. "We don't know the path that someone's mind is a-taking. We just don't know."

Chapter 31

Sunday Afternoon, Sheriff's Apartment

Miranda called Sheriff Larson at home to report her findings about the situation between Jennifer and Howard. Felicia answered and said that he wasn't there, but could Miranda come over and give an expert opinion on something?

Driven by her curiosity, Miranda was standing in the sheriff's apartment within twenty minutes. He hadn't yet returned.

"What is it you want me to see?"

Felicia bit her lip. "I'm dying to show it to you, but it's not worth the grief I would get from Richard if I let you see it without him to witness your reaction."

"No problem, I can wait."

They sat on the comfortable modern couch and Felicia prompted, "You said you had news?"

"Did you know that Jennifer was pregnant with Howard's baby at the time he disappeared?"

Felicia's eyes raised in surprise. "No. Wow, that's completely out of left field. Pregnant." She thought for a moment. "But what happened? Did she get—"

"No, no, no. She had a miscarriage the week after Howard disappeared. But that's got me concerned about Howard's temperament."

"Why?"

"Given the way Jennifer is acting, do you think there could have been some violence between them?"

"Oh, I see what you mean. Maybe he didn't want to get married," said Felicia. "No, I don't think that's the case. Good to bring it up though."

"Yes. It's a contradiction because the promise bracelet he was carrying meant that he was going to ask her. Probably the next time they met."

"Well, I wouldn't have thought about this angle five years ago, but things change: the violence might not have been from Howard."

"You mean it could have been from Jennifer?"

"I've seen that more times than I am happy to think about." Felicia rubbed her ear. "But, again, it doesn't seem to be the case here. Neither Howard nor Jennifer have any history of physical violence against anyone. There would be a history. There's always a history. That reminds me. I got an update from Dr. DuPont. She has discovered evidence of hairline fractures in Howard's hands."

"Fractures?"

"Yes. They could be the result of either defense wounds in a fight or hiking-related fractures. Dr. DuPont thinks they could be from a fall, but Sheriff Larson is convinced that he hit someone or something."

"Well, a blow to a pregnant woman's stomach wouldn't cause a fracture," said Miranda.

"No, but if you strike someone on the jaw, it could result in an injury to your hand as well as your victim could fall into something. She also found damage to the bones where the voice box would be."

Miranda winced. "So he might not have been able to yell for help."

A long silence followed.

Sheriff Larson came into the apartment and hung up his hat on the coatrack by the door. He walked over and gave Felicia a peck on the cheek and frowned at Miranda. "What's this?"

"I thought she should know about the microfractures and could help us identify this last artifact."

A half smile showed up on Sheriff Larson, which was an improvement from his habitual eye roll. "Fine. I haven't turned up anything on the internet or from the university."

"What is it?" Miranda's curiosity kicked into high gear.

Felicia got up and opened the lap drawer of the desk placed against the far wall of the living room. She pulled out a clear plastic pouch and handed it to Miranda. "We found several scraps of this material. The others are degraded beyond recognition, but this one is interesting."

Miranda turned the pouch over. It contained a two-inch square of fabric with inked lettering and squiggly lines. "These look like contour elevation lines. It's a map."

"Good," said the sheriff. "That's what I think. What is the fabric and what was used to draw on it?"

Miranda stood and held the pouch up to the light coming in the window next to the front door. She turned the pouch in all directions, including front to back. "This is old."

"Well, I figured that out, but how old?"

"This probably dates to around the time of the lost silver mines."

"You can tell that from just this little scrap?"

Miranda nodded. "That's what a fine arts degree will get you. Most museums have thousands of artifacts that will never be seen by the paying public." Then she turned the pouch over in her hands once more. "But things like this are available for scholarly research. In fact, most museums will give students a stipend to catalog and research unknown pieces in their collections."

Felicia stood beside her. "And you got one of those grants?"

"I did. I was assigned to the Donald W. Reynolds Museum and Education Center at Mount Vernon. That's where I got my love of big cities. It was so close to Washington, DC. Anyway, they had some original survey documents that were drawn by George Washington. I had a chance to study them closely. This is from the same era."

Felicia glared over at her husband. "See, I told you she could be helpful. She has a first-class education."

"Right, but how does that help us?" He put his hands on his hips. "How does an old map help find Howard's murderer?"

"If this is from the same time frame as George Washington's surveys, then this could indeed be a fragment of the maps Jonathan Swift created to find his way back to the silver mines that he discovered here in the Daniel Boone National Forest."

"If Howard had managed to find an authentic map, he was the perfect person for locating the mines."

"Where would he have found a map?" Miranda sounded frustrated.

"Maybe on one of his survey expeditions he found one of the mines that Jonathan Swift used for smelting silver coins. Those coins would be worth millions to private collectors. It's a reasonable theory since he was exploring drilling sites for his company."

"I reckon it makes a bit of sense."

The sheriff paused. "It makes as much sense as anything else. He was good at following animal trails, plus he was a degreed geologist familiar with the history of this area."

Miranda sighed. "He was also in need of money to provide for his new family."

Chapter 32

Sunday Afternoon, the Farmhouse

Miranda returned home to hear her mother scolding Sandy from inside the farmhouse. "Now you've done it. Your mommy is gonna be mighty mad with you. Don't you give me those puppy eyes? Bad dog. Bad dog."

Miranda tilted her head back to look up at the sky, blew out a puffed breath, then opened the screen door to go into the front room. "What has Sandy gotten into now?"

Her mother pointed to the remains of an expertly ravaged hiking boot. Its untouched mate was only a few feet away. "I can't believe how fast he managed to do that. I was only out of the room long enough to make a pot of chamomile tea. He was asleep on the rug. I'm sorry. Was that your only pair?"

"Don't apologize. I knew what I was getting into with

a puppy. Yep, those boots are fantastic, but expensive. I'll have to wear my high-tops. I may also have to choose a flatter trail for my tour on Tuesday. I'll order another pair tonight. With any luck I can get a rush order delivered by Monday evening. Thank goodness for online ordering." She picked up Sandy, gave him a nuzzle, and bopped him on the nose. "You're a bad little puppy. No chewing on my favorite boot, only on chew toys." He was far too young for much scolding, but you could never tell if puppies understood you or not, so she always tried to tell Sandy how she felt.

She followed her mother into the kitchen. "Ugh. We're a long way from the end of his teething phase. I'd better order more chew toys, too."

Dorothy poured two mugs of tea and motioned for Miranda to sit at the kitchen table. "What happened with Sheriff Larson and Felicia?

Miranda briefly summarized her meeting.

"Anyway, next I need to get a handle on Stephanie Brinkley. I texted Austin to come over and help me with the online searches, but he hasn't answered. He might be busy." Miranda heard the disappointment in her voice.

"Text him that I'm making thick-sliced pan-fried pork chops with a blackberry sauce, twice-baked potatoes with fresh creamed corn. He'll be by."

Miranda texted and got an instant thumbs-up icon from Austin.

She fired up the laptop in her office and checked her business email first. After all, without clients, she couldn't pay her bills. After responding to queries, processing payments, and scheduling tours for the week following her distillery training, she finally typed Stephanie's name into the search engine.

The first entries listed her as an associate pharmacologist working for Saint Joseph Hospital in Lexington. She had received her license from Frankfort, Kentucky, only a year ago. There were no links to any of the most popular social media sites. Apparently, Stephanie valued her privacy more than the rest of the Risky Business Adventurers.

Miranda sat back in her office chair and wondered how nice it would be to opt out of the promotional posting she did for her business. It was a tempting thought, but pharmacists didn't need to advertise. Tour operators who wanted to establish a moonshine distillery needed to be savvy users of social media. It was part of the deal.

She pulled out her murder notebook and updated the page for Jennifer. She wrote all that she had learned but wasn't satisfied that she had captured the complexity of the lady. Miranda still didn't know much about Jennifer's relationship with Howard and why they kept it secret.

Miranda flipped the pages to Stephanie and wrote down the few sparse facts.

A knock on the screen door alerted her that Austin had walked down the road for their meeting. She stood in the open door of her office and waved at him. "Come on in. You have perfect timing."

He smiled. "And that's a wonderful aroma coming from the kitchen. Is your mom cooking?"

Miranda bopped him on the arm. "She's not the only fantastic cook in this house."

He pretended to be hurt and rubbed his shoulder. "I know that. It runs in your whole family. That's why your moonshine is going to be a wild success. You have to be a good cook in order to make a good ole mountain dew."

She returned his smile. "You're forgiven. Look, I'm

trying to get some online information about Stephanie. I'm not having much luck; maybe your search phrasing will catch better results."

He sat down in her office chair and tapped in a few words. When the results had spilled out onto the screen, he pointed to an entry that declared she was a heavy contributor to a charity in Lexington that supported pancreatic cancer research. She was listed not only as a board member but also as a charter member of the newly formed organization.

"Well done. I wonder why she's supporting that particular cancer."

A crunching of gravel in the driveway alerted them to the arrival of a visitor. They went out on the front porch, and Stephanie got out of a bright red Porsche.

"I hope you don't mind an unannounced visit." Stephanie smiled. "I heard from Jennifer that you're trying to find out what happened to Howard. She confessed all that she had been holding back and said you were gentle and sympathetic. I want to thank you for that."

"Come on in. We're about to sit down to supper."

"Oh, no. I didn't mean to barge in on you like this, but I really want to help."

Miranda waved her hand. "Come on. You know how we cook around here. There's enough for an army. I'm glad you're here." Miranda looked at Austin. He raised his eyebrows. "Yes, you're going to save us from a run up to your cabin. Apparently, you don't like social media. We haven't been able to find out very much about you."

Stephanie pressed her lips together. "That's right." She walked up onto the porch. "I had a good friend in the pharmacy program with me. She had been an online activist pretty much like any person her age. You know, 'day in the life of a pharmacology student' kind of thing. Nothing overtly controversial at all, just friendly and chatty." Stephanie paused. "Then it got ugly with some followers who found her in real life. They found out that she was gay."

Miranda slapped her forehead. "That wouldn't go over well in some ultraconservative parts of West Virginia."

"That's exactly where she was. They began stalking her and it was a nightmare. She finally had to resign, leave the state, and enroll into another pharmacy program. It cost her a least a year's delay in graduating, an expensive year, mind you. I'll never be on social media."

"Thanks for explaining." Miranda led them into the dining room and popped her head into the kitchen. "Hi, Mom. One more for dinner. Can you manage?"

"Sure, sure, honey. I'm just taking a plate out to the barn for Ron. Set your friends up in the dining room. It'll be much nicer there."

Miranda grabbed another plate, napkin, along with silverware. She added it to the three settings her mother had already laid out. "Would you like a cocktail? I'm working on a new one to pair with our pan-fried pork chops."

Stephanie smiled. "Wonderful. I'm feeling quite the guest."

Miranda went over to the dining room sideboard.

"What are you going for?" asked Austin.

"I thought I'd go for something a tiny bit acidic to offset the sweet blackberry sauce, so I'm starting with a jigger of 'shine over some muddled lemongrass. Then I'll add ice and top it off with 7UP." Miranda mixed the four cocktails. By the time she garnished the mason jars with a

sprig of lemongrass and placed them on the table, her
mother had returned with a tray laden with serving plat-
ters and bowls.

With due appreciation to the wonderful dinner, Miranda resisted asking Stephanie any questions until the
meal was finished. "I have a dried-apple pie to reheat if
anyone's interested." That was followed by a unanimous
yes. "Good, I'll just pop it in the oven for a few minutes
and we can go out to the porch. It's such a nice evening,
we can talk out there. No one will mind a side of vanilla
ice cream?"

Another unanimous yes followed.

Miranda brought out the desserts and joined Stephanie
on the porch swing. Austin and Dorothy sat on the
wooden bench along the front of the house. After the last
fork had scraped against each empty plate, Dorothy gathered them up and left to clean up the kitchen. "I'll clear
up the kitchen, sweetie. Then, I'm off up to bed. I've got
a fantastic book that I simply must finish."

After a few moments of companionable silence, Stephanie cleared her throat. "I'm not sure how to start with
this, but I'm going to say that Jennifer couldn't possibly
have harmed Howard. She's too kind."

Miranda sighed. "I've gotten confirmation now that
Jennifer and Howard were romantically connected. What
I'm failing to understand is your friendship with Howard.
Did you two get along?"

Stephanie shifted her position in the swing and caused
it to squeak. "I'm sorry, but that's why I'm here. It's not
something you'll find out from the others. Howard and I
didn't take to each other from the very start of freshman
year."

"Why?" asked Austin.

"Nothing that I could do anything about. At first, he claimed to have an aversion to redheads. I have no idea why as he never admitted the real reason in the beginning beyond a blunt 'I don't like red hair.' Although we were outwardly friendly, eventually he began to avoid me when we gathered as a group."

Miranda lifted her hands in a why gesture.

"Okay, okay. It was because I'm gay. He figured it out back in college even though at the time I was still in the closet. Later, I was living in Lexington with my lover, who recently became my wife. Anyway, I'd been approved to adopt a seven-year-old girl from China as a single parent. He was livid. I wasn't out at the time, but he was hopelessly prejudiced and threatened to tell the adoption agency."

Miranda looked at Austin and then back at Stephanie. "You understand that you've just confessed to a powerful motive to get rid of Howard?"

"It's not like that; the agency knew about my partner. In fact, it was an advantage as they were seeking diverse candidates. Besides, I have an alibi."

"What?" Miranda raised her voice, and Sandy yipped and pushed through the screen door to run to her. Picking him up, she said, "Why haven't you spoken up? Sheriff Larson has been checking everybody out. You could have saved him a lot of trouble."

"I've been burned many times by so-called well-meaning officials, so I'm pretty cautious about sharing my personal life with any man, no matter how progressive he claims to be." Stephanie glared at Austin.

Austin took Sandy from Miranda. "I'll settle him in and get your notebook. It needs an update."

Miranda placed a hand over her heart. She appreciated

that he'd figured out that Stephanie would obviously be more comfortable sharing her secrets alone.

After Austin and Sandy had gone, Stephanie's words tumbled over each other in a rush. She wanted to get it over with. "I didn't finish the hike on the day that Howard went missing. I had an emergency phone call from my adoption agency in Lexington. They needed another set of my fingerprints for the final application. I barely made it to the police station in time."

"You got them done in Lexington? Why?"

"The Chinese orphanage doesn't have the ability to deal with scans like our agencies. I needed the physical-ink-on-paper type of fingerprint card to send. The Lexington officers were the only ones qualified to do them properly. Then I dropped the document off at the agency minutes before the paperwork was picked up by their courier." Stephanie gently folded her hands into her lap and sat silent.

Austin returned with Miranda's notebook, and she quietly copied down the name of the adoption agency.

"Thanks for letting me tell you in private. I'm still not comfortable with the other members of Risky Business Adventurers knowing about my wife."

"I'm sorry, but if you don't mind, I will let Sheriff Larson know. I'm not obliged to since I'm only the victim's cousin, but it would be a generous act of kindness to Howard's family if you make things easier." Miranda scanned Stephanie's face for signs of agreement. "I'll ask him to keep this information in confidence. He will likely confirm that your fingerprints were taken that day."

"Fine." Stephanie got out of the swing. "Thank your mother for a lovely meal and thank you all for being so kind."

Stephanie had nothing else to say as she was leaving except to repeat that she and Howard had accepted that they would stay out of each other's way. A short argument now and then was unavoidable, but they usually controlled themselves when they were around the others. They both thought the friendship of the group was worth it.

Stephanie was nowhere near Battleship Rock on that day.

Chapter 33

Sunday Night, the Farmhouse

Standing at the end of the porch looking at the plume of dust that followed Stephanie's red Porsche, Austin folded his arms across his chest. "That's not what I expected to learn, but honestly, it's got to be true."

"It will be easy for Sheriff Larson to verify."

"Why would anyone confess to hating someone so freely?"

"Maybe to divert suspicion." Miranda opened the screen door. "She took a big risk to share her private life with us. Apparently, she doesn't trust others very often."

They went into the living room.

Austin added, "But it feels suspicious for her to be that honest. Then there is the fact that it doesn't make her look like a bad person. It makes Howard look like a bad person. She probably thought that the sooner suspicion is away from her, the sooner she can go back to living her life. It's a smart move."

Miranda led the way through the dining room into her office. "The situation between Howard and Stephanie proves that he was more complicated and prejudiced than anyone in my family knew or acknowledged."

"Let's get our online searches done for the last of the Risky Business Adventurers. Kurt Smith is the final member. I'm sick to death of punching a keyboard."

"So, you think detection should be more—what? Glamorous?" She giggled. "Sorry, I'm thinking of TV detectives who tap a few keys and have an identity flashed up on a big display in seconds."

"Or even better, they have a horde of minions that do all the work behind the scenes and an answer is presented to the hero—"

"Or heroine."

"—naturally, it could be a heroine, within seconds." Austin sat in the guest chair. "Tap away."

Miranda jiggled the mouse to wake her sleeping computer, entered her PIN, and typed a search for Kurt Smith. Immediately, the screen filled up with advertisements for his plastic surgery office. The ads were polished and sophisticated, for beauty services at a clinic in the most exclusive area of Lexington.

"Wow," said Miranda. "He has a really big practice in Lexington. It looks like his reputation is so good he can support an entire staff who each specialize in youthful beauty treatments."

Austin looked over her shoulder. "Look, there's more. He's been on national television for some of his radical treatments. It looks like they're controversial."

"He also is one of the movers and shakers in Lexington's horse-racing crowd. Looks like he bought himself into the game by purchasing a training complex. Then one of his horses won the Kentucky Derby only a year later."

"That probably doesn't set too well with the established families of the racing world." Austin straightened up in his chair. "He must be a bit older than the others. I wonder how he became part of Risky Business Adventurers?"

Miranda rubbed her eyes. "I'm not sure, but it looks like there was some trouble the next year with a drugs scandal with his racehorses." She clicked on one of the entries. "As a surgeon, he would have easy access to performance drugs. I'm not sure how that would connect him to Howard in any way."

"Nothing obvious from these search results."

"All I know at this point is that I'm too tired to think about it anymore." Miranda covered her mouth over a barely suppressed yawn.

"Let's stop. I've got an early staff meeting at headquarters. I need to get some sleep before I fall asleep walking home." He put his hands on his thighs and lurched up. "Tomorrow will bring something new."

"Right. I've got to get Sandy out back to the chicken coop. Your dog-scent trick seems to be working to keep the critters away."

"Have you decided what to do about Ron?"

Miranda rolled her eyes.

Chapter 34

Monday Afternoon, the Farmhouse

Miranda flopped down on her back into the cozy sofa. "Whew! This has been a busy week."

Her mother came into the front room bearing a cold bottle of Ale-8 soda. "This might perk you up."

"Oh, yeah." Miranda sat up and swigged about half the drink. "The. Best. Soda. Ever! I really missed this for the whole time I was in New York City. I could occasionally get it in the deli around the corner. Thanks, Mom."

"An old farm truck came by yesterday. I was surprised that they would be out on a Sunday."

Miranda took another sip. "That must be my replacement ingredients for my first batch of moonshine. Lots of my farmers have jobs in Lexington or even up in Cincinnati. They deliver whenever they get a chance. Their timing is perfect."

Dorothy sat in one of the rockers by the window. "What have you decided to do about Ron? It's not fair to keep him hanging on. Although he's getting quite settled in the barn's loft."

"I know. I know." The phone rang, saving Miranda. She recognized the Lexington number illuminated on the screen. "Hi, Tyler. What's up?" Miranda pointed to the phone and went into her office to take notes in her murder sketch book.

"Sorry to interrupt but I've uncovered the background situation on Alfred. The plagiarism incident occurred a few months before Howard's disappearance. It involved Alfred's best friend from childhood, who . . ." Miranda heard Tyler cover the mouthpiece and speak to someone. "Sorry, I'm getting close to deadline here."

"No problem, I'm listening."

Tyler continued, "The friend is the nephew of the publisher who has since sold the newspaper and the John Latchy who turned out to be a no-talent weasel so he left not long after. Alfred, however, is still stuck with the suspicion and will carry this stain for life. He might still be mad. I know I would be spiteful."

"Do you think he could have been capable of murder?" asked Miranda.

"That's a huge leap to go from ruined reputation to murder."

Miranda paused a moment. "To my mind, Alfred doesn't seem to be the grudge-holding type."

"You do have the advantage in that you've met him."

"Right, I have. So far, he seems to be a well-adjusted person who obviously overcame a bad chapter in his life. He's got friends, hobbies, and a career he obviously enjoys. I'm glad dirt digging is not a normal part of my life.

That's your part of this investigation. I love digging up the puzzle parts and fitting the pieces together."

Tyler's voice lowered a notch. "You may be right. I've got a bug for the chase. Okay. Got to go."

The call ended before Miranda could say anything else.

She returned to the front room, and Ron was sitting in the second rocker by the window, chatting with her mother. He was on his best behavior. His hair was slicked down, still wet from a shower. He had on a clean flannel shirt under a newish pair of clean bibbed overalls.

He stood up. "Your mom suggested that I come on in and have a talk with you about building out the barn loft. Have you decided? I hope you'll consider how important it's gonna be to have good security after you start distilling your uncle's moonshine recipe."

Miranda picked up her half-finished soda and downed the rest of it. She felt pressured by both of them, but it was also a practical point to have someone in the building. She sat on the sofa and looked at Ron.

"I've been giving this some thought. Although I've up-graded the barn with modern plumbing from our spring, it is still a barn. It wouldn't keep out a determined seven-year-old."

Ron raised his eyebrows but remained silent.

"There are still some issues that we need to work out, but I'm coming around to the idea."

"Thank you, Miss Trent. You won't regret it."

Miranda was pretty sure she would regret it at any moment, but it was an ideal solution to her barn-turned-distillery security problem. A person of any sort would be a deterrent. "One of the first things we need to do is figure out how to keep track of your hours."

"Oh, I can do that." Dorothy answered so quickly that Miranda suspected that there was more to her friendship with Ron than Miranda thought. "I'll start a ledger book so we can tally up both the security tasks right along with the handyman tasks."

Ron piped up, "That's a great idea, Dorothy. You have such a clever way of thinking."

Dorothy continued, "We also need to figure out how many hours a week would go towards board and lodging."

"You're a wonderful cook, Dorothy," said Ron.

Miranda sighed. She needed to ignore this blossoming situation. Nothing she could do or say would help. "I basically think that any work towards getting the barn livable would be in trade for living up there."

"That sounds fair to me," said Ron.

Miranda looked at her mother, who tipped her head forward. "That's good for now. We'll get back to you on when guard duties should begin. For now, we need to get ready for the electricians that are coming early tomorrow morning. It should only take about an hour."

"Great. I'll get my work clothes on and get started." Ron smiled his thanks, flashed a wink to Dorothy, and left by the back door.

"That was very generous of you, sweetie."

"We'll see." Miranda decided not to challenge her mother's motives. A love interest might become complicated later, but her mother needed a little love in her life, even if it was temporary and would probably end in disaster.

Miranda changed into her paint-spattered work jeans, a T-shirt, and slipped on one of her uncle's old flannel shirts. When she walked into the barn, it was easy to see that Ron was trying hard to be neat. All of his tools were tucked away on one side of the tool stall, while the original barn tools had been neatly hung on the opposite wall. *Nice,* she thought.

Ron climbed down from the loft. "I worked a bit in the tool stall, and then I put everything from the shipment you got yesterday in your storage area. Look a'here, I tried to make it easy for you to grab what you need."

Miranda tilted her head. "You enclosed this? Just since yesterday?"

Ron stood a bit taller. "You need to protect your supplies."

She opened a newly hung door to the horse stall that she had set aside for the storage of the ingredients she needed to make moonshine. Inside, Ron had installed a ceiling, and everything was already placed on the shelving. She was just about to comment on the lack of light when Ron reached around the wall and flicked a switch. He had run a bare bulb from the ceiling. He had also installed a bracket and found a padlock. Miracle of miracles, it also had a working key on a nail next to the doorway.

"Fantastic, Ron." She could hear the appreciation in her voice. "I've got some conduit for you to install before we have anyone in here. Great job. I know you're not properly licensed, but if can you get the conduits all run before the electricians get here tomorrow morning, that would be absolutely fantastic. Feel free to say if you are unsure. I don't want to get on their wrong side."

"Sure, I'll take care of that right now. Where's the conduit?"

Miranda told him where she had it and was happy that he seemed to take her direction with ease. Must have something to do with being an employee and also having a place to live with running water, heat, and light.

The situation between Ron and her mother was worrying and increased the unease already in her mind. The fact still remained that Ron had a drinking problem. It might be complicated if not impossible for him to live in a moonshine distillery.

Was the risk too much for her mother to handle?

Chapter 35

Tuesday Morning, the Farmhouse

The electrician arrived in a vintage black Ford pickup at seven in the morning, just as he had promised. She led him into the main distillery area. She avoided any issues in the supply room by making sure the padlock was secure.

The electrician was ancient in Miranda's eyes. His walk was bowlegged and his back was bent over. He was the color of worn leather. and his hands were knotted and veined. *He must be over ninety.*

"Now, don't you worry about me, Miss Trent." His eyes twinkled at her reaction to his appearance. "I've been wiring things up in the country since before your mama was born." He carried a well-used open-topped toolbox that was organized as tidily as a shop window display.

"Yes, sir. The equipment supplier will be here at ten to

finalize the installation and start my training. Will you be done by then?"

His face crinkled in a smile. "Now, don't you worry. I'll be clear out of here."

Without another word, he sat his box by the circuit breaker box and began wiring in the fermenter. As she turned to go back into the house, Ron appeared at her side.

"Do you want to see what I've done so far?"

Oh, he's never going to have a good sense of timing. He will always want my attention at the worst possible time. Never mind that, I still need a security guard.

Miranda tilted her head and smiled. "Absolutely. I would like to know what you have in mind."

They climbed up to the loft area, and Ron had started to frame out one end as the bathroom. "I figured this was the best place to start. That way I won't have to bother your mama when I want to clean up. I don't mind the out-house, but a warm shower is mighty nice."

Miranda looked at the taped-off area. "It looks rather small. Can you get a toilet, sink, and shower all in this small space?"

Ron shifted his head back with a quizzical look on his face. "Do you need a sink?"

"Absolutely, yes." She looked down at the masking tape. "If we move the tape over, say about a foot, there's room for a shower stall. Then you can put the toilet and sink across from each other. Still tiny, but it will look good in the online photos."

Ron twisted his lips sideways. "Yeah, I can do that. It will take more pipes, you see. I would be happy to use the kitchen sink for washing up."

Miranda shuddered from her chin to her toes, "No, no, no. The kitchenette sink can face the back wall of the barn and still be close to the other pipes. We'll have to find an old farmhouse window at a salvage place."

"I know several sites where folks dumped stuff when they fancied up their houses. If you want an old-timey claw-foot tub, I know where there's one that was tipped out the back of a truck."

"Sorry, there won't be room. A walk-in shower would be better. Anyway, I'm good with you living here while this place is under construction, but the long-term plan will be for it to bring in more cash."

She left him to reconfigure the plumbing and went into the farmhouse for more coffee. She sat down to her computer to attack her online work. By the time she had gotten down to the last cold dregs in her cup, she heard a knock on the front door.

"I'm all finished, Miss Trent." Her elderly electrician stood out on the porch. "I can take payment in cash or a check. None of them fancy plastic cards work for me."

Miranda smiled. "No problem, I'll bring out my checkbook."

She had no sooner ripped out the check and handed it over when she heard another truck making its way down her gravel road. It was her equipment supplier with, for once, perfect timing.

It looked as if she would finally be finished with the installation of her distillery and move on to the actual making of her uncle's moonshine.

The supplier was careful, deliberate, and meticulous in checking each piece of equipment. He checked the wiring, stability, gauges, and safety features of everything. He was patient with her questions, approved of the quality of her ingredients, and seemed excited that she was attempting to commercialize her uncle's famous recipe.

By the time he left several hours later, Miranda had a notebook full of notes as well as all the installation and instruction manuals for her new distillery. The instructor declared her to be more than ready to start up her first batch of moonshine.

That was exactly what Miranda wanted to do, but she resisted the urge. She was overwhelmed by the amount of information that she had just been given. It would be far better for her moonshine if she waited a day or two to make sure her first batch was perfect. You couldn't go back in this part of the country if your first batch was terrible. It would ruin her reputation beyond recovery.

"Whee-hoo! It's finally done." Miranda hollered out to her mother when she went back into the farmhouse. "We need to celebrate."

Dorothy was in the rocking chair by the window working on some embroidery with Sandy asleep in her lap. "That's a great idea. Let's go get our favorite pizza from Miguel's Mystic Pizza. I've been hankering for that since I got here."

"Perfect." Miranda lifted Sandy high into the air and twirled around the living room. "We're gonna be making moonshine. We're gonna be making moonshine."

Sandy yipped and licked her nose.

In no time, they had gathered a few essentials and were in the van and on their way. Miranda and her mother sang all the verses they could remember for "Mountain Dew" at the top of their lungs. Sandy joined in with his crackly puppy howls, which left the women in tears of laughter.

Miguel's Mystic Pizza was a rustic part-diner, part-camping-ground for the many expert and beginning climbers that came from all over the world to tackle the Red

River Gorge's famous cliffs. What had started as a free pasture for backpackers had grown to a modern camping complex with showers, laundry, grocery, and, of course, the best pizza ever.

Miranda ordered while Dorothy and Sandy scouted around the outside to nab a picnic table. The place was packed for lunch, and they were lucky to get a small table close to the parking lot. Dorothy pulled Sandy's travel water dish out of her enormous hobo bag and poured a bit of water in it from her ancient thermos.

Miranda walked up while Sandy was slopping water everywhere. "Thrifty habits run through our family, don't they?"

"Well, I could never see the sense of buying water when we have a wonderful spring on our farm. Don't get me started on those expensive water bottles. No need for any of that with just a little planning."

"That spring is the basic reason for Uncle Gene's great moonshine. Fingers crossed that I can pull this off."

"Just as good as I remember," said Dorothy as she polished off the last of the pizza. "I'm so glad some things never change."

They cleaned up their table and were standing by the van when the Wolfe County Fire & Rescue truck came speeding down the road deeper into the forest, lights flashing and siren blaring. Miranda was startled to see Austin sitting in the passenger front seat.

"Mom, look! Austin in the fire truck? There must be a forest fire, right?"

"That would be one reason, but it could just as well be a rescue mission. He's one of the leaders and usually gets called out as soon as an alarm comes in."

Several climbers and hikers gathered in front of Miguel's, and Miranda picked up the mumbling that raced through the growing crowd.

"I heard he fell."

"Where is the rescue?"

"Somebody fell!"

"Who was it?"

"A lawyer. His name is Ben."

Chapter 36

Tuesday, Indian Staircase

Miranda and her mother drove out to the Gladie Learning Center and parked next to the Wolfe County Fire & Rescue truck. Austin and the volunteers were unloading climbing gear and a wire litter.

Miranda walked over. "I heard that the fallen climber is Ben DeBerg. Is he all right?"

Austin turned to Miranda, his face stiff with concentration. "No one so far has spotted him. He went down into some dense undergrowth." Austin hefted a large pack onto his back and grabbed on to one end of the litter. "We'll know soon. I'll call as soon as there's news."

Miranda watched them trudge up the trail that led to the Indian Staircase. She turned to her mom. "There's so much that doesn't make sense. Ben was considered to be an expert climber."

"Do you think it's got something to do with Howard's death?"

"Yes. It can't be a coincidence that one of the Risky Business Adventurers has an accident where Howard was killed." She rubbed the back of her neck. "I think I'm going to tag along, I really want to know more about this."

"That's the right thing to do, honey."

Miranda grabbed her backpack from the van. "Well, no matter how this turns out, they're gonna need some coffee and sandwiches. Can you handle that?"

"Of course. I'll take the van and have Ron help me load up the fixings and set up one of our folding tables. We'll have everything ready when you get back off the trail, hopefully with your curiosity satisfied."

Miranda kissed her mother on the cheek. "Thanks for understanding. I've got my emergency pack, just in case the weather traps everyone up there again."

She raced up the trail. It took much less time to reach the spot than when she led the tour. She heard the rescue team on top of the cliff.

Pleased with her speed, but completely out of breath, she slung off her pack, sat down, and leaned against the Indian Staircase rock face. She didn't want Austin to see her gasping for breath. A stray thought rushed by. *Am I safe? Could I be in danger from whoever wanted to hurt Ben?*

As she recovered, she resolved to be more careful and make smarter decisions. She turned her head a fraction, and a glint down by the trail's edge caught her eye.

More trash, she thought, shaking her head in frustration. Why couldn't people pick up after themselves? As soon as she felt ready to tackle the climb, she bent over to pick up the litter.

It wasn't litter. It was a climbing piton. Chips around the base indicated that it was freshly installed. Miranda wasn't sure why it would be in this unlikely spot over-looking, well, not anything.

Puzzled, she put on her pack and carefully climbed the ancient carved steps up onto the clearing. The rescue team of two stood by the litter, and Austin was talking to a pair of day hikers.

"Again, you're sure you heard a scream?" His voice was higher pitched than normal, thought Miranda. He was frustrated.

The taller hiker folded his arms. "Look, this was not in our plan for today to abandon our hike to call you guys out on a goose chase. We heard a god-awful scream that sounded like it came from right here. We were only a few yards down the back trail."

"How did you know it was Ben DeBerg?" Austin asked.

"We met him at the trailhead and he asked us where we were hiking today. He seemed chatty and not that anx-ious to start. I thought it was because he said he was going to go solo cliff climbing and maybe he wasn't sure of his skills. He started out ahead of us. He knew the trail because we didn't pass him until we climbed the Indian Staircase."

"How long after you left him did you hear the scream?"

The hiker looked over to his buddy. "Maybe about five minutes. No longer than ten. I had stopped to tighten my bootlaces so we were pretty close." His buddy smiled his agreement.

Miranda joined the group. "What's wrong?"

Austin's eyes lit up. "Miranda, why are you here?"

"I thought I might be able to help. What's wrong?"

The hiker spoke quickly. "We've told you everything we know. Can we go now?"

Austin scrunched his mouth sideways and looked at his rescue partner, Andrew Perry, who gave a tiny nod. "Sure, we can always reach you at Hemlock Lodge if anything else comes up."

The hikers turned to go, but the taller one stopped just before they rounded the next bend. "I hope you guys find him. If I ever get in trouble, you're the ones I would want to be looking for me." Then they disappeared down the trail.

Miranda approached Austin and Andrew. "What's happened? You found Ben, haven't you?"

Austin huffed and looked over to Andrew. "That's what's wrong. We can't find any sign of Ben either falling off or climbing down." Austin walked over to the edge of the overlook. "There would be signs of a fall through the trees, and you can actually see an outcropping just below here. If he's unconscious or injured, we should see his gear."

"But I don't understand. I thought it was illegal to rock climb within the boundaries of this park?"

Austin frowned. "That only keeps the climbers who obey the rules from trying these cliffs. It does nothing to prevent the rogue climbers."

"Wait," said Miranda. "I saw something on the trail down below the Indian Staircase. It was a fresh piton. Could Ben have fallen from there?"

"Absolutely, the echo effects of these cliffs and canyons makes determining the direction of sound unreliable. Show us."

"Great." Miranda took them down to the piton.

Austin squatted down to finger the stone chips around the piton. "That's fresh." Austin stood up and rubbed his hands together. "I think I see a glimmer of another one, but it's shrouded by that pine limb." He raised his eyebrows. "Would you be willing to take a look?"

"Me?" Miranda's voice squeaked. "I can't climb. What about either of you?"

Austin and Andrew exchanged a look. "It's just that you're so much lighter. If you don't, we'll have to wait until someone arrives who can climb down that cliffside."

"How dangerous is this?"

"Nothing is without some risk, but if I didn't feel confident that the both of us can handle any problem, I wouldn't suggest this. We'll use a rescue harness on you and make sure you don't fall. It's not really as steep as it looks, and I'll be down right here with Andrew. We only need to eliminate that this might be a possible location. It won't take long."

"If you're sure I won't break my neck."

Austin started to laugh, but suppressed it when he saw the look on her face. "I'm sorry, but you're so adventurous. A little climbing seems like it should be a piece of cake for you." He lowered his voice. "I promise I won't let you fall."

Reassured, Miranda followed their instructions and was guided down the cliffside as safely as a baby in a carrier. She felt elated when her foot landed on the ledge at the base of the cliff.

Austin spoke to Andrew. "She's down. Keep everything in place. I'll let you know if we need to come right back up." Austin went to Miranda. "Where is this piton?"

She led him to the far side of the trail and pointed to it. "It's pretty well hidden. If the sun hadn't caused it to glint right when I was passing by, I don't think I would have seen it."

Austin bent over the hardware. "You're right. This has been put here just a little while ago."

Miranda pointed. "There are trace remnants of rope left in it. Could he have fallen from here?"

Austin looked down over the cliff. "I don't see any sign of a fall. No broken branches, but there are some faint marks. Let me get my binoculars."

"I've got a pair also. The two of us looking should cut down the time. You take the left of the piton and I'll take the right."

They both got binoculars from their packs and lay down flat in the trail to focus on the trees farther down the cliff.

Miranda felt her heart thudding in her chest, willing them to find something that would indicate that Ben could be down there. Not only down there, but alive.

"Okay. I've got it." Miranda lowered her binoculars and pointed to a tree. "There's where things went wrong. You can see a bright splash of yellow right over there where that branch has been broken."

Austin followed the direction of her outstretched arm. He refocused his binoculars. "I see it. That's where he started to fall. We're going to need a lot of help. The terrain here is brutal."

Miranda laid her binoculars down and cupped her hands around her mouth, "Ben! Ben DeBerg! Are you there? Please answer."

The only sound that came back was the echo of her calls.

Austin repeated calling out Ben's name, but again, nothing.

Miranda felt a sickening clutch at her gut. Ben was a superb climber. If he wasn't moving with all this commotion, she didn't think he was alive.

"What's going on down there?" said Andrew.

Austin got up, then pulled Miranda up as well. They dusted themselves off, and Austin yelled up the Indian Staircase, "We found where he fell. Gather everything together, then I'll come up and help you bring down the equipment. This is where we're going to stage our search and rescue."

Miranda put her hands on her hips and scanned the area. "There isn't much trail space, but at least we've found the right spot."

Looking grim, Austin pulled out his cell phone. "I'll call in for helicopter support at Gladie Learning Center, and we'll call in the next level of rescue volunteers."

"I'll go down ahead of you and see how Mom is doing with a refreshment center." Miranda started to go but turned back and kissed Austin full on the mouth. "See you down there. You stay safe."

Chapter 37

Tuesday Afternoon, Gladie Learning Center

Miranda scurried down the trail, determined to help with the rescue efforts. *I probably need to officially volunteer so that I can be better prepared for emergencies like this. As a cultural-tourist business, I need to have solid connections within the community. But first I need to get my distillery up and running, then I'll reach out.*

It was easy to spot her mother. The canopy emblazoned with the Paint & Shine logo stood front and center in the parking lot. Next to it was another canopy with a Fire & Rescue symbol on each side. The small parking lot was packed with emergency vehicles from neighboring counties along with farmers' pickup trucks and fancy knobby-tired off-road buggies. There was a flavor of routine about the place that Miranda took as a sign that mountain rescues were ordinary rather than rare.

"Hi, Mom." Miranda gave her mother a big hug. "Thanks for getting this organized. I am truly impressed with what you've done in so little time."

Dorothy was standing behind a table serving coffee from an enormous stainless-steel coffee urn. A smaller urn was filled with hot chocolate. She was also offering doughnuts and cookies to the volunteers from the large serving trays that had come from Miranda's kitchen.

Dorothy flashed a shy smile. "I had a lot of help. The church is always ready for these emergencies, so I picked up the big coffee maker to keep the volunteers warm. The Dunkin' Donuts shop sent out their normal supply, but your canopy is fantastic. Ron helped me get it here and set it up. Do you want yours with just cream?"

"Yes, please. I'm desperate for some caffeine."

Ron popped up from under the table bringing out another stack of paper cups to set on the table. "Have you found any sign?"

"Yes," said Miranda. "We think we've located where he went over the cliff. He had hammered in a new piton to belay down. I can't figure out why. It's illegal to climb within the park."

"That would be part of the attraction for Ben," said Kevin Burkart. He was dressed in camouflage hunting gear with a bright orange vest and carrying a rifle case slung over his shoulder. "He's always been willing to break the rules then apologize later."

"Are you here to volunteer in the search?" Miranda was surprised to see Kevin here when she knew that their rental of the cabin had ended. "I thought you would be back down in Florida by now."

"I normally have quite a few business appointments to keep with my financial customers, so I stay at Hemlock

Lodge. As soon as I heard that the missing hiker was Ben, I came right out to see if I could help."

Miranda waved to Austin as he and Andrew entered the tent and she could hear Austin asking for everyone's attention.

Dorothy pointed over to the Fire & Rescue tent next door. "They're organizing the search now. Sign up and they'll put you on a team." Kevin went into the tent.

"I'm hoping Ben's using some basic rules of keeping put and trying to make some sort of noise so we can find him." Miranda had to yell the last few words as the Fire & Rescue helicopter started up its rotor.

"He could also wave a white T-shirt at the helicopter," said Ron.

"Only if he's conscious. Any kind of fall in that part of the park could be serious and possibly fatal." Miranda looked at her watch. "This time of year, the sun goes down pretty early."

The helicopter took off and sped down the clearing to begin the first of the search patterns that the pilots had been trained to execute. Everyone stood and watched until the sound subsided.

The next car to pull into the crowded parking lot was the Wolfe County sheriff's patrol vehicle. The sheriff was the first to make a new parking row in the grass. It appeared to be a routine move. Sheriff Richard Larson and Coroner Felicia Larson got out and headed toward the tents.

"Any good news?" Sheriff Larson asked one of the volunteers.

"Not yet. The helicopter just left for its first pass."

Felicia nodded. "What about the ground search? Who's leading that?"

"We have two separate teams that will be searching the ravine. Each team is coming from opposite sides to cover the ground as quickly as possible. If we get lucky, the helicopter will spot him and direct the rescue teams right to the spot."

Sheriff Larson fiddled with the zipper on his jacket. "The most successful rescues are usually when the victim is found within the first few hours after getting into trouble. How long has it been?"

The volunteer replied, "We think he fell about two hours ago. We're still within the time frame for a quick and successful rescue."

The two teams started up the trail. Ron joined the first team led by Andrew. Miranda and Kevin joined the second team led by Austin. It seemed to Miranda as if the trail were increasing in steepness each time she tackled it. Other trails seemed to get easier, but not this one.

They were about fifteen minutes up the trail when Austin received a transmission from the helicopter that they hadn't seen a single sign of Ben. They were going to refuel and make one more pass before darkness fell.

"That's not good," Austin said to his team. "Our best chance was finding him at the bottom of the ravine where we found the piton."

"Where will they search next?" Miranda asked.

"They'll start on the downhill side of the ravine. It's the natural path for lost hikers."

"But Ben isn't exactly a beginner," said Miranda. "Why wouldn't he respond to the sound of the helicopter? He knows what to do. I don't understand unless he's out cold."

Austin quickened the already rapid pace. "Let's get

down to where he might be coming out. I have a bad feeling about this."

Miranda focused on speeding her pace to trot next to Austin. "I'm getting a bad feeling, too. He knows the best way to get rescued. He's an expert climber. He must be unconscious or dead."

Austin glanced. "But what is going on that experienced sportsmen are ending up in trouble?"

"What if he doesn't want to be found? It's possible that Ben has faked the fall and he's in hiding? That would answer everything."

Austin nodded. "We need to hurry."

Chapter 38

Tuesday Evening, the Farmhouse

They had driven home from the Gladie Learning Center after darkness had fallen. The search had to be abandoned until first light.

Miranda had asked Austin to stop by the farmhouse for a cold supper. Ron also came in from the barn to join them around the dining table. They shared a simple meal of cold sliced ham with biscuits and apple butter.

Their disappointment was deeply felt. So was their frustration at not being able to locate Ben safe and sound with nothing but a few scratches and hunger to remind him to never climb alone.

"What's the plan for tomorrow?" Miranda passed the plate of biscuits to Austin. "How early can we resume the search?"

Austin took two biscuits and passed the plate down to Dorothy. "We're set to continue the search at daybreak, but we will meet at the Gladie Learning Center at seven to flesh out our first round of searches."

"You don't sound confident that he'll be found," said Ron as he took three more biscuits.

Austin scanned around the table and finally his gaze rested on Miranda. "Miranda and I have concluded that Ben is either seriously wounded—perhaps dead—or he doesn't want to be found. In other words, he's clever enough to have faked the fall and he's in hiding."

Dorothy served herself a thick slice of ham and put the last one on Ron's plate. She frowned. "He has always been a bit of a maverick, but why hide? Who is he hiding from?"

Miranda was spooning out more apple butter and pointed the spoon at Austin. "I wonder if he thinks he's in danger?"

"From who?" asked Ron. "Why would he need to hide?"

"Because he killed Howard?" Miranda raised her eyebrows. "That would be a reason to stage his death."

"He would need to hide from us if we found proof that he killed Howard," said Austin.

Miranda glanced at her mother. Dorothy seemed calm but hadn't touched the food on her plate. Miranda thought this discussion of her nephew as if they were arguing over an episode of *NCIS* must be upsetting. Finally, Miranda took a deep breath and spoke her mind. "He would need to disappear if he knew who killed Howard. Especially if the killer discovered that Ben knew."

Austin eyed the empty ham platter with regret, then helped himself to the last two biscuits. "I think that's a likely situation, but who would he be hiding from?"

Dorothy forked her slice of ham and put it on Austin's plate. She also gave him a look that said, *Don't mess with me.* "Why doesn't he just go to the sheriff and tell him so that the killer is caught and everyone is safe?"

Ron huffed. "I wouldn't tell the sheriff anything."

Miranda piped up, "The sheriff wouldn't pay attention to you anyway. But it's true that he's been hot and cold with the investigation since we discovered the bones. Not at all his normal behavior."

Austin grinned his thanks to Dorothy. "Of course you wouldn't, Ron. You two have history. But Ben is a criminal defense lawyer."

"But that doesn't mean that he's as innocent as a lamb either. I mean, who really completely trusts a lawyer?"

Miranda rubbed the back of her neck to loosen the knot that seemed determined to become permanent. "There must be some reason for this elaborate ruse. There are three possible outcomes." She ticked them off on her fingers. "One, he's injured or dead. Two, he's plotted this as his escape because he murdered Howard. Three, he knows Howard's killer and this will ramp up focus on the investigation so the killer can be caught."

Dorothy handed over her biscuit to Ron, then stood up. "This is too confusing. I feel like we're all just running around in circles, and it's given me a terrible headache. I'm sorry, I'm going up to bed." She left the table and headed up the stairs. "Good night. Lord a mercy, I pray that things are clearer in the morning."

"Where's Sandy?" Miranda scanned the room. "Sandy! Where are you?"

She heard a distant yipping that sounded as if it was coming from the back of the farmhouse. When the three of them made it out the back, Sandy's yip had turned into a growl. He was standing in the pool of illumination shed by the motion-sensitive light attached to the back porch.

His front paws were as close to the edge of the circle as possible. He looked up at Miranda and growled like a big dog.

"Sandy, what's the matter?" Miranda picked him up, and she turned to Ron and Austin. "He's never done this before. Barked and yipped? Certainly, but not growling. Can you see anything?"

"I'll go get the big flashlight," said Austin.

Since she lived so far from town, Miranda kept a flashlight in every room. Power outages were as common as fog down this little dirt road. She didn't have a high priority in the repair list with the electrical company. That might change once the distillery business caught on and she became a high-volume customer.

Austin returned with the high-beam spotlight. Before he could turn it on, Sandy lifted his head back and howled as if he were being murdered. That was followed by the distinctive sound of a chain saw starting up.

Ron yelled, "Hey! That's my favorite saw. I'd know the sound of that baby anywhere. Someone took it from my tools." He bolted out towards the sound. "Stop! Thief!"

Austin switched on the high-intensity lamp and illuminated Ron's back as he sped up the hill toward Miranda's neighbors, Roy and Elsie Kash. In seconds, the sound of the chain saw was replaced by the piercing crack of splitting timber. That was followed by a loud ground-thundering thump and a shriek of whipping wires that ripped away Miranda's circuit breaker panel that was mounted on the back outside wall of the house.

All power went out in the house and the barn. An intense fountain of sparks spouted from the transformer that was on the ground crushed under the utility pole. Next, they heard the engine of an all-terrain vehicle take off down the hill away from the farmhouse toward a small ravine.

Austin took off after Ron, closely followed by Miranda, carrying a yelping and howling Sandy. Austin and Miranda easily overtook Ron. She yelled, "Go back and check on my mom. She's alone and is probably terrified. Stay with her."

Ron looked angry but terribly relieved.

Using the flashlight, Austin was able to spot the point in the dense brush where the vandal disappeared.

When they reached the escape opening, they ran along a cleared path, but the sound of the escaping vehicle became faint and then died away altogether. They just couldn't outrun it, and Austin's ATV was too far away, still in his outbuilding.

They were panting like ruined racehorses, and Miranda was the first to speak. "We . . . need to . . . call . . . the sheriff." She plopped down in the pathway still holding Sandy, but also rubbing her side. "That kind of vandalism was a deliberate warning. Who would do that?"

They trotted back to the house to find Ron sitting on the low stoop at the back door. Dorothy was sitting beside him trying to get him to drink some water. He refused because he was still puffing and gasping like a steam engine. "Why?" was all he could say. He wasn't in as good a shape as Austin and Miranda, who hiked in the hills nearly every day.

Austin's breath was almost normal. "I think this was a deliberate act to interfere with Miranda's investigation."

Ron finally recovered his breath. "It coulda been the barn on fire with me sleeping off a drunk. I'd be a goner for sure." He shot an alarmed look at Dorothy. "Of course, I'm not drinking like that anymore."

Dorothy patted his shoulder and forced the glass of water into his hand.

Miranda sat down next to her mother, still holding the wiggling Sandy tight. He wanted to chase the four-wheeler. "I agree. Somehow, we're getting close." She looked back toward the dark in which the house and barn should have been lit up like a cozy cottage painting. "This is certainly quite a distraction." She sighed in frustration and realized she was close to tears. A pit of fear was in her chest, along with an oppressing feeling of defeat. "Someone could have been killed."

"No one was near those wires," said Austin.

Miranda shot back, "But we don't know if this vandal looked around to see that. That transformer could have sparked onto the roof. It could have set the farmhouse on fire."

Austin lowered his voice to a softer whisper. "But none of that happened."

A silence fell among them all. The relief of their escape felt welcome.

Miranda cleared her throat. "You're right." She lifted her head and pressed her lips into a thin line. "I was hours away from starting my first batch of moonshine. This will put me behind. Again."

Austin put his arm around her and pulled her into a side hug. "Let's concentrate on what we still have. Not that it might have been so much worse." He waved the beam of the flashlight back toward the farmhouse. "It truly looks like interference was the intention, not injury."

"Thanks, Austin. That makes me feel *so* much better."

Miranda leaned her head onto Austin's shoulder, then Sandy licked them both in the face.

Chapter 39

Tuesday Evening, the Farmhouse

Miranda's property looked like an emergency-vehicle auction yard with bucket trucks, repair vans, and ambulances parked in every little corner of her yard. The fire department was here making sure the transformer fire was out. It had burned a black ring in the sparse grass, but the firemen had drenched the area to kill any residual embers.

The electrical department arrived to assess the damage so they could determine what kind of replacement parts were needed. They had brought a new utility pole with them and laid it next to the hacked-off stub of the original.

Sheriff Larson had arrived and walked over to Austin's place to fetch his ATV. They were going to patrol the dirt path to look for any evidence of the vandal, but mostly to make sure he wasn't hanging around to cause more trouble.

Miranda left a message with the distillery equipment supplier to cancel tomorrow's final inspection. They wanted to reschedule right away since the last payment on the equipment was due when that was finished. She didn't know what time to tell them she would be ready, so she promised to call back when the electricity was back on. That was the best she could do.

Her mom had come downstairs right after the transformer exploded. After the excitement of the chase, she had set to work immediately. She lit the coal-oil lanterns and brewed up a large pot of percolated coffee on the gas stove. She had arranged a tray of paper cups filled with coffee. Sugar, cream, paper napkins, and a heaping plate of cookies were also on the tray. She wandered around in the yard serving up everyone, completely comfortable in her flowered nightgown with its matching floor-length robe and pink slippers.

"Mom, you need to go back to bed. Everyone has had more than one cup of your coffee, and the electrician has scarfed down at least a dozen of your cookies."

"Don't be silly. I wouldn't think of it until everyone is gone. You know I couldn't sleep a wink with all these folks traipsing everywhere. Besides, we don't have power yet."

Miranda shook her head from side to side. "It's going to be a long time before we get power." She gave her mom a big hug. "Thanks for setting out the emergency lamps in the downstairs. You can take the one in the kitchen up with you."

"We'll be fine. This house didn't have electricity when it was built by your grandfather."

"Hopefully, everyone will be gone soon."

Miranda had barely got those words out of her mouth when the firemen came in and said that the grass fire was completely out. Then the electrical company also made their way down her dirt road after a sincere promise to be back the first thing next morning.

Austin and Sheriff Larson drove up to the farmhouse from the back and joined Miranda and her mom in the kitchen.

"He didn't leave anything behind on the trail," Austin said. "I'll come back in the morning and walk it in daylight, but I don't think he left a trail we could trace."

"What about fingerprints on the utility pole or on the chain saw?"

"Unlikely," admitted Sheriff Larson. "That pole was taken down by someone who knew that there would be a chain saw in the barn and knew how to use it. He or she probably wore gloves so they'll be no fingerprints. I know I always wear 'em when I'm running mine. It feels like they planned to cause a disruption, but I think finding the chain saw was an extra opportunity to cause more havoc than they originally thought about."

"It's working, too. We're all out here trying to recover and not investigating Howard's murder," said Miranda.

The sheriff inhaled a deep breath. "On that point, you need to get back to running your business and leaving me to handle mine."

"But—" Miranda interrupted.

Sheriff Larson yelled, "No buts. This could easily have resulted in a tragedy. As it is, lives were threatened and property was damaged. I can't have you running around interfering with official investigations. Back off. I mean that." He stomped out of the farmhouse, got into his patrol car, and sped down the road.

Miranda flushed a bright rose and folded her arms over her chest. "If he thinks that will put me off, he's wrong. Aunt Ora asked me to look into this, and that's what I'm going to do."

Chapter 40

Wednesday Morning, the Farmhouse

Miranda stood at the edge of the porch holding a steaming mug of coffee and watching the sun rise over the trees across the valley. She had crept out of the bedroom in her pj's without waking Sandy, lit the oil lamp in the kitchen, and brewed a big pot of coffee. The morning stillness was beginning to fill with the dawn chorus of birdsong as the sunrise approached.

"Penny for your thoughts." Dorothy walked out to the edge of the porch and kissed Miranda on the cheek. "I barely slept a wink last night. After everyone finally left, I kept hearing all kinds of sounds that I imagined to be the return of our vandal. But with Sandy and Ron with us, one of them would have called out an alarm. I finally dropped off about an hour ago. Thanks for starting the coffee." Dorothy turned. "Why the long face?"

"I'm feeling odd. Not odd exactly. More like balancing on a tightrope with no clue on how to get off the stupid thing."

"I know just what you mean. You know, it's that sensation when you're searching for a word but it just won't appear. It's odd."

Miranda sighed. "I feel like I should know who killed Howard, but the clue that resolves everything is just out of reach."

Dorothy smiled and her shoulders dropped. "That's good. You always get like this just before there's a breakthrough. No matter what you've tackled, your education, your painting, even these investigations, there's been a time when you've been on edge."

Miranda pressed her lips tight. "I know that it always happens, but it still drives me crazy." She downed the dregs of her coffee. "I've got to get dressed before the utility company arrives. They've promised me first priority. Oh, I've canceled the tour."

"Well, don't hold your breath, it's easy to promise."

In short order, Miranda raced through her morning chores: caring for Sandy, tidying her bedroom, fetching water from the well, checking the lamps for oil, and setting out fresh batteries in case they were needed.

She drove down to the general store and got four bags of ice. Then she emptied the contents of her refrigerator into two coolers with an ice bag each and crammed two bags into her freezer. That should hold things until at least tomorrow. After that, she'd be on her way to the Walmart for a generator. She had too much meat in the freezer to risk losing to spoilage. She should probably have a generator to support the distillery anyway.

Fortunately, Ron was actually being helpful today. Her mom had decided to take charge of his task priorities. The two of them had patched the screening on the back porch, remounted the circuit breaker box that had been ripped off the back of the farmhouse, and raked up all the burnt grass debris.

By that time Miranda heard the heavy-duty engines of the power company truck making its way up the road. The truck had a large bucket, apparently for the pole installation.

She exhaled a sigh of relief. She hoped it wouldn't take long to get power back up. Someone must have added his or her influence to ensure that she was at the top of the power company's priority list. She would have to find out who it was so she could thank the person. For now, she was enormously grateful.

Austin pulled into the driveway and joined her on the porch. "Why aren't you with the Search and Rescue?"

"I called and told them to continue without me." He tilted his head. "I got a strange message just as I was about to leave about someone signaling in Morse code. I think it was from Ben."

Miranda led him back to the kitchen and poured him a cup of black coffee. "What? Spill it. How did you get a message?"

"One of my fellow rangers was patrolling down a fire road looking for poachers." Austin drank from his cup. "Wow, this is really good. You need to make coffee like this every day."

"Come on, life is more than good coffee." She sipped from her cup, then rolled her eyes. "Well, maybe not. The message, please?"

"Sure. He saw a flashlight up on one of the cliffs, and at first he thought it was someone walking down one of the trails hoping to surprise a sleeping deer and shoot it."

"Oh, really? Like it's that hard to take deer around here. That's criminal."

"Yeah, but that's why we patrol. We charge them with poaching. Anyway, as he watched the flashing, he started to figure out that the beam was stationary but the flashing was in a pattern. The pattern was a continuously repeating message in Morse code."

"The message?"

"Hang on. He doesn't know Morse code, but he took down the repeating pattern." Austin pulled a notepad from his top shirt pocket. "Even I recognize an SOS, but I don't know anything more either. However, I think your uncle did. He was a ham radio operator for decades."

Miranda snatched the notepad from his hand. "I was a Girl Scout all through elementary school. And Uncle Gene taught me to copy code from his radio set during the summers I lived down here. Let me see if I can still read it." She looked at the dots and dashes.

— — —   · · ·   — — —
— · — — · · ·

"You're right. Give me a minute."

She ran into her office and rummaged in the desk and pulled out a pencil and fired up the computer.

Austin followed. "What are you doing?"

"I don't remember each individual letter anymore, but the entire code is online."

Miranda found the Wikipedia Morse code chart in a few seconds. The problem with the symbols on the notepad is that they were just one after the other with no indication for the gaps that might signify the end of a word. Luckily, the message was short.

She found a translator and typed in each dot and dash as they were written in the notebook. She didn't include the SOS sequence, but instead entered the intervening code. She looked up at Austin. "This is going to take a few tries. Hovering isn't going to help."

Austin looked at his feet. "Fine, I'll be outside helping Ron and your mom. I think they're up in the barn."

Miranda returned her focus to the screen and went letter by letter. It was tedious and frustrating, but she finally teased out the message.

Miranda stood up so quickly she knocked her knee against the edge of her desk. "It's Ben!" she shouted as she ran out the back of the house. "The message is from Ben."

Austin ran out of the barn. "He's alive?"

"Yes. We need to get to him before he dies at the hands of the murderer."

She showed him the translated message:

SOS Ben

"It repeats?" said Austin.

"Ben is hiding from Kevin." Miranda could hear the strain in her voice. "Let's call Sheriff Larson, and if we can get him to believe us, he can broadcast to everyone that Kevin should be picked up."

"Right," said Austin. "But we also need to find Ben. I know where my buddy was when he saw the flashing light. Let's start searching there for a starting point. My buddy couldn't see any landmarks in the dark, but we should be able to guess where the signal came from." Austin looked around the farmhouse at the number of trucks and the activity swarming around them. "Can you leave?"

"Of course. Let me print off this chart and grab my

backpack. I'll also leave a note to tell Mom and Ron what's up. They need to be warned about Kevin." She hit the print button.

"My outdoor pack is in the truck." Austin rubbed his chin. "You can call Sheriff Larson as soon as we have cell service."

"As soon as we verify that we have something to tell him. He hasn't been a fan of my involvement in this investigation. But now that we're tracking down Ben and Kevin, he needs to know what's going on. I certainly feel better about Ron hanging around now."

Austin smiled. "I don't think I've heard that from anyone about Ron."

They got in the truck and were nearly to the main road when Miranda said, "You know, it could be that Ben is the killer and wants us to believe that Kevin is after him."

Chapter 41

Wednesday Morning, Daniel Boone National Forest

Austin stopped the truck at a small widening of the single-track fire break that also served as an access road. "This puts us at almost a match for the GPS coordinates where my buddy noticed the signal. I'll park back here in this little turnout."

They walked down the middle of the road, and Austin stopped in his tracks. "Here's the exact spot." Austin put his cell away and they both got out their binoculars. "Let's scan the cliffs. If the flashes were coming from the east, that means Ben was up there." Austin pointed to a red sandstone bluff.

"Wait." Miranda fished into the side opening in her backpack and pulled out a makeup mirror. "Maybe he'll see this." She stood in the middle of the road, looked at the angle of the sun, and started to twitch the mirror in the direction of the cliff. "This might take a little time. We don't know if he's actually up there, and even if he is, he might be asleep or might have gone somewhere else entirely."

She kept up a nonstop flashing of the mirror while Austin continued to scan the cliffside with his binoculars. He said. "I think this is worth at least a try."

"Sure."

After ten long minutes, Miranda stopped to relieve her cramped hands. She stretched her back and shoulders as well. She sighed. "That's disappointing. I was hoping—"

"What was that?" Austin trained his binoculars on the cliffside. "I saw a flash of light. I think we should try sending him a message?"

"Sure. Let me get out the chart." She pulled it out of her back pocket. "I'll send the general all-purpose CQ. It means 'calling all stations,' but sounds a bit like 'seek you.'"

Miranda flicked the mirror to the section of cliff where Austin had seen the flash. She had time to repeat the CQ twice before she got a response. It was short and simple: *Ben*.

"It's him!"

"Ask him where he is."

"Of course. I don't remember what the shorthand is for 'Where the hell are you?' A simple 'where' is going to be it. Get ready to copy down what he says. I don't know code well enough to read it on the fly."

Miranda referred to her chart and flashed the code. In only a few seconds, the returning flashes began. Miranda called out the dots and dashes to make it easier for Austin.

"Let me ask him to repeat it so we don't make a mistake." Miranda signaled the abbreviation for "repeat."

As soon as she finished the signal, Ben flashed the message again, only a tiny bit slower. He signaled an *EOT* for "end of transmission" then Miranda sat down in the road to transcribe the message.

"He says he's in a hidden cavern above the Indian Staircase. It has to be the one where we spent the night. He wants just the two of us to come and get him. He says don't contact the police or rescue groups." She looked up at Austin.

"He must think that Kevin would know where he is through the police radio frequencies and could find and kill him."

She scrambled up and brushed the trail dirt from her trousers. "Let's get up there without telling anyone. He must be desperate enough to stay out there overnight."

"He may be fully aware of his danger." Austin turned the truck around in the little turnout and they made their way up to fetch Ben.

"Do you think this could be a trap?"

Austin exhaled a frustrated breath. "It could be, but the only way to know is to investigate. Do you want to stop?"

"No way."

As soon as the forest ranger truck was spotted at the Gladie Learning Center, the coordinator latched on to Austin, assuming he was there to take over a shift.

Austin waved hi. "I've got another lead that I want to confirm before I modify your search plans. It might come to nothing, and you guys are doing what has to be done so effectively, I don't want to divert your focus."

After a bit of fast talking, Austin and Miranda were on their way up the trail.

"I'm finally getting good at this climb," Miranda commented from atop the Indian Staircase. "Not the kind of practice I was expecting, but it's good."

Austin reached the top and they stood for a moment. "I don't think we should shout. The cliffs and ravines will distort the sound and could possibly alert Kevin that we think Ben is here."

"What if we tap Morse code with something?"

"Smart," said Austin. "I never know what you're going to come up with."

Miranda took a Swiss Army knife out of her pack and tapped out CQ on the face of her watch. "It's not very loud. Let's walk the perimeter and see if he'll come out."

When they were close to the entrance of the cavern, Miranda increased the sound of the CQ a little. Then she heard a rustling on the right side of the cavern.

"Ben," she called quietly. "Ben. It's me and Austin. No one else is here. You can come out."

A sharp tapping carried on the wind.

Miranda motioned for Austin to be silent, then she moved in the direction where she heard the tapping.

A small game trail was off to the side, and she stepped onto the narrow path. She pointed to some crushed leaves, which indicated that someone had recently been here. A few more yards down the trail and a thicket presented what looked like an impasse. Miranda bent down and followed a small opening through to a sheltered clearing on the other side.

She stood up and waited for Austin. There was enough room for him to stand beside her. "Have you been in here?" she asked.

"I had no idea this was even here."

They heard the tapping. It sounded much louder now.

Miranda whispered, "I'm getting nervous. What if this is another trick? This group has been a constant source of surprises. I don't really want another one up here."

"Good point. We need to be extra cautious." Miranda used her fingers to follow the cliffside toward the sound of the Morse code. In about twenty feet, they came upon a waist-high cave opening. The sound was coming from inside. She signaled for Austin to respond.

"Ben," said Austin. "Are you in there?"

A faint response reached them from inside. "Yes. Yes. Are you alone?"

"We are," replied Miranda. "It's just me and Austin." She mouthed to Austin that it was definitely Ben. She recognized his voice.

"Come on in," said Ben. "We need to talk. I need your help."

Austin and Miranda got out their flashlights and examined the entrance. The cave was not entirely a natural opening. On one side were marks left by a pickax that had been used to widen the opening. Miranda thought the excavation had been some time ago since the marks were worn smooth.

As she started to go into the cave, she felt Austin pull on her shoulder. "I should go first in case he has a gun."

"But if you follow me, you can pull me out if things get dangerous. I can't pull you out as easily as you can pull me out. I'm strong, but I wouldn't be quick about it."

He scrunched his brow. "Right." He motioned for her to go ahead.

She pointed to the marks and whispered, "This was mined at some point."

Austin nodded yes. "Mined for what? It's pretty high up for coal."

"Silver?"

"That's possible."

"Hey, are you guys coming in here or not? What's going on?"

"Hold your horses," whispered Miranda. "It's a narrow passage."

They crept into the opening on hands and knees, dragging their backpacks behind them in a slow, steady progress. After about ten feet, the passage ended up in a roomy cavern about the size of a small living room. Miranda stood up and shifted over to the left to give Austin enough space to get in.

Miranda panned her flashlight from left to right and finally it lit upon Ben, who was sitting on the floor of the cave next to a small backpacker tent. He had dragged in pine needles for underneath the tent and had a small pile of firewood ready to feed the tiny fire that had mostly burned to embers.

Ben got up. "I'm so glad to see you. I've been in here for what seems like forever. It hasn't even been twenty-four hours. I've never gone this long without talking to someone." He stumbled forward but didn't appear to be injured. It looked as if he was simply stiff and sore.

Miranda stood her ground. "Why did you stage a fall? Everyone turned out to search for you. You were right here?"

"Yes, I needed help to prove that Kevin killed Howard. He knew that I was getting closer to proving he killed Howard. I wanted to not only draw him up here, but I wanted witnesses, too. It was risky to expect this result, but here you are."

Austin shook his head. "Well, you are a charter member of the Risky Business Adventurers."

"How long have you suspected Kevin?" asked Miranda.

"I've suspected it from the start. I deal with criminal behavior every day, and I've seen a nasty arrogance grow in Kevin. It started right after Howard disappeared. Without a body, I couldn't make a case."

"What changed?" asked Austin.

"He got careless. That's part of the arrogance. He thinks he's untouchable." Ben paused. "You can sit, this is going to take a while. I'm fine if you want to stay by the entrance. I'm not sure I would have the guts to come up here and find me." He picked up a twig from the tiny fire and lit a candle he had placed next to the side of the cave. Behind it was an aluminum pie tin to reflect the light. "Please, sit."

Miranda and Austin each sat on one side of the entrance.

Ben continued, "This cave is the reason Howard was killed."

"Why?" Miranda swept her flashlight around the cavern. She stopped the beam when a reflected glint winked at her. "What's that? Is that what I think it is?"

Ben chuckled. "Oh, yes, it is. It's a silver vein. A mighty fine one with a mixture of copper. This was very likely one of Swift's lost silver mines."

Miranda started to stand up but didn't. She panned the flashlight in every corner of the cave. The light was reflected back at her in small light patches. "I can't believe it. No one has found a single one of his silver mines."

"No one has claimed to have found one," said Ben. "I believe that Howard found several while he was working for the oil company. Somehow, he got tangled up with Kevin and had to share the locations. At some point, Kevin decided he needed to keep Howard from sharing that information with Jennifer."

"But silver isn't worth all that much nowadays. Not like it was in the early 1980s." Miranda continued to pan the cave with her flashlight. She stopped the beam near Ben's tent. It illuminated a small black cast-iron pot, a ladle with a long shaft, and the remnants of a stone fire ring. "What's that stuff?"

"That's smelting apparatus. This is most likely where Jonathan struck his silver coins."

"The famous counterfeit coins?" Austin's voice rose half an octave. "Those would be priceless to collectors."

Miranda felt a tingling in the hairs on the back of her neck. She felt vulnerable even though she was accompanied by two men. "Hey, guys. This might not be safe for us all to be in here at once. Maybe—"

They heard the sound of a match striking at the entrance to the mine.

"What's that?" Miranda felt a tremble run up her spine. She was pretty sure she knew what it was. She grit her teeth in frustration—too late. "Who's there?" she yelled into the tunnel. "Kevin, is that you?"

"Good guess. I think a terrible accident has just happened on the mountain. Bad news, it's your accident."

They heard a sizzle and the sound of something bouncing in the entrance tunnel. Then everything happened at once. A flash, a crash, and then a blast of dust flew into the cavern, snuffing out the candle and throwing everyone to the floor.

Chapter 42

Wednesday Morning, Indian Staircase

Miranda screamed, grabbed Austin's arm, and plunged them both to the other side of the cavern. She landed akimbo on top of the cushioned tent. The dust clogged her throat and she started coughing and spitting out the flying dirt. She flung out her arms. "Austin," she yelled, then coughed again. "Austin, are you hurt?"

"I'm fine," he said, which started his own coughing spasm. "Are you hurt?"

"I don't think so. My ears are ringing like fury. What about you?"

There was a short silence. "I'm good. Where's Ben?"

"Ben!" Miranda yelled, and began feeling around herself in the absolute pitch black. "Austin, I can't find Ben."

"Hang on." She could hear Austin fumbling in his pockets. In a few seconds, a match sputtered to life, and

Miranda could see that their cavern was only half its original size. The dirt from the cave-in was still flying around and caused her to sneeze and she blew out the match.

"Damn. Sorry, Austin. Do you have another one?"

She heard another strike, followed by Austin's face behind the heavenly light. "Where's Ben?" He looked around with the match and poked around in the debris where the candle had been. "I found it. Thank heaven." He lit it and held it up.

Off to the left they saw a mound just behind the collapsed tent.

"Ben," Miranda shouted. She scrambled over and was rewarded by a low groan.

"What happened?" Ben sat up and then screamed. "My leg!"

Austin brought the candle closer and they saw that a large slab of rock had pinned his leg. "Can you feel it?"

"No, I can't—" Ben let out a high-pitched yelp and fell back lifeless.

Miranda felt her heart sink. She placed two fingers at Ben's neck and found a pulse. "He's passed out. Probably best." He was pinned by a large rock that looked as if it had just peeled itself off the side of the cavern. "Do you think you can lift it up far enough for me to drag him out?"

Austin played the candlelight all around the rock. "Let's see if I can even budge it at all. Here. Hold this." He handed her the candle, and she watched while he squatted next to the rock's edge and gave it a mighty heave.

Ben woke and screamed like a wild animal. The boulder didn't budge an inch.

Miranda turned to Ben. "Did you bring an ax?"

"Sure"—he panted in reaction to the pain—"but I know where you're going with this. It's a short-handled one. You can't use it as a lever." His voice faded away and he passed out again.

"Damn." Miranda looked around and then back at Austin. "I appear to be fine. Are you hurt?"

"Something hit my right arm. I thought I was fine, but now it's throbbing like fury."

"Trying to shift that rock didn't help. Here, let me see." Miranda felt his arm from shoulder to wrist. "It feels fine, it might just be wrenched. Hang on, I have a first aid kit in my backpack. All I have to do is find it, right?"

Austin cradled his arm. "Yep, I've got one in mine as well."

"You're gonna need to get some painkillers working before that arm starts to swell. Both packs should still be where we were sitting."

"Yep, I'll see if I can find them." Miranda crawled toward the entrance and searched through the rocks and dust for her backpack. Her fingers found a strap so she cleared away the rubble and pulled it free. "I found mine."

She crept back to Austin and Ben, pulled out her first aid kit, and by the light of the candle found a package of Excedrin. She flicked three out into her palm, then handed Austin her water bottle and the tablets. "Take these now to get a jump on the swelling."

Austin downed the tablets in one gulp.

Miranda scooted over to the wall and stacked up a couple of flat rocks. She cleaned off the top rock, then let the candle wax drip into a soft pool. She stuck the candle in it. "If we find Ben's tin plate, that would be great."

Austin began to massage his shoulder. "Thanks, having a little light feels better." He looked toward the entrance. "How bad is the cave-in?"

"I've got a flashlight in here somewhere." She rummaged down one of the pockets and pulled out a tiny black one. She twisted it on, and the brightness caused them both to shield their eyes. Miranda turned it down and pointed it at the entrance. "No light is coming through. It must have collapsed."

Austin crept closer, using only his good arm in a three-legged-dog action. "That sizzle we heard before the explosion meant that it was probably a stick of dynamite."

"Well, since we're not completely buried, there must have been a problem. We should be dead."

"If we're not found, we'll be dead anyway."

Miranda poked at the rubble in the tunnel. It was loose and she scraped at the material with her cupped hand. It came away easily. "Look, this isn't hard packed. We might be able to dig our way out."

"This might be ridiculous, but let's check anyway: Do you have a cell signal?"

"Oh, God, that would be our salvation." Miranda pulled out her phone from her back pocket. "I don't. But we only need a single bar to text Sheriff Larson."

"How's the battery?"

"It's at seventy-nine percent. What about yours?"

Austin pulled out his cell from his back pocket. The screen was shattered into a web of cracks. "It's smashed." He blew out a frustrated breath. "My radio won't work until it's completely away from the cliff."

Miranda shone her flashlight over at Ben, then focused on the water bottle. "We've only got enough water for a few days at best. Ben will be in big trouble if we can't get help. Our only choice is to dig ourselves out."

"This is going to take hours, so we need to pace our-selves. If you can drag out the debris, I can use my left hand to shift it away. We each need to rest in between."

"Yep. That'll work. Let me wedge the flashlight so I can see what I'm doing." Miranda used a couple of rocks to illuminate the opening. Then she started pulling at the rubble with both hands. She created a pile then moved aside to lean against the cavern wall while Austin used his good arm to move the pile out of her way.

After about three cycles of digging, she realized they both stopped talking in order to save oxygen. The thought of dying from lack of air was worse than dying of thirst. She headed back into the tunnel, which she had cleared to a depth of about three feet—nine feet to go.

The toil was beginning to wear on Miranda and Austin. After another three cycles, they both lay panting and decided to rest for a little longer. In seconds, they were both asleep.

Miranda awoke to the sound of groans coming from the back of the cavern. It was Ben. He was beginning to stir, and in a moment he would realize that he couldn't move his leg. She raised up on one elbow and nudged Austin.

He snuffled and snorted. "What?" Then he adjusted to sitting upright.

"Ben is beginning to stir. See if you can get him to take some painkillers as well as some of our water. He needs to stay still until we get rescued. I'll get back to the dig-ging."

"Right." Austin grunted and slapped his shoulder. Crad-ling his sore arm, he moved toward Ben.

Miranda wiggled back into the tunnel and began shift-ing more dirt. She was at least halfway and was grateful for her gloves. She came upon a rock about the size of a loaf of bread wedged against the ceiling. Pulling on it didn't work, so she ran her fingers around its edge, removing as much soil as she could.

She repeated that two more times, and on the third try the rock came away in a flurry of gravel and dust. She began coughing but managed to shove the rock out into the cavern. "Austin, this huge rock has opened up a nice chunk of the tunnel. One or two more sessions and we might break through."

"Fantastic. We need help or we're going to lose Ben."

Miranda wiggled back into the tunnel and removed another backpack-load of dirt. She shoved the pack down and used her feet to kick it out to Austin. He emptied it and gave it back. On the next excavation, Miranda saw a tiny chink of light. "Austin, holy cow, I can see daylight." She inhaled deeply to draw in the fresh air. "We're nearly through."

"Thank God. We can't be quick enough for Ben."

She started digging another load into the backpack, and her gloved hand felt a soft resistance. She frowned. This wasn't dirt or even brush. She explored the area again with a firmer grasp. She felt a face.

"Austin! I've found a body. It's Kevin. He's dead."

Chapter 43

Wednesday Evening, the Farmhouse

Miranda let her mother fuss over her and Austin as much as she liked. Dorothy ordered them to take hot showers using the newly restored electrical power. Austin was wearing her uncle's clothes from the bag that never seemed to make its way down to the charity shop. Then Dorothy tucked them side by side onto the couch in front of the fire, wrapping them in a heavy vintage quilt. Miranda noted that it was her grandmother's beautiful wedding-ring pattern. Hot cocoa was accompanied by a large plate of fresh gingerbread cookies.

"Thanks, Mom. Do you have enough for the sheriff and Felicia? They should be along any minute."

"I have a mountain of cookies. I've done nothing but bake since the Fire and Rescue volunteers noticed that the two of you were missing and called the sheriff, who then called me."

Austin grinned sheepishly. "I've never missed a rescue callout. I've been a little late sometimes, but never completely missed one. The search for Ben was scheduled to continue at about the same time we were climbing the Indian Staircase."

Miranda took another cookie. "We had been able to text the sheriff over Kevin's body." Her body shuddered under the quilt. "We were rescued in short order after that."

They heard the crunch of gravel on the driveway. Dorothy opened the door and let the sheriff and Felicia in. "I've got hot cocoa and gingerbread cookies. Set yourselves down and I'll fetch a couple of mugs for you. Marshmallows or plain?"

Felicia and the sheriff had weary eyes and looked a little pale around their lips. "Plain for me, marshmallows for the sheriff," said Felicia as they collapsed into the rockers by the front window.

Sheriff Larson let out an involuntary groan as he stretched out his long legs. "You guys are looking a damned sight better than you did a little bit ago. How's the wrist?"

Austin automatically waggled his hand to test it for pain. "Fine. Doc Watson gave me a pain shot, and I'll need to rest it for a couple of days and take some anti-inflammatory pills. Good news. Nothing broken."

Sheriff Larson and Felicia accepted the mugs that Dorothy brought. "I know you want to question these kids, so I'm off to bake something else. I don't know what yet. I'm still figuring out what Ronny's favorites are." She blew a kiss to Miranda and went back to the kitchen.

Miranda raised her eyebrows and eyed Austin. "Ronny?"

"Looks like Ron might have met a woman who can straighten out his life."

"Isn't that a bit of a risk?" Felicia asked. "I mean, you're going to have a working distillery here. Isn't that like having the fox watch the chickens?"

"I've found a local intern who will be helping me with that. His name is Lance Campbell. Apparently, he helped Uncle Gene from time to time. He's an enthusiast among the local 'shine crowd, and he can make those underground connections that I can't."

Felicia cleared her throat. "I have Kevin's body in the morgue, and I wanted to let you know that he died instantly in the collapse of the tunnel. He didn't suffocate."

Miranda sighed. "Thanks, that's a relief. I was worried that suffocation was going to be our fate as well." She glanced at Austin. "Or starvation. Or thirst. And even worse—in the dark."

Sheriff Larson took another cookie, gave it a quick dunk, and popped it whole into his mouth and made quick work of the delicious treat. "Just perfect." He paused and drew out a notepad and pen. "Now, let me get this down for my report. Austin, you got a call from another ranger that he had seen a pattern of flashing lights."

"Yes. He was patrolling for poachers out on our system of firebreak back roads. He copied down the pattern of lights and I brought it over here."

Miranda added, "My uncle was an amateur radio operator. I decoded the message and we concluded that it was Ben asking for help. We took off and found him."

Austin adjusted the sling on his shoulder to give his wrist more support. "But, unfortunately, we led Kevin right to his hideout."

"Did you two know that silver mine was back there?"

Austin and Miranda said, "No," in perfect unison.

Miranda continued, "Did Ben tell you why Kevin killed Howard?"

"I had a chance to question him before they took him to Lexington Hospital. He said that he was suspicious of Kevin from the moment he heard that Howard was missing. Ben and Howard had been quite close, and he took the disappearance hard. He started his own investigation."

Austin gave Miranda the side eye. "Well, that sounds like someone I know. Probably why he vandalized your power. You're getting a reputation."

Miranda shushed him. "Let him finish."

The sheriff continued, "When Ben discovered that Kevin was making so-called hunting trips to this area, he said it didn't make much sense. Kevin could afford to go anywhere. In fact, prior to Howard's disappearance, Kevin had made several trips to Africa for big-game hunting. So, he thought there must have been something else."

"What was it?"

Felicia blurted out, "He discovered that your cavern was one of Jonathan Swift's lost silver mines."

"Yes, that's what all that old smelting stuff was for," said Miranda. "That's where Jonathan Swift must have struck his silver coins. Kevin must have tried smelting a limited number of coins after he spent the ones he killed Howard for."

"Right," said Sheriff Larson. "Coins struck by the legendary Jonathan Swift would be worth a fortune."

"What happened to them?"

Sheriff Larson stood. "I'm pretty sure there are a few private collectors holding on to counterfeit Jonathan Swift counterfeit coins. That's real justice." He motioned to Felicia. "Let's go home. I'm beat. Tomorrow will be filled with reporters, paperwork, and reports."

Miranda walked them out to the porch, and Austin stood beside her and watched with her as the sheriff and Felicia drove back to town. "I'm glad we were able to help, but it feels like we actually just increased the circle of pain. Kevin's dead. Jennifer's emotionally frozen. Alfred will get a career boost. Nothing really changes for Stephanie or Kurt. Not very satisfying."

"But we found Howard and his killer."

Miranda pulled her shoulders back. "You're right. I'm looking at this from a purely negative view because this will be so hard to share with Aunt Ora."

"You've never been reluctant to do the right thing," said Austin softly.

"But, knowing that doing the right thing will hurt someone is a new burden. I know my aunt will be extremely grateful that we fulfilled her deepest wish and gave Howard peace."

Miranda felt Austin's good arm steal its way across her shoulders, and he drew her into a side hug. "We make a good team."

She lifted her head to give him a soft kiss. "A very good team."

Recipes for Moonshine Cocktails

Cherry Mimosas

Serves 4

Equipment
1 cocktail shaker
4 champagne flutes

Ingredients
Ice
¼ cup Cherry Ale-8
¼ cup clear moonshine
Prosecco
Maraschino cherries

Directions
Fill shaker with ice.
Add Cherry Ale-8 and moonshine to shaker.
Shake and pour into flutes.
Top up the flutes with prosecco.
Garnish with maraschino cherry.

Lemonade 'Shine

Serves 4

Equipment
Vegetable peeler
2-quart pitcher
Lemon juicer
Spoon
4 mason jars

Ingredients
6 fresh lemons
2 cups water
Mint leaves
½ cup turbinado sugar
1 cup clear moonshine
Ice

Directions
Peel off four lemon skin curls.
Muddle mint in the bottom of a 2-quart pitcher.
Squeeze lemons, add juice to pitcher.
Add sugar, stir all until sugar dissolved.
Add moonshine.
Fill mason jars halfway up with ice and add water.
Stir and pour into mason jars.
Garnish with mint and lemon curls.

Cola Moon

Serves 4

Equipment
    2-quart pitcher
    Knife
    Spoon
    4 mason jars

Ingredients
1 fresh lemon
¼ cup turbinado sugar
1 cup clear moonshine
2 16-oz. bottles RC Cola (or any cola on hand)
Ice

Directions
    Peel off four lemon skin curls.
    Squeeze lemon, add juice to pitcher.
    Add sugar, stir until all the sugar dissolves.
    Add moonshine.
    Add cola.
    Fill mason jars halfway up with ice.
    Stir mixture and pour into mason jars.
    Garnish with lemon curls.

Recipes for Snacks

Cheesy Bits

Serves 16

Equipment
- Baking sheet
- Aluminum foil
- Parchment paper
- Cutting board
- Measuring cup
- Small mixing bowl
- Spoon
- Knife
- Spatula

Ingredients
- 1 cup grated cheddar cheese or use a packaged cheese mixture
- 1 cup chopped white onion
- 1 cup mayonnaise (here in the South, we use Duke's mayonnaise)
- 4 slices of sourdough bread (or any sliced bread on hand)

Directions

Preheat oven to 375° F.

Wrap baking sheet in aluminum foil. Cut a piece of parchment paper to fit.

Mix grated cheese, chopped onions, and mayonnaise in the bowl until thoroughly blended.

Cut bread slices into fourths.

Heap about a tablespoon of the mixture onto each piece of bread, covering the slice to the edges.

Place on baking sheet with about a half an inch separation.

Bake in the oven for 15–20 minutes, checking frequently until topping is bubbly and browned around the edges.

Let cool for a few minutes.

Old-Fashioned Corn Bread

Serves 16

Equipment

Seasoned cast-iron skillet
Small mixing bowls
Measuring cups
Measuring spoons
Mixing spoon
Knife
Spatula
Aluminum foil

Ingredients

1 tablespoon bacon drippings
2 cups cornmeal *or* 1½ cups cornmeal and ½ cup flour
1 teaspoon baking soda
1 teaspoon salt
1 tablespoon sugar (optional)
1 large egg (optional)
1¼ cups buttermilk
6 tablespoons unsalted butter, melted

Directions

Put the bacon drippings in a 9- or 10-inch well-seasoned cast-iron skillet and put the skillet into the oven. Then turn the oven on to 400° F with the skillet inside. (If you don't have an iron skillet, you can use an uncovered Dutch oven or a metal cake pan.)

Whisk together all the dry ingredients (cornmeal, baking soda, salt, sugar if using) in a large bowl. In another bowl, beat the egg (if using) and buttermilk until combined, then mix that into the bowl of dry ingredients. Stir in the melted butter.

When the oven is hot, take out the skillet (carefully, as the handle will be hot!). Add the corn-bread batter and make sure it is evenly distributed in the skillet.

Bake at 400° F for about 20 minutes, or until the edges are beginning to brown and a toothpick inserted in the center of the bread comes out clean.

Let the bread rest for 10 to 30 minutes in the skillet before cutting it into wedges and serving.

To store, let the corn bread cool, then remove from pan and wrap in plastic wrap or transfer to an airtight container. Store at room temp for 2 to 3 days.

Bean Salad with Tart Dressing

Serves 4-6

Equipment

Can opener
Large mixing bowl
Measuring cup
Mixing spoon
Measuring spoons
Saucepan

Ingredients

1 16-oz. can of green beans, drained
1 16-oz. can of yellow wax beans, drained
1 16-oz. can of red kidney beans, drained
1 cup chopped celery
1 cup chopped sweet onions
1 cup chopped green bell pepper
1 jar (4 oz.) chopped pimento peppers, drained
½ cup vinegar
¼ cup extra-virgin olive oil
¼ cup white sugar
¼ teaspoon salt
¼ teaspoon black pepper

Directions

Mix green beans, yellow wax beans, kidney beans, celery, onion, green bell pepper, and pimento peppers in a bowl.

Combine vinegar, oil, sugar, salt, and pepper in a saucepan; bring to a boil. Cook and stir until sugar is dissolved, about 5 minutes. Remove saucepan from burner and pour dressing over bean mixture; toss to coat.

Refrigerate until flavors blend, 8 hours to overnight.

Pickled Beets

Serves 4–6

Equipment
  Knife
  Scrub brush
  Saucepans
  Colander
  Mixing bowl
  Measuring cup
  Measuring spoons
  Mixing spoon

Ingredients
1 lb. small beets (about 7 beets)
½ cup white vinegar
¼ cup sugar
¼ teaspoon salt
½ teaspoon black peppercorns
2 bay leaves

Directions
  Trim but leave the root and 1-inch stem on beets; scrub with a brush. Place in a medium saucepan; cover with water. Bring to a boil. Cover, reduce heat, and simmer 45 minutes or until tender. Drain and rinse with cold water; drain again. Cool slightly. Trim off beet roots. Rub off skins. Thinly slice beets. Place in a large bowl.

  Combine vinegar and sugar in a small saucepan. Bring to a boil. Cook 5 minutes. Remove from heat. Stir in salt, peppercorns, and bay leaves. Pour vinegar mixture over beets. Cover and chill. Discard bay leaves.

Acknowledgments

This second book in the Paint & Shine series has been a lovely trip down memory lane. My parents are both from the area where this story is set, Wolfe County, Kentucky. My grandfather built the farmhouse that's featured here from a Sears Catalog kit. I've spent most of my summers as a child running barefoot in the soft grass, gazing up at the Milky Way in the evenings, and hiking the hundreds of trails in the Daniel Boone National Forest. Although I'm a good cook, I'll never reach the standard of biscuit perfection that my grandmother achieved every single morning of her life. I can still taste the biscuits. I hope I have done justice to an idyllic part of my upbringing.

I have so many people to thank for getting this book out of my head and onto the page. It was a long journey, and sometimes the path wandered into the weeds or disappeared completely. Luckily, I have a tribe of supporters.

I thank my parents for a wildly original raising. Mom and Dad thought that children should be shown how to live their best life, not lectured into it. My mom taught her two girls and two boys how to cook, clean, knit, sew, paint, draw, and not be afraid to tackle something new. She praised the trying—not the result. My dad taught us all to hunt, fish, camp, track, shoot, and garden, and how to use power tools. Both parents instilled in me a work ethic that I still bless them for today.

My mother's parents let me run loose on their little truck farm most summers. I loved the feel of rich soil on my bare feet, the smell of freshly cut hay, and the warm acceptance of all their neighbors as "Della's oldest grandchild." I relished the freedom to play in the creek, climb the big hill, pet the cow, run through the tall corn, and generally make a huge nuisance of myself. My mother's parents are buried in a peaceful cemetery overlooking the bend in the road above the tiny village of Trent, Kentucky.

They were hardworking, generous, kind, and clever backcountry folk. My grandma Buchanan was the best biscuit maker in Wolfe County. That was an important skill in those days. She made at least one cast-iron skillet full every morning from the time she was a teen until way into her eighties.

My mother's middle brother, Harold Gene Buchanan, inspired the Uncle Gene character in this series. He parted this life too early but managed to leave behind an inspirational, spiritual, and scientific legacy to his family and friends. He was a big personality full of boundless energy, curiosity, and drive. He showed me, by example, that your background doesn't limit you in achieving your dreams.

My independent editor, Ramona DeFelice Long, was an amazing award-winning writer, editor extraordinaire, and refined woman with deep roots in the southern heart of Louisiana. She knows what makes a good story and could tell me in a way that didn't scare the ever-loving bejesus out of me. Sadly, she lost her four-and-a-half-year battle with cancer in the fall of 2020.

She will be sorely missed by the hundreds of writers that she inspired to join her Sprint Club. The rules were simple: Sign in. Write for one solid hour. Enjoy the rest of your day knowing that your favorite job is done. My condolences to her lovely sister and the oft-mentioned menfolk, her husband and twin sons. Rest in power. Thank you.

First readers are important, and I have a powerful one. We exchange pages every month and meet to rip them apart, so we can put them back together in better shape. Sam Falco, you're my hero.

I'm crushed to report that my wonderful agent, Beth Campbell, has left BookEnds Literary Agency to pursue the next stage in her publishing career. She inspired me to write better and try harder to produce the best writing I can. I wish her the very best. I know we'll hear about her soon.

My new agent is James McGowan, a member of the cast of rock stars that make up the fabulous staff that Jessica Faust of BookEnds Literary Agency has gathered. He's enthusiastic about this close-to-my-heart series and my new projects. I'm grateful I can count on him to be my champion in negotiating the twisty passages of modern publishing.

My extraordinary editor at Kensington Publishing Corporation, Elizabeth Trout, has managed to take my jumbled plot threads and wibbly-wobbly emotional crises and guide me to a much better story. Larissa Ackerman has been proactive in consulting with me to brainstorm new promotional and marketing themes with creative and fresh concepts. Last year, I finally met Michelle Addo, who rocks Kensington's new Cozy Club Mini-Cons, held all over the country. When I appeared with the other cozy mystery writers at Poisoned Pen Bookstore in Scottsdale, Arizona, it was a bucket list event for me.

I wouldn't be published at all if not for the Sisters in Crime organization and their online group, the Guppies. The fishy name comes from the following: The Great Unpublished. The group started out as a collection of unpublished writers sharing information about the confounding world of publishing. The secret to its success is that after reaching that revered status of published, Guppies stay in the group and reach back to help others. The split is now about fifty-fifty published to unpublished of more than nine hundred members. If you have any inclination to follow the writer's journey, you need to sign up right now. Here's the link for national organization: https://www.sis tersincrime.org.

I am grateful for the dedication of booksellers everywhere who love readers and are kind to writers. My local bookstore in downtown St. Petersburg, Florida, is Haslam's Book Store at 2025 Central Avenue. The owners have welcomed me with unstinting support, and I've even been specially honored to meet all four of the bookstore cats: Beowulf, Teacup, Clancy, and Emily Dickinson.

My next-favorite local bookstore is owned and managed by the irrepressible Nancy Alloy of Books at Park Place. I enjoy talking all things bookish with her and her dog, the very skeptical Watson, who greets me with subtle and rare affection.

The newcomer to the local bookstore scene is Tombolo Books. They opened only a few months before the COVID-19 pandemic and managed to support readers and writers during a difficult time.

In today's online world, book bloggers are markedly influential on who discovers your books. At Malice Domestic I met my first real live book advocate. Dru Ann

Love, who runs https://drusbookmusing.com. She posts her personal reviews, reveals new covers, announces new releases, and publishes author interviews. Her main feature is "A Day in the Life" essays in the voice of the character of the featured mystery. Thanks, Dru—I'll hug you in the hotel lobby at the next mystery conference.

My muse of many years, Joye Barnes, is completely responsible for my lack of writer's block. Every time I get a little stuck, I mentally look her in the eyes and ask, "What would Joye be thrilled to have happen next?" Thank you, Joye, for your unfailing support.

Many writers struggle through their writing process hideously alone without the support of their families. I'm not one of those. I have the devoted encouragement of my husband, sons, daughters-in-love, grandchildren, parents, brothers, sisters, and a large extended family, all cheering me on to finish the next book.

I am ever so grateful to you, the readers. There is no greater reward than to hear that one of my books helped someone get through a difficult time by providing a few hours of distraction. That's one of the reasons I write. Other than that I'm completely addicted to writing.

George is my constant cheerleader, relentless taskmaster, overall handyman, and ever-ready book-bag carrier in support of my writing dream. He has earned the title Trophy Husband for this role in this adventure.

If you're from eastern Kentucky, you'll notice that I've used a large chunk of my fully paid-up artistic license. I have combined two famous trail locations into one for this book. I love the Indian Staircase and climbed it many times as a child. It's a wonderful adventure, but I'm not sure I still have the innocent confidence it takes to climb it. The other aspect I've altered is a view of Battleship Rock. I've moved the cliff to be seen from the top of the Indian Staircase. That's the scene that I want Miranda's clients to paint.

Thanks for your support. It means everything. It's worth repeating: you mean everything to me.

Read on for a special preview of the next book in the
Paint & Shine Mystery Series . . .

Death a Sketch

Forthcoming from Kensington Publishing Corp.
in summer 2022

Chapter 1

Late Friday Afternoon, Miranda's Farmhouse

"I have a bad feeling." Miranda Trent rocked gently in the porch swing, her hand wrapped around a cup of hot mint tea. "What a mess. I shouldn't have accepted a big contract from that horrible man and his horrible company. A four-day workshop is a big leap for my new business." She drew up a handmade quilt and tucked it around herself and Sandy, the sleeping puppy in her lap. "Have I made a dreadful mistake, Mom?"

"There's no way to tell, honey," said her mom, Dorothy Marcella, who was tucked into the other end of the quilt, one booted foot touching the plank boards of the porch floor to keep the swing moving. "You need the business."

"I certainly do. Tourist season is virtually shut down for the winter, and there won't be anything happening in these hills until spring. Well, except for a few Christmas events up at Hemlock Lodge."

"I've been so busy going back and forth to Dayton trying to sell my house and haven't paid much attention to you." Dorothy tapped Miranda's toe with her own. "What's so special about this? You've been doing your cultural tours for a couple of months now. I'm sorry to have been so preoccupied when you needed to brainstorm."

Miranda felt the warmth spread through her chest, and she began to relax. She had been upset by her mom's distance. It wasn't deliberate. Her mom had a lot of spinning plates at the moment. "I got a call a couple of weeks ago from a sportswear company headquartered in Lexington. BigSky Corporation is known for their popular graphical designs. They're really gorgeous. Anyway, they asked me to provide a four-day team-building workshop based at Hemlock Lodge in Natural Bridge State Park."

"That sounds like the kind of challenge you love. What's the format?"

"Basically, it's a series of games, competitions, and challenges. On the first day, we hike the trail to Balanced Rock and draw with charcoal. We lunch here at the farmhouse, then we tour the distillery and make up the mash for moonshine in my brand-new tiny one-gallon sampler stills. That's followed by a nature-photography event, then some outdoor stew preparation."

"That sounds like something that should suit you right down to the ground. I don't understand why you're so wrought up."

Miranda pursed her lips. "That's just day one. On day two, we tackle a rope-bridge challenge, have a boxed lunch followed by a watercolor lesson at Rock Bridge, then everyone makes chicken potpie here at the farm-house and checks the flavoring of the moonshine mash."

Dorothy shook her head. "My, oh my. That's a lot to get through. No wonder you're feeling stretched thin. What's on for the third day?"

"We start off with an aerial rope event at that zip-line roadside attraction over in Slade. Then we have an eco-friendly scavenger hunt, and for the artistic event, we make table centerpieces with the items collected. The cooking events are pie baking and then using your an-cient sourdough starter for dinner rolls."

"You mean Viola?"

"Yes, although I'll never get used to the way you treat that starter like it was alive."

"It is alive! Family tradition demands that you name it after the person who gave it to you. That's a pleasant way of sharing the love in the bread."

"Then on the last day, everyone pulls together to create a traditional Thanksgiving dinner where we celebrate the team and finish off with the moonshine that everyone helped to create."

"I'm exhausted just hearing about it. You do see the irony here, don't you?"

Miranda pouted. "What on earth are you talking about?"

"It's so funny. You, who is a world-class worrier as well as an introvert, is teaching a team-building work-shop when you're not sure if your Paint and Shine busi-ness will make it."

Miranda gave her mom a sad smile. "Nailed it. Well, it's also one of my strengths. I relate to loners. You re-member that's what Grandma used to say: 'What doesn't kill you makes you stronger.'"

"I think this might be a bit too far. Do you have enough

help? Should I postpone my trip to Dayton? I could do that."

Miranda grabbed Sandy and snuggled him up under her chin. "No way. You need to get that house sold. I won't risk it. You've gotten a really good offer for that house. I'll have the Hobb sisters for kitchen work and the BigSky Corporation is sending a manager to assist with wrangling the candidates. They're supposed to be in line for some sort of special fast-track management program depending on their performance in the workshop."

"So why are you worried?"

"I don't know. Sometimes I think I worry just to feed my habit of being a great worrier. You know that."

"Yes, but this business is all about what you enjoy. You should be enjoying it."

"When I stop to think about it, I am." Miranda paused for a few seconds. "I've been working on my people skills, and the art gallery job I had up in New York City was super for learning how to approach people and close sales."

"That's right, you are more confident. So, why are you so worried?"

"It lasts four days. Four whole long days. I've never done anything like it, but since the tourist numbers were falling, it seemed like a gift."

"This is normally a slow time for sightseers and tourists. It's the weekend before Thanksgiving, and lots of folks are already on their way to family gatherings, not cultural touring adventures."

"I did wonder why they wanted this particular time. Although most of the fall colors are still on the trees, one heavy rain will strip them down to bare branches."

"It's already cold up on the ridges and cliffs right now."

"Right, I'll know better when I've been in business for a couple of years." Miranda sighed deeply. "If I last that long. Who knows if I'll even be in business a year from now—or even a month from now? Most new businesses fail in the first year. These last few weeks have been a whirlwind introduction to cultural touring."

Dorothy patted Miranda on the shoulder. "Dear, I know you think you're the cause of the tragedies surrounding your new Paint and Shine business, but violence is a natural part of living out here in the highlands. We're from a rough and determined stock of Scotch Irish. The Hatfield-McCoy feud is not a fairy tale. There are some that say it's still running."

"I'm learning that." Miranda scratched Sandy's full belly. They sat swinging with the only sounds coming from country night. She picked out a barn owl, a coyote, and finally the cricket from inside the house. She had been trying to evict him for several weeks with no luck. Was he good luck or bad? She couldn't remember.

Dorothy took a long sip of her tea. "I feel bad about going back to Dayton right now. It's even worse since Ron the Handyman"—she stopped and smiled when she said his name—"has taken a big job over in Jackson. I think you are going to need all the help you can get."

"It's not a problem, Mom. You're lucky that the house sold so quickly. Going back and forth is just too much hassle. Especially since Ron proposed."

Dorothy began folding the quilt off her lap. "Are you sure?"

"Don't make me repeat that whole string of reasoning. We've already been through that. When is your closing?"

"Monday morning." Dorothy drained her cup. "In fact, I'd better get on the road. Friday nights are always a nightmare going through Cincinnati. It used to be that the backups were for those coming south. Now, it seems just as bad whichever direction you're going."

Miranda glanced at her wristwatch. "Right, if you leave now, you should be just ahead of the rush." She took Sandy in her arms and walked down to the driveway with her mom.

Dorothy tickled Sandy under his chin. "You be a good puppy now, okay? Watch over Miranda for me."

With a feeling of intense isolation, Miranda watched her mom's car drive away. She hadn't fully considered how much she would miss how her mom had been helping her with the tiny tasks that kept a household going while Miranda concentrated on her small business. Such as laundry, dusting, and keeping food in the refrigerator.

The phone rang and Miranda felt annoyed but pushed that aside. She was determined to secure her ownership of this homestead farmhouse. All she needed to do was keep her schedule full enough to make a decent profit. Her uncle's will stipulated that she needed to pay her taxes and establish a licensed moonshine distillery within ninety days of his death. She was close to achieving both so she could enjoy this wonderful country life. She went inside, put Sandy down, and picked up the handset.

"I've got more changes," said Mr. Tobin, vice president of human resources of BigSky, the world-famous manufacturer of sportswear.

"Good evening, Mr. Tobin. More changes? It's a little late, don't you think? The workshop starts tomorrow morning."

He paused. "What did you say? Is this connection bad? I need more changes."

Miranda sighed. He wasn't listening to her at all. "What kind of changes?"

"Two things. First, I want to split the workshop into two teams. Then I want them to compete against each other for a big reward. That should elevate the focus with the workshop participants. This is not going to be merely fun time in the mountains."

Miranda thought about the activities she'd planned for the workshop. Grudgingly she admitted to herself that those were good ideas. He might be annoying, but he was a creative businessman. "I agree, Mr. Tobin. A competition will add some spirit to the events, but won't there be some sort of scoring and evaluation tasks? I'm not set up for that kind of paperwork, and I couldn't just add that without significant extra fees."

"No, I see that. Don't worry, I'll handle those processes."

His tone made her feel like a dolt for mentioning it. It was demeaning.

Mr. Tobin continued, "Also, since there's going to be some scoring and assessment tasks, I'm going to send my administrative assistant. She'll handle all the paperwork."

"That's good. Who is it?"

"Rowena Gardner."

"Rowena Gardner? That's an unusual name. I think I know her if she's from Dayton, Ohio."

"She commutes into the plant from Winchester, but if I remember from her application, I think she got an associate degree from a junior college in Dayton, Ohio. Anyway, she doesn't have a local accent and she's an efficient admin."

"Rowena was the star organizer of our class back at

Colonel White High School. If I'm remembering right, she was president of the Honor Society, captain of the cheerleaders, and also our class president."

"That sounds like her."

Oh my goodness, if this is Rowena, it's bound to be an omen that this workshop will be a fantastic success. She's a little odd, but a good organizer. We were great friends.

Miranda frowned. "Wait, that means you're adding a person to the total participants?"

"You don't need to charge me for that, she won't be participating in the events."

That weasel, he's trying to lowball me on the price. He's not getting away with it.

"Well, that's fine, but she will need to eat if she's going to tag along with the competitors to make scoring assessments. In fact, it will be the same as your special-meals-only fee. Right?"

There was a short pause. "Oh, very well. That won't cost much. She'll join you tomorrow morning for the eight o'clock orientation meeting at Hemlock Lodge." There was another pause. "Hold for a second. I've got another call."

He switched her on hold before she could agree. She thought that if this was how corporate types ran things, she was glad she didn't work for a big company. Not her cup of tea at all.

"That was bad news, so I won't be coming out tomorrow to lead the workshop. I've got a labor union emergency over at the manufacturing plant in Louisville. They've chosen the holiday rush because they know that we can't afford any production losses leading up to Black Friday. I've got to handle it in person."

Miranda raised her eyebrows. This would go much smoother if he wasn't around. "That's too bad, but I've got everything all lined up. It will be fine."

"Oh, not to worry. I'm sending over a substitute manager to take my place."

Miranda gritted her teeth. *Just many last-minute changes was she supposed to deal with?*

"Perfect! Who is it?"

He ended the call.

Miranda replaced the handset into its charger. "It would be nice to know who this new supervisor is," she said to the empty room.

As she started back out onto the porch, the phone rang again.

"Hello, this is Paint and Shine, your source for cultural tours in the Kentucky Highlands."

"Hi, Miranda. It's Rowena Gardner. You sound just the same as you did in high school. Way more professional, though."

Miranda laughed. "Hi, Rowena. It is you. I couldn't believe it when Mr. Tobin mentioned your name. You sound the same, too."

That voice brought back a memory of them trying out for the cheerleader team in their high school gym uniforms. Rowena's long dark hair and olive skin in the school's salmon suit fit her curvy shape in all the right places. On the other hand, back in those days Miranda's figure had yet to appear. She didn't blossom until the following year.

"It's great to hear that we'll be working together. Although Mr. Tobin didn't seem to know much about your past."

"I am not surprised. He doesn't see any of his under-lings as worth getting to know. Anyway, he's sending me over to help manage the workshop. Apparently Mr. Tobin is going to make this workshop competition a strategy for his recruitment goals for the new year. I'm not sure what he had in mind, but I'm sure it will be a passel of trou-ble."

"Are you staying up at the lodge?"

"No way. Mr. Tobin won't spring for the extra ex-pense. I'll be going back and forth from Winchester every day. It's not a problem, I'm used to driving to the Lexing-ton office. Driving to Hemlock Lodge would be fine."

"That's nonsense. You can stay with me."

Sandy had patrolled all the rooms in the farmhouse as soon as Miranda set him down. Now he was back at her feet and nipping at her ankles. "Stop that."

"Stop what?" Rowena asked.

"Sorry, it's not you, it's my puppy, Sandy. He wants some attention. Where was I? Oh, if you stay here, you'll be right on the spot for any problems that might come up. Plus, we can catch up on old times before the event gets underway. I think it going to be fantastic, but I expect we'll be run off our feet. Please come."

"Really? You mean that? Are you sure I won't be putting you out just when you'll be busy keeping all these candidates focused on your workshop?"

Miranda laughed. "Actually, I would be taking advan-tage of you in helping to keep everything running smoothly. My mom has gone back to Dayton to close the sale of her house. You could take her room."

"I'm not sure."

"Come on. We have so much catching up to do. It

would be more fun to do that before the madness begins. Please, come. Pretty please?"

"Well," chuckled Rowena, "how can I possibly resist a pretty please?"

"Great. Come on over tonight and we can have a nice long chat before the workshop starts. Mom's bedroom is upstairs, so it comes with some privacy. It also has a desk, and I finally have great Wi-Fi connectivity. You'll love it."

"Perfect, but I'll bring over some wine. Luckily, I brought my laptop home from work today. Somehow I knew I might be required at the last minute. Mr. Tobin is not big on well–thought-out plans, as usual. I'll pack up and be at your place in a couple of hours. Text me your address."

Miranda sent the text and then refreshed things in her mom's upstairs bedroom. She changed the sheets, replaced the quilt with a fresh one, and cleared out a space in the top drawer of the dresser. She also removed a few of her Mother's clothes to give Rowena a slim slot in the closet.

To chase the lingering scent of her mom's cologne from the bedroom, she opened the front window. It looked out over the dirt road that ran by the farmhouse. Her last touches were to set out fresh towels, put a carafe of water on the nightstand, and set a vase of wildflowers on the desk. Miranda dusted all the furniture, then gave the floor a quick sweep. All was in visitor-perfect shape.

Rowena arrived at the farmhouse a few hours later in a clean but elderly blue Ford Fiesta. Miranda ran to the car and they squealed their delight. She gave Rowena a giant hug standing right in front of the open car door.

"Rowena! You look wonderful. What have you done

to your hair? My memory might be tricking me, but I thought it was straight—stick straight in fact. Now it's curly and absolutely gorgeous."

"I stopped trying to make it stay straight. This is my natural hair, and I'm happier not worrying about it. It takes me no time at all to get ready for work now."

"I love it. It suits you. Let's get your luggage put away." Rowena pulled a small wheeled suitcase out of the trunk. She also had a backpack that held her work laptop and its electronic paraphernalia, and a large black handbag. Then, finally, a special office box containing hanging folders of papers for the workshop participants. Miranda picked up the file box. "Go right on into the house and up the stairs that are in the dining room. Go right on through the storage area. The bedroom is at the front of the house. There's a small desk right in front of the window for you."

Miranda followed a few paces behind. Rowena stood in front of the desk and looked around the room. "This is delightful. So cozy. Is that one of your grandmother's quilts?"

"Yep, I'm knee-deep in them. That sounds like I'm complaining, doesn't it? I'm grateful that she's still able to keep up with her main pleasure in life." Miranda placed the box on the small desk. "Would you like a worktable as well? I have several sizes."

"I can see you're used to working out of the office. Yes, please. I could use a small table, thank you very much." Miranda went to get it while Rowena opened her suitcase and stowed away her clothes in the mirrored dresser and in the small closet.

After she set up her laptop and work materials on the desk and portable table, Rowena pulled out a bottle of

Shiraz from her suitcase. "I just grabbed this from my wine rack. It's an Australian blend that most people like." Then she lifted her eyebrows for a moment. "Plus, it has a screw top and I don't have to show you how terrible I am at opening a bottle of wine."

Miranda smiled. "Perfect. I'll rustle up a charcuterie board. I have some local cheeses, sugar-cured ham slices, along with homemade peach marmalade and some crackers. Come on down when you're settled in. We'll snug up on the living room couch in front of the fire."

Rowena came downstairs. "This is a beautiful farmhouse. So cozy with real country touches." She pointed to a runner in the dining room and a matching circular rug in the living room. "They're gorgeous. They match everything perfectly. Your grandmother again?"

"Yep. She's a real dynamo. I just gave her the remaining fabric from my new curtains, and she braided these up in only a couple of weeks." Miranda smiled. "It's nice to have her so near. She loves her life at the Campton Rehabilitation Center."

"What? You mean a nursing home? She's happy there?"

"Yes, very happy, but this one is different. All the residents are from this area, and they all have known each other from childhood. Every time I visit, I drag her away from some kind of activity. I've learned to check the website before I visit."

After a couple of hours, most of the bottle was gone and they had polished off all the meat, cheese, and crackers. They caught up with each other's families, covered Rowena's training as a secretary, and Miranda's art education in Savannah. Then Miranda outlined her unsuccessful stint in New York City trying to make it big as a landscape artist.

Rowena frowned. "I've had my relationship trials. I broke off a five-year engagement last year, so I ran from that. Unfortunately, I also had to leave a good job in marketing. I was lucky to find work at the BigSky Corporation. Stupidly, I've fallen into a bad relationship again. At work again, of course. I'm such an idiot."

"You mean with someone you work with at BigSky?"

"I'm hoping not to repeat that experience anytime soon. Not the getting-engaged part anyway. I still like the going-out dancing. Never mind me. I don't want to talk about it. What about you?" Rowena raised her eyebrows at Miranda.

"Well, I'm not married, but I must say, there's a forest ranger next door who is not only a pleasure to look at, but he's kind. That and, of course, he makes me laugh."

"Is it serious?"

Miranda looked at her former classmate and scrunched her brow. "I think there's some sign of it, but I'm so focused in getting this business up and running, I'm not really thinking about that. That might be a mistake."

"It feels as though we graduated from high school last week. How nice to reconnect." Rowena looked down into her empty wineglass. "Let's not lose each other again."

Miranda collected their glasses, plates, knives, and napkins and piled them on the empty charcuterie board. "I feel the same and I don't intend to lose track of you either." She looked at the empty wine bottle. "Would you like to have a sample of my moonshine? It makes for a great nightcap."

"You make 'shine?"

"Yep. That's a condition of my uncle's will. In order to keep the farm, I need to have a distillery up and running within the first six months."

"What happens if you don't make the deadline?"

Miranda stood stone-still with her green eyes open wide. "Oh, for heaven's sake. I don't know." She pressed her lips into a thin line. "I've been so focused on getting things running, I haven't considered that possibility." She headed into the kitchen and looked over her shoulder. "Come on back. We'll drink in the kitchen."

Miranda put the charcuterie board on the counter. She motioned for Rowena to sit in one of the oak chairs at the little enamel kitchen table. After Miranda dealt with the dishes, she got out down two small mason jars and put two ice cubes in each. She got a lime from the refrigerator and sliced it into wedges. Then she filled the jars with equal measures of Seagram's ginger ale and her latest batch of moonshine. She swiped each rim with a lime wedge and dunked it in as a garnish.

Sitting down at the table, Miranda raised her jar. "A toast to a rediscovered friendship. May we not get lost again." They clinked their jars and each sipped the cocktail.

Rowena's eyes widened. "This is wonderful! It's smooth, fresh, and not a bit harsh going down."

"Thanks, that's exactly what I was going for. I've finally replicated my uncle's famous recipe, and I've gotten the making of it down to a manageable job."

Rowena took another sizable sip. Then leaned back in her chair. "It's just lovely and I'm not a real fan of hard liquor. I prefer my red wines. What are your overall plans for the property?"

"Nothing simple, of course. I'm struggling to finish

getting the distillery in the barn approved. There are still some licensing issues, but I'm making do with my uncle's original still until the construction stage is complete. Big projects out in the country are a complete nightmare."

"Better you than me. I'm happy to work for my bread in the corporate world. It's safe and predictable." Rowena downed the last of her cocktail. "I'd better try to get a little sleep. I'm happy for the overtime, but the workshop will be stressful. Everything is always stressful with this company."

"Really? I had hoped for a nice group of outdoorsy types eager to learn something about art as well as cookery."

"Not this time. . . . Hey, is that your boot?"

Sandy was standing in the doorway to the kitchen with a hiking boot hanging by its tongue from his mouth. He tilted his head sideways and the boot clomped to the floor.

"Oh, Sandy!" Miranda lurched out of her chair and grabbed up the boot. "Oh, no. This is one of my new boots."

Sandy looked up with adoring puppy eyes.